To Lucy

from

Frank Hickey
a local writer

SOFTENING
FLATBUSH

BY THE SAME AUTHOR

BOOKS

The Gypsy Twist
Funny Bunny Hunts the Horn Bug
Brownstone Kidnap Crackup
Can Showbizzers Crush Crime?

FEATURE FILMS

Spy, The Movie
(co-written with Charles Messina
& Lynwood Shiva Sawyer)

SOFTENING FLATBUSH

A Max Royster Mystery

by Frank Hickey

Library of Congress
Catalogue-in-Publication Data

Softening Flatbush / Frank Hickey
1. Fiction – Crime 2. Fiction – Mystery 3. Fiction – Hardboiled

Published by Pigtown Books, an imprint of
Hidden Pearl Books L.L.C.

ISBN: 978-0-9848810-6-2

For further information, please contact:

info@pigtownbooks.com

10 9 8 7 6 5 4 3 2 1

First Edition / First Issue

To Jane Hickey Sexton,
dancer, singer, actress, sister and friend,
who began performing in Flatbush.

Prologue

After roll call, we flowed down the Flatbush precinct house steps. My legs shook from fear in the rookie blue pants.

The burly black Captain Asphar pulled me aside.

"Royster, you got three civilian complaints in just two weeks after the Academy," he told me. "The Internal Affairs rats will grill you about these charges. They can find you guilty of not combing your hair. Or anything else they want. You're still on probation. I'm betting that you will be thrown off the NYPD and probably jammed by the Feds for civil rights violations. FBI already called me to say that they opened a case on your pink butt."

My legs wilted. I turned from him and coughed and retched and spat a dry heave into the gutter.

He nodded to himself.

"On paper, your arrests look solid," he said. "I don't know what happened out there. But all three mutts say that you stopped them for Walking-While-Black and then beat them for no reason."

"I got two guns and crack and a switchblade off them, Captain," I said. It was the truth. My voice cracked. "All three fought me. One bit my neck."

Even to me, it sounded like I was lying.

The Captain made a face.

"But before that, you got to appear before a Citizens Against Police Abuse meeting. This is a new wrinkle. This Flatbush, Brooklyn, precinct here is ninety-eight percent black. The meeting judges if white cops like you belong in Flatbush."

I shook.

"Never saw nobody get that many complaints so fast," my Captain said. "You got a problem with us black folks, Royster? Do you use the n-word about us?"

"I call all criminals 'clients', Captain," I said. "No matter what race. The clients here ruin lives of honest black families. Murders every week. Crime causes tragedy. Not racism. But nobody wants to hear that."

"Patrol tonight, but do nothing," he said. "Nothing, do you hear? I got to put you out there for our patrol stats. But leave us black fools alone."

✌

Twenty minutes later, I was freezing in the chill fall night. The cold cut through the dark blue NYPD uniform right through it to my skin.

They had given me a meal period. But I forgot what time the period was. Stress could do that to me.

This could be my last night walking around free, I thought. The FBI wanted to have me walking a prison yard in a different uniform.

The shuttered Flatbush shops in gray-black city shades mocked me. They remembered happier years, of a safer neighborhood.

Past midnight now, everyone was shut tight. Rap music pounded somewhere.

My shaky legs brought me across Empire Boulevard and up a side street.

A black man strode in front of me. He chanted something. Then he ripped off his white T-shirt.

Huge gladiator muscles bunched and swelled. He looked like a super-hero on the back page of a comic book. He stood at least five inches over me. His shaved head and thick torso said weightlifter.

Tearing off clothes meant he was on PCP. That drug gave the user superhuman strength.

"Seven-One David," I sputtered into the radio. "10-85 on Sullivan and Washington. Possible PCP suspect. Request a Taser and a sergeant-"

The radio squealed.

This was a dead zone. Nobody could hear me broadcast.

Huge apartment buildings loomed above me. They blocked my radio signal. The NYPD never spent cash on things like radios.

My belly heaved again. I wanted to run away. Let black cops bust black clients here. There was no reason for me to get bitten again and called a racist and sent to die behind bars.

This client saw me.

"Wawwww!" he hollered.

He charged at me.

I skipped backwards. Everything in me froze.

The law said that I could not shoot him. I had to arrest him without hurting him. Let the lawyers try it.

Nerves made me hop sideways. My fingers tore the OC teargas from my belt and manage to spray above his screeching mouth.

"Awww!" he shouted in a Jamaican accent "That's nothing but cheap aftershave!"

He knocked the can from my hand.

My other hand drew the plastic baton. It slammed into his thigh with everything that I had.

The Academy had taught us this thigh shot. They said that it would drop anyone.

It did not drop him.

I hit him again.

"Get back!" I shouted.

He was on me. I smelled the PCP chemical odor and his sweat. We went down together.

"Oh, no!" I gasped.

The big buildings spun on top of me. This was not supposed to happen. Cops were not supposed to be on the ground.

"Hey, look!"

"Po-po getting done up!"

Black men shouted. They gathered closer. They watched. I smelled beer and a cigar.

The client grabbed my throat. I swung the baton's butt against his skull. Blood flew. He kept squeezing. I swung it again. He blocked it with his free hand. He tore it from me. It flew away into the gutter.

My thumb went into his eye. He kept squeezing. I twisted my head and broke his grip.

"Help me!" I rasped out.

I did not care that I was a cop. He was winning.

"Help yourself, po-po!" a black man shouted.

A window went up.

"Somebody help that officer!" a man bellowed from the window.

A foot crunched against the client's cheek. The kicker kicked again. Spit flew from the client's mouth.

The kicker was a black guy, short and stocky. He kicked again and scored on the client's eye.

"Don't help him!" the cigar smoker hollered.

"Uncle Tom!" his buddy added.

"That's slave stuff right there!" another man said, waving a fat book.

The client tried for my throat again. His hands caught my neck and banged my head KLUMP! against the pavement.

"Don't mix in it!" the cigar smoker shouted. "Big boy come looking for you later, if you do!"

"No court for me," the man with the book said.

"I don't be helping no white po-lice!" the cigar man shouted.

Hands from the crowd got my belt. One tugged at my gun. I squealed in terror.

"This is worse," I whispered.

"Get that gun!"

I swung an elbow and hit the gun-grabber. But the client had heard. He let go of my throat. He unsnapped the gun from my holster. He held the black Glock.

Both my hands grabbed his hand holding the gun. We rolled over each other. I banged his gun hand against the sidewalk. He held onto the gun.

The kicker karate-chopped against the client's neck. I could feel the shock. The client still held the gun. He pointed it at the kicker.

We rolled against a stone plaque set on the sidewalk. I slammed his wrist against the stone. He gripped the gun. His finger went to the trigger. I beat his wrist against the plaque again with everything that I had.

He yelped. The gun dropped. I let it go and head-butted him against the plaque. More blood wet me. His head lolled back. I butted again. His eyes closed.

My handcuffs spun out of my new belt and onto his right wrist. Then I crammed the left one on. It caught his skin and tore it. But it clicked shut.

He was cuffed.

My fingers found the Glock and shoved it down into the holster. The holster closed and locked around it.

The plaque stood above a square of concrete with the words:

On This Site Was
Ebbets Field Baseball Park
1913 – 1958

This was the park where Jackie Robinson had played for the Brooklyn Dodgers. Flatbush had been safe then. The locals nicknamed the area "Pigtown". Some had raised pigs in their backyards here.

My kicker was pulling on my arm. His young black face twisted, searching me.

"I couldn't let him kill you!" he shouted.

"I couldn't let him kill YOU!" I screamed back into his face. "We only got each other!"

CHAPTER 1.

Dancing Cheek-to-Cheek

Years later, I was in the rich Manhattan neighborhood that I called "The Playpen." It ran from 59th Street to 96th Street on the Upper East Side.

Playpenners danced in the basement of St. Jean Baptiste Church, on 76th Street at Lexington Avenue, home of Stephen Dane's Manhattan group. I often went there to dance.

Cooper, a woman I knew only from dancing, had just finished a rumba when I came in. She wore a silk-smooth evening dress that echoed her ebony hair. Sinatra sang a slow foxtrot over the speakers, "All My Tomorrows."

"May we dance?" I asked her.

"Okay," she said. "It's my first night dancing this month. I just moved to Flatbush in Brooklyn."

Her pure white teeth split in a grin. Dark blue eyes heated. Dancing, she leaned her slim strong frame back. Her evening dress molded to her figure. The tip of her nose showed a spring sunburn. It gave her a wilder look, like a forest animal.

Her fingers gripped mine. I could feel their strength. When she inhaled for the next step, the suntanned skin between her breasts showed.

I tried to look away from this stranger and think of loves gone sour in the past. Avoiding trouble was becoming my new religion.

"Flatbush is a cool neighborhood," she said. "Stately old buildings. Great architecture, wonderful friendly people, next to Prospect Park. Each street and each house has a unique personality."

"I know," I said. "I used to work there."

"Really, Max? What did you do?"

"I was a gandy dancer on the choo-choo train of justice."

"Are you ever serious, Max?"

"I tried being serious once. All I could get was a job as a handgun target paster for the Ku Klux Klan."

"You never give straight answers. Every time that I dance with you, you say funny things that I can't quite figure out."

"Me, neither. Why Flatbush?"

"Why not?"

"Because you and I agree that it is a great neighborhood. Beauty and dignity and magic from years past. Ebbets Field baseball stadium, home of the Brooklyn Dodgers, known worldwide as 'Dem Bums'."

"So we both see Flatbush the same?" she asked.

I paused, spun her and stepped into promenade position.

"But Flatbush suffers," I said. "The honest black folks live behind chains and locks. It may be Brooklyn's most dangerous neighborhood. Murders run rampant there. After dark, the crack gangs run it."

We danced some more.

Good cooking smells wafted from the kitchen in back.

"You see the faded glory in those old buildings on Flatbush Avenue, near the Prospect Park stone gates," I said. "Even the street names have magic – Empire Boulevard, Beekman Place, Lenox Road."

"Is this an obsession?" she asked me.

I smiled.

The dance ended.

Another man, white-haired, dressed in a blue Hawaiian print shirt resplendent with golden surfboards, took Cooper to dance an American waltz.

Sgt. Al Lipkin came down the staircase, wearing a light grey suit and a tight look on his elfin face. Sandy hair crested back in an old-fashioned pompadour. His nose crooked, broken in street fights as a young patrol cop.

"Why the heck do you twist my arm to get me here?" he asked. His high voice roiled a city accent.

"You need to unwind after working One Police Plaza all week. Politics, back-stabbing captains, meetings, chest pains."

"So here I am."

"And the women are waiting to unwind you," I said. "Slowly and gently. You're not wearing a hip holster, I hope. They'll feel that old .38 Colt Detective Special of yours."

"Ankle holster," he said. "What-the-Christ kind of people come here, richy neighborhood, and why am I here, dancing inside a Catholic church, a Jew like me?"

"Just New Yorkers who like to dance," I said. "Secretaries, nurses, college couples, aging showbiz types, gigolos posing as dance teachers with older women."

"Where are your other friends that help you clear cases?" Lipkin asked. "You know. Barkeeps. Crazies. Good-time ladies."

"My friends, those Playpen Irregulars, are dancing through the doors now," I said. "Here's Tisa and her husband, Ivan."

Tisa's black hair, sleek and long, twirled around the high cheekbones of her laughing tan face. Her pearl teeth sparkled. Her smile echoed in her brown eyes

Ivan's bulk would make two of her. Jazzmen would call him "Mister Five-by-Five."

"She's beautiful," Lipkin said. "Mexican?"

"Ecuadorian Inca."

"*Buenas noches*, senora," Lipkin said. "I'm new in the Playpen Irregulars. So I don't know everybody yet."

"We Irregulars laugh together through everything," Tisa said. "Unemployment. Heartbreak. Cancer. No matter what."

Her husband, Ivan, a bulky youngster built like the village blacksmith, drew her into a waltz. Curly hair and glasses framed his cherub's face.

"That's her husband?" Lipkin asked.

"I'll save you time," I said. "Ivan is around twenty-two, Jewish like you. From Far Rockaway. Tisa is ageless. Some Indian women are like that. Maybe forty. They seem very happy together."

"Unusual group," Lipkin said. "Don't Irregulars sometimes bail out of your group?"

"Some do, sure. Some join looking for fast sex. Or to network with the rich. Or something darker. They forget how to relax. They don't last long."

"And you all dance?"

"Look around at them," I said. "A cop like you watches people for a living. Some dancers here are twenty-one. Others are pushing eighty. Some are beauties. Others look like me. Hopefuls who want to learn dancing. Uptight supervisors like you. Battered ex-cops like me."

Lipkin hunched his shoulders like a shy teenager at the prom and walked around the dance floor, scanning.

"Max! Mister Royster, sir!" Nancy said.

Her sky blue backless dress emphasized her tigerish shoulder muscles. Nancy stood about five feet tall, ninety-eight pounds of steel-wire strength. Her blonde hair lay brushed back from a heart-shaped face. Cherry-red-rimmed glasses gave her a small-town girl look.

We swayed into the waltz.

My own body arched down to hers.

Lipkin danced with another woman, across the floor.

"Why are Civil Servants so horrible to us taxpayers?" Nancy asked.

"Your lovey-dovey man busted again, Nancy?"

"Worse than that. I got jury duty! Did you ever hear of anything so stupid? I'm trying to run my own business. You think that it's easy to get a school like that up and running with students that pay their dues? If I get stuck on a trial, I could lose my school."

Her Kansas drawl honeyed her words, even when she was mad.

"Nancy, there's an easy way to get you out of jury duty," I said. "And without you informing on Santiago, your little honeybunch, slinging crack outside the fertility clinic, the angel that he is."

"Bribe them?"

"No, my way is different," I said. "Nancy, you remember that I used to be a cop?"

"How could I forget?"

"And I know that you love me" I said. "I'm your old honeybunch. With every diphthong and corpuscle. Even though your heart belongs to that celestial little crack-dealer."

"Forever, Max."

"When you're in court, tell them that you love an ex-cop," I said. "That ex-cop is me. Because of that, you would be biased. You think that every cop is a great guy who would never lie. The lawyers, defense or DA's office, will break their legs running to drop you from that jury pool."

"Oh, that's so neat!"

"And we love each other," I said. "That's the whole truth and nothing but right there!"

She hugged me. Those muscles crunched mine. Everyone on the dance floor eyed us.

For a minute, I forgot Nancy's last name. Maybe my memory was going.

The dance ended.

Lipkin chatted with his dance partner, a patrician woman in a green flowered dress.

Cooper smiled and nodded her head with a young blond man. It made me feel pudgy and old.

A Business Type, dynamic and strong, liquor blowing near me, took Nancy's arm as an invitation to dance. His hair appeared razor cut, designed for power breakfasts. His healthy face looked destined to rule. His eyes said that he knew it.

Nancy smiled her glowing cat smile at him and shook her head. He made a face and stepped away.

"I know that smile," I said to her. "It means that you are vexed with that gentleman for touching you."

"A woman's body is a woman's business," she said.

"With your training, you could smile sweetly," I said, "then take off his head and make him eat it with Brussels sprouts."

Her smile glowed again.

"It IS tempting," she purred.

"But that would hurt Stephen Dane's Manhattan Ballroom friends. You wouldn't want to do that."

"No way. Stephen hosts the best ballroom in Manhattan."

We both watched Stephen, agile and cheery, bring shy couples together to dance. He never stopped teaching, spinning around the floor behind his smile and immaculate dark suit.

The music changed to an Argentine tango, something slow and gliding. Violins pealed in the song.

Cooper appeared again.

"Dance, Max?"

"I'd be a fool to say no."

Nancy smiled and moved off.

"How do you know my Flatbush so well?" Cooper asked.

"I told you," I said.

She went into my arms.

My belly sucked in. She smelled of scented soap and light perfume. Cooper looked like a young and lithe thirty. I was hoisting forty-eight years around with me like a broken suitcase. 220 pounds on six feet of old injuries weighed me down. The injuries had scarred me as a knock-around guy first and then as a cop.

"Hey, Patso," I said.

A burly man with a sagging choirboy's face lit by baby blue eyes lurched onto the dance floor.

"Another Playpen Irregular comes to call," I told Cooper.

"What's 'the Playpen'?'" Cooper asked.

"The Upper East Side, from 59th Street to 96th Street," I said. "One of the richest and safest neighborhoods in the universe. Protected like a baby's crib. You could live and die here without ever seeing the outside world."

"So he's another one of your secret club members?" Cooper asked. "Maybe I should join."

We danced more.

"What are you thinking about?" she asked.

"Contrasts."

"Excuse me?"

"And liabilities."

Someone tapped my arm. Business Type leaned in closer, blowing Scotch breath on us both.

"I'm cutting in," he slurred.

Cooper shook her head.

"Sure you are," I said. "But some other dance, some other place, some other partner."

"I'm in software," Business Type said, touching Cooper's shoulder. "Been up for three days for today's conference. Had some dinner, drinks. Now I want to dance. And I'm going to. With you."

I stepped away into the tango basic, holding Cooper. Then we went into the movement called 'an ocho'. Her heels spun.

Business Type touched my arm.

"Now you got me mad," he said.

CHAPTER 2.

O, Let's Go Over To Brooklyn!

Business Type loomed over both Cooper and me. His fists closed.

My feet shifted from tango to fighting stance.

My chin tucked down in fear. I felt very small.

"You may be software," I said. Nerves cracked my voice. So I pitched it low. "But I'm hardware."

"Max!" Nancy asked, dancing over. Her voice climbed and held a high note. "If the judge asks me in court if I love you, do I have to swear under oath that I love you? Can't they arrest me for lying?"

Business Type gaped at Nancy. So did Cooper.

I kept my eyes on Business Type and my hands loose and near my face. It was an old trick from Patrol. With my hands there, I could block or strike.

"Nancy," I said. "It's very tough to prove legally that you don't love another person. They are not filling up jails with perjurers about who loved who."

"Hey, I know you," Business Type said to Nancy. "You didn't want to dance with me."

"Oh, yes, I did," Nancy said.

She beamed that same smile.

"Sometimes, when a girl sees a real man like you, she plays hard-to-get," Nancy said. "You are just too much."

"Want to dance?"

"Sure thing, lollipop. But first let's go out on the street. Where we can be alone."

"No," Cooper said.

"It's all right," Nancy purred. "Let's go right now."

"Why?" Business Type asked.

"So I can show you something that you never imagined. We're wasting time here."

She strode towards the door in her heels. Business Type threw me a harsh look and followed her swaying hips.

"Max," Cooper said. "That little girl."

"That little girl knows Japanese Ninjutsu. Deadliest martial art, if you work long enough at it. She has. Nancy runs her own school. Sometimes she trains me."

"That man bothers me," she said.

"Not for long."

"I never saw a drunken fool like him at a ballroom dance before," she said.

"You're right. It just does not happen in ballroom. He's a white buffalo. Excuse me a minute."

℃

I went up the stairway and stepped outside the church door.

Across the street, Business Type put his arm around Nancy. She came in closer. Her foot stomped his. He bent. She elbowed his gut, fisted his groin and slammed the same hand up into his throat.

Business Type dropped.

He started crawling away.

Nancy kicked his bottom and then returned to the church. She smiled her secret smile as I held the door for her.

℃

Buzz Edwards hunched inside the church doorway, moving his beer belly with grace. Black and cheery and carefree at seventy, he made pop eyes at me and smiled. Convicts in Attica had smashed out most of his teeth, when he had been a Corrections Officer. Only a few of them remained.

"Dancing, dancing," Buzz said. "Yessir, buddy. Life is good."

Lipkin moved past us, holding a slim Latina woman with rhinestone glasses and tinted blonde hair.

"I don't know how to dance," Lipkin said. "But I sure know how to fake everything. The Job teaches us how."

"Especially at One Police Plaza," I said.

"Tonight, I need a place to dump some stress. I'm not drinking anymore. This is a good place to dump it."

"Que dice?" Al's partner asked in Spanish. "What does he say?"

I answered her back In Spanish. "He says that you are wonderful, Señorita. And a good dancer."

She beamed. Her face changed. She was a teenager once again.

Stephen changed the music to another foxtrot. Mel Torme sang "Cast Your Fate to The Wind".

Lipkin and his partner glided away.

"Who is that man?" Cooper asked.

"That's Al Lipkin. My protector. Hook. Connection."

"No, not him. The big drunk one who wanted to dance with me. So obnoxious."

"He's just a *frotteur*," I said. "Pay him no heed, my dear. I have rescued you."

"Your ninjutsu friend rescued YOU. What does that word, *frotteur*, mean?"

"It's French" I said. "But we also use it in English. You can read about it in old law books. The New York Penal Code had a section on it, long ago."

"But what is it?"

"It's a psychological disease as well. It comes from the French verb 'to rub.' Those unfortunates who need to rub up against another person to achieve erotic friction and thereby sexual release are called *frotteurs*."

"At least by you."

"Psychiatrists also use the term," I said.

"Ugh! So 'frotteurs' are those perverts in the subway?"

"Those who have a weakness," I said. "In fiber or spirit that you can see in their eyes."

"Max, you can tell just by looking in their eyes?"

"Better than that. I can go into the suburbs, look at the architecture and announce that *frotteurs* live here.'"

We danced through some more songs.

Leo, the Playpen Irregular, danced past. He was a lean, graying grandfather with a smile that never dimmed. Three fingers were missing on his left hand and two on his right, from a boyhood disaster. He smirked at Cooper.

"*Gna oy nay*," he said.

Then he twirled away.

"What's he saying?" Cooper asked.

"I taught him how to say 'I love you' in Cantonese," I replied. "He's Puerto Rican, without much English. That's his way of saying 'Hello'."

"Now, that man, Al, who protected you," she said. "From what? How?"

Her clear voice, with no New York accent, made me hang fire.

"It's complex," I said. "And you and I just know each other on the dance floor. Nowhere else."

"Are you trying to tell me that I'm too stupid to understand you? I can dance with somebody else in that case."

I bit my lip.

"Your Flatbush neighborhood was my training ground," I said. "And I'm slow to tell some people because it weirds them out."

"Why?"

"Good question. It probably goes back to their childhoods. I used to be on the cops, the NYPD, in Flatbush."

She stopped dancing and reared her head back.

"You were really a cop?" she asked.

"I don't know how real. But I tried."

"That's why you are so conflicted about my neighborhood."

"It's not yours yet," I said. "Where were you raised, Cooper?"

"White Falls, in northern New Hampshire."

"Catchy name. There's a message in there somewhere. Are there a lot of black folks in White Falls?"

"Hardly any." She paused. "Is that bad?"

"No, it's okay. You can catch up in Flatbush. Make up for lost time. My point is that you didn't grow up around much black culture."

"I've been in the city for four years."

"Where?"

"West 72nd."

"That's another pink area. Flatbush is maybe ninety-five percent black and five percent pink. No Latinos. And the only Asians there live upstairs from their bulletproof-window take-out restaurants and seldom venture out."

"So you can teach me about the neighborhood. I'm renting now. But I may want to buy."

"Cooper, I like everybody. I do not care about skin color or looks or accents. It took a long time to convince Flatbush that I felt that way. Everyone needs to be treated right. Civil rights means being able to walk your street without getting mugged. Sit on your front stoop with your family on a warm spring night."

Her mouth quirked.

"Now you're making a speech," she said. "You sound so cute."

❧

After dancing, we wound up in the Green Kitchen on First Avenue and 77th Street.

"Do you miss being a policeman?" she asked.

"Yup."

"How much?"

My body squirmed on the plastic seat.

"You're making this tougher," I said. "Whenever I talk about it, nightmares about missing it return."

"Why?"

I could not answer.

"I sure didn't know that," she said at last. "I'm sorry."

"I miss the Job more than I have words for. And, as you said, I have enough words for a speech."

"How strange. A man like you wanting to stay a policeman."

"I'm screaming to get back in. By law, this is the last year that I can re-apply. In six months, it will be too late."

"Caesar salad," Cooper told the smiling, bearded waiter. "Blue cheese dressing. And a black coffee, please."

"Buffalo Bill burger, well done. Toasted bun. Coffee very light, no sugar."

The waiter left.

"Here's a Flatbush expression for you," I said. "Right now, we're having 'coffee and'."

"Coffee and what?"

"That's just it. 'Coffee and' means 'coffee and whatever you want with that coffee'. The expression started in Flatbush and moved around the whole country in the Depression."

"'Coffee and'. You certainly have your own expressions. Do *frotteurs* ever take coffee and?"

"Too much so. They live nervous."

"What was it like, being a cop in Flatbush?"

"One fifteen-year-old girl wanted to change the TV channel, argued with her sister and threw a cup of bleach in her eyes. The judge had to tell her to stop laughing about it.

"A man named James grew somewhat vexed because his baby's mama stopped giving him what passed for love. Another baby mama drama. He torched her house with her and his son in it. They died screaming. He had named his son Semaj because it means 'James' spelled backwards, and he said that a son should never get ahead of his father. Whatever that means.

"Once, responding to a lover's quarrel, my cop shoes slipped on hanks of the woman's hair on the dining room floor, bloody and torn out by her lover."

Cooper listened, wide-eyed, and prompted me to tell more police stories.

The food came. Our coffees cooled.

"I hear that some women regard policemen as father figures," she said. "Protectors. Have you come across that?"

Our eyes met.

My smile stretched. I was enjoying tonight's games.

"Sounds unlikely," I said.

She regarded me.

"I've even heard that some New Yorkers are afraid to start a new love affair," I said. "Afraid of getting hurt."

"The things that one hears!" she replied.

I paid the bill, and we headed for the subway on Lexington Avenue.

&

A squat Latino clerk in an MTA vest was tying a pink cord across the subway entrance.

"Track fire at Grand Central," he muttered. "No IRT service in Manhattan. Take the F train to Borough Hall, Brooklyn."

"Yessir, absolutely," I said.

"No trains?" Cooper asked.

"Not unless we build them," I said. "Cab!"

&

I hailed a yellow cab cruising down Lexington.

"Where you go to?" the driver asked in an East European accent.

"128 –" Cooper started to say.

I grabbed her arm and pushed her into the back seat.

"Tell you in a second," I said. "Got it written down."

We piled inside the cab's back seat. The driver twisted around, a balding delicate man with a hawk nose.

"128 Lincoln Road," Cooper said. "That's in Flatbush, Brooklyn."

"I can't take you to Brooklyn," he said. "It's late, and I am nearly out of gas."

I took a deep breath and leaned forward.

"My dear Bogdan Porytko," I said, reading his hack license. "Your gas gauge reads half a tank –"

"Is broken."

"– and you will please to take us where we wish to go. Anywhere in the city."

"Flatbush is trash place. I pick up those people, they rob and kill me. The gas is okay. But I don't want to go there."

"Then drive us to the 19th Precinct police station on 67th Street," I said. "A reunion with my old comrades tonight would feel sweet."

He drove, grumbling what sounded like filthy words, in his native tongue.

"Why didn't you give him the address when we were outside the cab?" Cooper asked.

"Taxi laws. The rules say that he has to wait until you are seated inside before he can ask you where you're going."

"I didn't know that."

"Most New Yorkers don't. Trying to get to Brooklyn at night, you better learn. Welcome to Flatbush."

We came down past the floating, shifting East River, spun through curves and went up onto the Brooklyn Bridge, cables flashing shadows across her face.

"It's amazing," I said. "Brooklyn is just across the river but so very different from Manhattan. Two miles and ten minutes across the water. Smaller buildings. Much more quiet. A feeling of neighborhood."

Cooper nodded, looking away.

Maybe my Brooklyn talk was boring her now.

Our driver snorted.

"A true romantic up front, there," I said. "Beaudelaire, Oscar Wilde. Or Liberace."

Spinning down Brooklyn's Flatbush Avenue, we saw nobody walking the streets.

Prospect Park flashed past our windows.

I kept stealing looks at Cooper in the cab's half-light.

"*GOVNO!*" our driver cussed.

He hit the brakes. The cab fishtailed. I went against Cooper. She felt wonderful against me.

"Flatbush embrace," I said.

The cab's fender missed a teenager racing across Flatbush Avenue. His legs pumped. He threw a scared look over his shoulder. Shadows hid his body.

A black guard in a dark blue uniform ran after him. He waved a baton.

"Look, Max! Why don't you do something?"

"I am doing something. I'm bringing you home."

"Flatbush always this crap," Bogdan the Romantic said from his perch.

Another guard ran down Flatbush, shouting into a walkie-talkie.

A jeep with a flashing red roof light bumped up from another street and came into the triangular square.

The first guard hurled his baton at the runner. It went wide of its target and spun end-over-end and pinwheeled into a clothing store's display window, shattering the glass into a million crystallized jewels of light that caught the jeep's red roof lights and our own headlights. Shards fell between steel window bars.

An alarm bell split the night. It rang like an old-fashioned fire bell.

Above us, windows opened. A siren sounded.

An NYPD blue-and-white patrol car roared up. Roof lights danced. Another cop car zigzagged in front.

"Running down Lincoln!" another guard shouted out.

"I live on Lincoln," Cooper said. She sounded shaky now. Flatbush was fast losing its charm. We stopped to let three more NYPD cars pass.

Our cab waited at a red light. The light stuck. We kept waiting.

"Stay inside the cab until it's over," I said. "When I say 'Drop!' you drop below the windows. They may shoot."

"No! I want to get inside my place now."

"How sweet," I whispered. "Our first quarrel."

The cab slewed down Lincoln, a dark two-way street shaded by trees.

A broadly-built black man lay draped over a car hood. Syrupy blood covered his face and shoulders. He lay limp. His arms and legs hung over the car's hood.

I bolted out of the cab and thumbed his neck pulse. There was nothing to feel. I shook my head.

Cooper heeled out of the cab.

"That's Lutz!" Cooper screeched. Her face came apart. "He's my friend! Just a local comedian! Why would somebody kill him?"

She reached out to him.

I blocked her arm.

CHAPTER 3.

Call Me "Birdie"

"Cooper, don't touch him," I said.

"You did!"

"I had to. Please put your hands in your pockets. Don't speak, please."

I scrunched down and checked under the cars nearby. Sometimes limber and skinny clients hid underneath cars.

The siren noise faded. Cars stopped, their tires screeching.

Blood had formed a pool on the left side of his head. He had thick, square hands and lay on his gut, a big friendly belly. Fat cigars spilled from his shirt pocket onto the sidewalk.

He wore a blue denim work shirt, short-sleeved with pearl-white snap buttons, brown corduroy pants, thin black belt and tan running shoes. A wristwatch had left an imprint on his left wrist, but there was no watch there now. No wallet bulged in his pants. I touched a finger lightly to his pockets but felt nothing solid inside.

About four feet from his body, the letters "OB" looked fresh-painted on the sidewalk. But the letters were not painted. Someone had dipped a finger in the blood from Lutz's head and written with that finger on the sidewalk. The letters "OB" lay still wet and sketchy on the sidewalk.

The killer had left a message all right.

I was trying to figure it out.

Cooper took action and paid the cab fare herself.

Bogdan tore off.

Making sure that Cooper stayed still, I went thirty feet down the block, scanning.

Tomorrow must have been garbage pickup day. All the cans stood in the gutters.

I lifted someone's garbage can and put it on the sidewalk. Going another thirty feet past Lutz's body, I checked the sidewalk and rolled another garbage can onto it.

On my cellphone's notepad, I wrote down the license plates on the parked cars. Then I put down the street numbers of the homes that had lights on. Somebody was awake in them.

Circling the body and taking photos and notes with my cellphone I glanced at Cooper, who still stared, weeping at Lutz.

"Why are you doing all this?" she asked.

"Once you open up a crime scene, you lose it forever."

"Shouldn't you call the police?"

"Right now I'm my own police."

Sniffing the air around Lutz's body, I smelled hair oil mixed with sweat. He might have been running from someone before he was killed.

I dialed 911.

"911 Operator 637, what is the emergency?" the woman operator asked in the growly city accent, looking for an argument.

"Dead male body," I said. "Former MOS Maxwell A. Royster, tax number 547376, last Ten Card Command One-Nine Precinct. Have one, I say again, one RMP, give me a 10-85 on 90 Lincoln Road."

RMP was cop slang for a radio motor patrol car.

"Where is the body?" the Dispatcher asked.

"As I say, meet me at 90 Lincoln Road. Notify Sgt. Albert Lipkin, Chief of Detectives Office. And Brooklyn South Homicide and the Seven-One Precinct."

"Sir, you expect me to do all that?"

"You better. You're on tape."

"Are you trying to be a wise guy?"

"No. It comes naturally."

"I can't make these calls," she said.

"Yes, you can, Operator 637," I said. "New York Penal Code 153.3 mandates it."

I was making it up. She probably did not have a judge standing by at the next swivel chair.

"Thank you," I said. "I'll be standing by."

Nobody was looking out of their windows yet. That was going to change.

An RMP pulled silently up to the corner of Lincoln Road and Flatbush. The two officers inside waited. Their hands were probably touching their holstered Glock 9mm service guns as they scoured the street with their eyes.

I had done the same thing on calls. Years ago, less than a mile away, some client with a shotgun had made the same call and blasted Police Officers Dockery and Fleck The client did it because they were white and cops.

Keeping my hands high and visible, I stepped into the middle of the street. Eye contact was important to street cops. Many claim that they could tell when it was safe to approach a person due to eye contact. They were often wrong. They paid with their lives and their families, jeweled with wet-eyed children, grouped by the flag-draped casket at their funerals.

"Royster," I said as they approached me on foot. "I'm off the Job in the One-Nine."

Cops in the 19th Precinct still called me crazy, a "funny bunny", for hunting a rape-killer on my own time.

"What the hell you doing in this house-of-crud command?" one cop asked.

"Chasing women," I said.

Still keeping my hands in sight, I jerked my chin towards Cooper. She was still standing by Lutz's body.

The cops relaxed. They could trust what I had just said.

"Now I know that you're one of us," the first cop said. He was black, with a gold hoop earring on the left side to match his yellow plastic eyeglasses with baby dinosaurs on the temple bars. His sergeant probably told him never to wear them on patrol.

"Like women, huh?" the other one said. She was a wiry white woman with jagged front teeth.

"Guilty," I said.

"Well, so do I," she said.

"Where's the stiff?" the other cop asked. "I'm sorry, *corpus delicti*."

"Down the street."

"Why did you tell 911 to meet here?" the woman asked.

"To avoid gacking up the scene," I said. "Contamination. Scraps of paper. Lieutenants putting their fat fingers all over the car where the body is and smudging any other prints."

"Lieutenants," the man said, like it was a curse.

"We sure seen that happen," his partner said.

"You got blood letters over by the body," I said. "They say 'OB'."

"You think that maybe the mutt signed his work after he cooled this brother here?" the black cop said.

"It's possible," I said. "I didn't write it."

"Yeah," he breathed out.

"Let's just stand back and let the carnival come," I said.

The carnival of bystanders came out from the houses.

A couple of young sergeants showed up to give orders and contradict each other. It was the same old Job. More uniforms rolled. Some of the faces looked familiar but I could not place them. My memory was skipping tonight.

"Who put these garbage cans here?" a young black cop with a Caribbean accent asked.

"I did," I said.

"That's changing a crime scene. We could lock you up."

"Go ahead," I said.

That stopped him.

"Those cans are not in the crime scene officer," I said. "They protect the crime scene from outsiders gumming up the evidence so we can never get a conviction."

"It's still messing with our scene."

"Check your New York State Criminal Procedural Law," I said, winging it. "Twenty-five feet or less is considered the crime scene. Check the case of Nick Charles versus Asta Amalgamated Dog Food. It's all there on paper."

Another unmarked car slanted to a stop. Piva clambered out and swiveled his big head around until he saw me. In Flatbush, my red hair and green eyes made me stand out from the crowd.

"Royster, what the Christ are you doing here?" he asked.

He stood a bit larger than me, with graying hair combed back in a pompadour and a broad-cheeked face. Foxy eyes took in everything, unblinking. He always talked about his Department bench-pressing medals, and his body showed the years of disciplined pumping iron. The forearms looked like huge turkey drumsticks, swelling towards the elbow and tapering towards the wrist. He wore a short-sleeved dress shirt, shield on his belt and a suede hip holster holding his Glock.

A wispy moustache showed vanity over a mouth that was always ordering a scared underling to do something. He moved at ease through the Department, cajoling some and bullying others. Rookies feared him because he would dress them down in public. He said that it made them better cops.

It had taken me months to learn that Piva did not care about making anyone a better cop.

Piva cared about Piva.

Sergeants and bosses respected him because of his years in the street and his high arrest and summons numbers. They also knew that he could channel gossip against, shaping the truth for himself. So they avoided ruffling him.

"Piva," I said. "You're out of the Bag. Congratulations."

We New York cops called our uniform "the Bag".

"Just Temporary Duty," he said. "TDY with the squad, Royster. I don't have your polish."

"Me, neither."

"Don't tell me that you moved into this precinct with those other silly white people. Think that they're gonna gentrify here and turn it into Greenwich Village. You and I know better. Am I right?"

Cooper probably fit into his category of silly white people. I hoped that she was not listening.

"You sure are, Piva," I said. "The initials 'OB' are over there by the body.

The uniforms slopped around the crime scene. A couple more detectives that I did not know got out of a Buick Regal and knocked on doors of homes closest to Lutz's body.

Another detective spoke to Cooper. She might have to make the official identification. Her face muscles forked between stoic and agitated.

"Did you know this CUPPI?" Piva asked me. He was using the old term for "Circumstances Undetermined, Pending Police Investigation" for any death without a doctor's signature.

It did not strictly apply. Maybe Piva was using it to remind me that once upon a time we worked as cops together.

"Just saw him dead tonight," I said. "Name is Lutz."

"How does a black guy get a Kraut name like Lutz?"

"G.I. babies on the G.I. bill, I guess," I said.

"But the initials 'OB' are in his blood. They must mean something."

"They mean that I got a mutt named Obadiah Bernet," Pia said. "He's done strong-arm and gun robberies all over Flatbush. His nickname is 'OB'. He's already whacked one turd and did just six years for Manslaughter One. Everyone hates him. How come you don't remember OB, Royster?"

"Been out for years, remember?"

"You were never in," Piva said. "Always a weirdo cop. Full of book ideas that don't work on the street."

My breath blew out. It tickled my moustache. Piva was always quick to slam anyone who disagreed with him.

In the back of my ears, where all street cops feel the way the wind is blowing, my intuition was sounding alarms. I could sense the uniforms listening harder now.

Pulling it up from somewhere, I tried a glad-hander smile on Piva.

"The sale begins when the customer says 'No'," I said. "Here's my notes on the license plates at the scene and what homes were awake. You can door-knock them now and get what they heard and saw. But don't assume that it was OB who did this. Keep an open mind. You say that everyone hates him. Maybe someone framed him."

"You're reaching," Piva said.

"Sometimes you got to."

"Royster, I'm trying to make detective!" Piva barked. "Not wind up like you, off the Job, no pension, as a 'birdie'."

His tone drew the Crime Scene Unit techs, civilians in windbreakers. They were taking photos of Lutz and the two-way street and the buildings nearby.

"You a 'birdie'?" one of the uniforms, a stout lad with a necklace of chins covering up the collar brass reading "71," his precinct number.

"*Mucho loco*," his partner added. He was a balding Latino with a shaved head and smoked a stogie in violation of crime scene rules. The smell traveled.

"So take off, Royster," Piva said. "We got the ID from that crotch that you're with. We don't need you. You're worthless."

"Take a memory course, Piva," I said, tightening up. "I ain't worthless yet."

"I said take off, Royster. This is a straight Rob-One murder. No wallet, cash or wristwatch on him. No need for your bull. I don't owe you anything."

"Yes, you do," I said. "Sunday, March 3rd. The last tour that we worked together."

"I don't know what you're farting out, Royster," Piva said. "You got no friends here, champ."

"I got myself," I said. "That call you and I rode together on that Sunday. Where I got hurt. Then you wrote up the report. Called me careless. And started a whispering campaign to cover yourself."

He rushed me, fast for such a big bruiser, and grabbed my shirt. It ripped. He pulled me past the RMP, past Lutz and into the alley next to the Crime Scene van.

"Lighten up, Piva," Necklace-of-Chins said.

"No names," his partner said. "Watch what you say."

Piva used his arm muscles to slam me against the building wall. My head went back KLONK!

CHAPTER 4.

Among Old Friends

The uniforms crowded the alley so that nobody passing could see what was going on.

I shook my head and came away from the wall.

"Piva," I said. "You going to make detective? Get your gold shield this way? This solves nothing. Cool down."

"I don't care."

"Nothing's happened. Drop it."

"I'll drop you!"

Piva stepped in and threw a jab. But I dodged the punch, moving my head in a circle under his left arm. I came up balanced and ready for his right hand.

It came fast and grazed my left ear. I bent at the waist and moved more to my right. My circling threw him. He had to keep throwing more punches to his own left side, his weaker side. His right hand rode over his left forearm.

That was why smart boxers circled to their opponent's left.

I had to keep dancing. One punch from those turkey-leg arms, and I could get concussed against the wall for keeps.

Brother Lutz might have me for company on his Voyage to the Imponderable. Street cops had seen it happen before. It would not help my memory problems.

He threw a long left, stepping in. I weaved underneath it and came up on his side again. All he knew was boxing. That was good for me. If he tried some karate or a kick, I would get hurt. But he kept throwing punches. I knew Piva. He never switched tactics. He could not.

Three more punches went past my head. His cheeks took in air. I came back up in a perfect spot to blast his kidney. He scared me. But I did not want to hit him. I wanted to tire him out.

His breath chopped some more.

"That's enough, pal," one cop said from the shadows. "Bosses will get here soon."

"You can't reach that guy," another uniform said.

My legs cramped from the twisting around. I ducked, and his breath came out again. Whiskey rode on it. He had probably sneaked a few shots earlier that night while typing up reports.

"He's under!" Piva said. "Take him!"

Three cops grabbed me. I stopped. Fighting them would be stupid.

"Piva, you arresting me for something?" I panted. "I would sure like to know what."

"This."

The cops held me. Piva threw a short punch into my gut. I jackknifed upwards. He was that strong. My feet left the ground. Pain corkscrewed all around me.

My knees bit the alley sidewalk. Then I flopped face down. I tried rolling in case he kicked.

"That's it," Necklace-of-Chins said. "You got him for Resisting. What else?"

"Nothing," Piva panted. "Forget it. No arrest. I just voided the arrest."

"Hey, hey," Latino Baldy said. "Play the game fair. You said he was 'Under'. Don't leave us hanging here. We could get jammed up."

"Not by Royster," Piva said. "He's no rat."

"Try me on a Monday," I wheezed.

"No problem, guys," Piva said.

He shook his big arms and turned his back on me and stepped away. I just watched him. My body was paralyzed, and my right ribs felt broken. When I breathed, the ribs stabbed with short sudden spurts of pain.

"Royster's too scared to complain," Piva went on. "Too scared not to. Too afraid to do just about anything, Right, Royster?"

"Don't let me interrupt your monologue," I said. "Just keep ranting."

Piva snorted and strutted away. I watched him go.

୧୬

From the alley mouth, Cooper's slim shape threw a shadow. I twisted in surprise. My ribs knifed me with pain. When the uniforms saw her, they cupped palms over their name-plates and stepped away.

Again, I had done that same thing years before.

"Is this some kind of nightmare, Max?" Cooper said.

"Funny that you should ask that."

"Lutz dead and the police beating you up for finding the body."

"Typical civilian," I said.

"What?"

"Sorry. What I mean is, it's more complex than that."

"The man that hit you. You and he used to work together?"

"Let's get out of here, Cooper. My resume would depress you. Just like it does me."

"He can't just hit you and walk away."

"Things were clearer in your old neighborhood," I said. "But you picked this one. Welcome to Flatbush."

"How can you let him do this?"

"I'm abashed and embarrassed that you saw that. It was not the Department's finest moment."

"How you stand this?" she asked.

"Maybe because I loved working as a cop. And I want to fight for truth and justice again. Without bums like Piva."

The media vans were arriving. News camera persons were setting up their angles. Someone had covered Lutz's body with a tarp.

"See that skittish-looking TV reporter interviewing Piva?" I asked. "She should have been in the alley a few minutes ago, watching him in action."

"Really?"

"Yeah. She missed out."

"Now I know how some cops bully people," she said.

We moved away from the TV vans and RMPs under the trees along Lincoln Road.

"You don't know what you moved into," I said.

"Oh, stop."

"I don't mean the crime today. This used to be an enchanted neighborhood. The wealthiest and most secure Brooklynites wanted to live right here, next to Prospect Park and Ebbets Field for the baseball games."

"That's just history," she said. "I can't get that officer's face out of my mind. And you want to re-join those people?"

"Name me someone else who can fix up a neighborhood," I said.

"Maybe tomorrow I will," she said. "If you like. They're called Flatbush Secure."

Cooper turned into a three-story house shaded by solemn trees, painted brown wooden shutters set against cream walls. It reminded me of Dutch houses.

"Coming down this driveway to get inside a back door is not the safest idea of the week," I muttered to Cooper. "What if some client falls in love with you at the market and is dying to whisper sweet nothings to you in private?"

"You sound like Lutz. He tried super-super hard to improve this hood, this Flatbush neighborhood. He was a genuinely funny comedian who waited tables, waiting for Flatbush to become safe."

"I don't know if Flatbush can," I said.

She snuffled some more.

She unlocked a door and we walked up a staircase. My ribs ached with every step that I took.

"I've got what used to be the servants' quarters," she said. "I'm renting now, but I want to buy here."

Being alone with her clipped my breath shorter in a galloping excitement.

She opened a wooden door to a large living room. A client could easily kick it in.

"That policeman called you a 'birdie'," she said. "Is that something that I should know about?"

She scrutinized me.

"The Job loves their slang," I said. "Do you really want to know?"

"Very much."

"The slang 'birdie' comes from putting some official words together. It's an acronym for 'By Virtue of Mental Disease'. 'By-R-Dee'. Shorthand that some witty locker room cop coined, and old partners told me about. They told me about it because that's why they threw me off the Job."

"You said before that this year is your last chance to rejoin the Police Department."

"It is," I said. "By January, it will be too late."

"I want to ask if you ever killed anyone but I don't want to know right now."

"It's a deal," I said.

"Can you sleep on the floor tonight, Max? I don't think that you should subway home. Tomorrow, you should get X-rays for that punch that he hit you with."

"Please forget about that punch, Cooper."

"But he had no right to do that."

"You and my ribs agree."

"Max, you're too old for me. And way too tangled."

That one cut. The rib pain eased off and met her words. The two pains would race around all night in my head. I was that kind of fool.

The floor creaked under my foot. The house was probably built in the 1870s, when Brooklyn was a separate city. A comfortable kitchen adjoined a bedroom door.

Cooper had tables and chairs already established in the dining room. It looked as if she had lived here for years. The furniture looked pricey to my eye. Cooper was risking her life in an expensive manner.

"Goodnight," she said.

She opened the bedroom door, went inside and closed it behind her.

"Modern woman," I said to myself. "That's the style. No long talks or agonizing re-appraisals."

❧

With some of her hard plum-colored pillows under my head, I tried to get comfortable. My soft contact lenses came out of my eyes, and I fingered them into the carrying case.

My ribs still burned with pain.

"Seems to be a lot of different pains swirling about now," I muttered. "But our hero must stay cheerful."

Sleep slipped away from me.

ᥴ৲১

A nightmare flickered behind my eyelids. January had already passed. I wandered around One Police Plaza in frosty Manhattan. Big calendars seemed to be everywhere. They accused me of letting paperwork slide. I had lost my chance to become a cop again.

"But I tried," I kept saying. "I really tried."

Nobody cared. Whey-faced clerks in windowless cubbyhole offices shook their heads and pointed to their calendars.

"Like it says in Latin," one clerk said. His spotty face said that he was trying to be witty. "Snooze 'em, lose 'em. If ya snooze, ya lose. Or 'Snus-sum, loose-sum'."

The big calendar read "January" in scarlet letters.

Then the nightmare shifted.

I was naked on a Flatbush street corner and trying to cover up. A bright red sports car pulled to the curb. Pink letters read "Leshyde Hughes, Deputy Acting Medical Examiner."

My fingers kept stabbing my cellphone to call my Playpen Irregulars. But the phone kept melting in my hand.

Behind me, the Playpen Irregulars grouped. Tisa, Patso, Leo and Buzz pointed at my stomach.

"You're getting fat," Tisa said. "Why are you in Flatbush without us?"

A rail-thin, black scarecrow of a man leapt like a dancer from the driver's seat of the red sports car. He wore a soft felt hat, tipped forward and an immaculate dress suit with a dancer's shoes. He did a dance routine, leaping and compacting himself into an old-fashioned number, complete with a cane. His shoes fluttered in perfect time to the music.

The music kept coming from somewhere. It was a mournful jazz tune with a trumpet and a piano.

"Nobody dances as good as that Leshyde Hughes," a paunchy black man in a pink alligator sports shirt said. He held an open can of El Modelo malt liquor, in violation of the NYC Municipal Code. "He the su-preme, yo."

Then Leshyde Hughes spun around so smoothly on his heels that it made my ribs ache with fresh pain. He did a high kick, a kick-ball-change step and then sprang to the side.

Behind him, Lutz lay still humped over the car's hood, with the same syrup of blood caked and dry underneath his head and painful open mouth.

ళ

Sweat washed me.

I woke up, lifted my head and banged it back against the wooden floor. My ribs still ached. Maybe I was getting soft.

Perhaps other white cops had transferred out of Flatbush after dreams like that one. And they never looked back.

"Now, I got Cooper's nightmare," I said aloud. "Her problems are my problems."

CHAPTER 5.

Meeting the Friends of Flatbush

During the night, I could hear Cooper crying in her room. I was not far behind.

Daylight filled the windows. She showered and then came from her bedroom dressed for the street.

Lutz's dead body seemed to travel alongside us as we strolled in the pre-autumn sunshine.

"You have to meet my buddies in the Friends of Flatbush Group," Cooper said. "Then we'll get breakfast. Can you wait that long?"

"Are they going to use words that are too big for me to understand?" I asked.

"Stop faking this dumb-cop routine," she said. "You have an awesome vocabulary. Sometimes you speak like those poets that *The New York Times* prints on the editorial page."

"Naw," I said. "I'm nobody great. Just another police blue-suit slopping across life's great stage, dragging that piece of lumber behind him.

"You're a fraud," she said. "A loveable old fraud. Got to realize your potential."

That word "old" made my breath suck in. But maybe Cooper called me "old" without thinking. After all, brickwork from oldish Dutch buildings still rose above the bargain stores lining Flatbush Avenue.

೧

Cooper swayed her body into a doorway marked "Friends of Flatbush: Flatbush / Lincoln / Ignatius / Parkville / Parkside / Empire / Rugby Road / St. Paul's Place." Something about the sign turned me to wisecracking again. The tan building rose three stories. The small lobby smelled of hot curry sauce from some nearby Indian takeaway restaurant.

"This is a neighborhood watch group?" I asked as we mounted the battered linoleum stairs. "Like the Sons of Liberty or the Mothers' March on Airplane Glue?"

"Much, much more. It's the first group that I've felt close to since high school. We all get each other through the day."

"Kind of like my Playpen Irregulars."

"Different. We have clear goals and myriad talents in the private sector."

"So do we," I said. "Ivan can sing all the verses of 'Eli, Eli' in Hebrew."

We entered the headquarters on the third floor. The room held Black, Latino, Asian and pink professionals. Their clothes and their words showed that they were well-off but not making much noise about it.

Yellow waxy painted walls clashed with a reddish carpet that reminded me of Lutz's blood. I shook my head to clear it. Wide windows looked out onto Flatbush Avenue.

A biggish man with very high shoulders unhooked himself from the magazine rack and smiled at Cooper. Lank black hair fell over a scarred forehead. His smile died when he saw me.

"Hiya, Coop," he said in a New England accent. "How ya been?"

"Sad about Lutz" Cooper answered.

"Look at the weapons that our guards found when they cleared out a building for renovation," he said.

Nickel-plated handguns with white bone grips gleamed on a folding table. A black Army .45 automatic lay with the slide back. Someone had fired the last shot many years before. Chunky brass derringers nestled alongside the other guns. On top of a Nazi dagger with a bloody blade was a Colt Single Action pistol, a Peacemaker, the gun that won the West. I wondered how that cowboy gun ever got to Flatbush. A Malaysian kris, a dagger with a wavy blade dwarfed the gravity knives on the table. They boasted handles of reddish woods, black plastic and imitation stag colors of cream and brown. One was wrapped in green Army parachute cord. I wanted to curry favor with Cooper's group.

"I can bring these weapons to the Precinct," I said.

"No," Cooper said. "That's Manry's job."

Whoever Manry was, her saying his name turned me jealous.

A blonde woman with a gymnast's body and a smile so bright that it looked fake, pointed a blue-painted fingernail at the weapons. She shook her head.

"This shows the fear in that one building," the blonde woman said. "Nobody there trusts the government to protect them."

"Brigden, this is my dancing partner, Max," Cooper said.

Today Cooper made me analyze her words. Maybe I was too sensitive, wanting her too much.

The term "dancing partner" sounded like Cooper was distancing herself from me.

Brigden stepped away.

It was time to restate the bidding.

"Cooper, I don't want to be just your 'dancing partner'," I muttered. When anything turned me shy, my city accent came back.

She coquetted me a smile.

"What do you want?" she asked.

Someone bellowed to my left.

"That's Skip Cossee, our director," Brigden announced.

A black man, wide and short like a budget refrigerator, rolled across the room to us. He carried what some called "hard fat", where the muscles mixed with the skin tissue. He looked solid. Nothing jiggled.

His face beamed round with boyish happiness. His skin was the color of cherry wood. His mobile face changed as he stomped across the room.

The suit was generously cut to allow him to grow wider in future years. It looked handmade to my shopper's eye. I could never afford a suit like this one. His white-on-white shirt put him in the rich part of the clothing boutique. Dull cufflinks of hammered gold adorned his sleeves. His hair and brief moustache looked recently trimmed. Cologne wafted from somewhere near the designer necktie. He looked like an oil painting that someone had stayed up late to finish.

"I'm mourning Brother Lutz in my own heathenish kind of no-churchy way by raising six kinds of hell," he boomed in a deep voice that rolled like a bowling ball smashing into pins.

"Called that boys club masquerading as a police precinct, and some desk jockey sergeant would NOT put me through to the captain, and when I asked him for his name, the line went DEAD! My next call was to the inside line at Gracie Mansion where the Mayor lives, which number I got for years because this is MY town!"

That was the way that he spoke. His words exploded into capital letters with ease. He commanded everyone inside earshot to listen to him.

"I told that Mister White Boy Desk Sergeant that murder rates are climbing back up again in this precinct," the black man said. He trod his stage. Again, his voice carried.

"Surprise, surprise," he went on. "The white power structure don't cry no real tears when another Flatbush darky stops breathing ahead of schedule. Well, they gonna feel my feet on their friggin' tummies when I give them these weapons."

Skip waddled to the bathroom door and tore it open.

"Hey, there, Captain Asphar!" he boomed. "What you doing, sitting on the mother-hugging floor there? Sucking your thumb. Or something. Come on out here; help the old shot-to-hell fat man here!"

The bathroom was empty. Some giggled.

"Skip," Cooper asked. "Do you curse this much in court?"

"No," Skip replied. "More."

"More?" she asked.

It was time to upstage this performer, Skip.

Cooper was paying him way too much attention.

"Anybody would cuss," I said. "Myself, I been there too much to be normal. You're a lawyer?"

"You betcha booties I am," he said. "Best criminal defense lawyer in Brooklyn."

"And shy," I said. "Diffident and self-effacing. Modest."

"I am an ample individual," Skip said. "Even my white tailor calls me larger than life."

"And you represent this Friends of Flatbush group?" I asked. "Excuse me. But I'm still trying to figure out the setup here."

"Cool, baby, cool," Skip purred. "Like the lady said, I'm the group director of this lash-up here. Bringing this hallowed ground of Flatbush back from the dead is an awesome responsibility."

"I bet that you're great with juries in summation," I said.

"Baby, I'm so great with lady jurors that I lost my wife!" he roared.

It seemed to pain him. There was something of a hurt, massive buffalo in the way that he minced across the floor.

"Donut delivery!" Brigden shouted from her desk. "He's double-parked downstairs. I'll get it!"

This was a chance for me. If this group liked me, Cooper might fall right in with them.

"I'll get it," I said. "Robbed another bank yesterday. So rest easy."

"I'll go with you," Skip said. He slung a black coat of soft leather, elegant and stylish, over his shoulders. "This way, I get to eat the best ones on the stairway."

Clambering downstairs to the street door, I looked back at Cooper and banged into the wall. She looked beautiful.

∾

On the street, a tan Ford with a cracked windshield and ruined fender pulled away from the curb.

"Hey, donut brother!" Skip wailed. "Come back, baby! We starvin' hungry here, baby!"

A crew of black teenagers came from nowhere and circled us. I never saw them coming.

"We gonna take you off," the Leader said. He had gold-capped teeth, bling neck chains and a red baseball hat and sneakers. That red color meant he belonged to the Bloods gang.

Dizziness hit me. I staggered.

Skip smiled like a saint.

"Whoa, man!" the Leader shouted. He pointed a wide hand at Skip. "Lookit, dude! We got us a leather coat!"

Skip kept showing his teeth in a joyous smile. His own hands went under the coat crosswise.

He drew twin silver-plated .45 Colts with walnut grips. He thumbed back the hammers.

"Yeah, baby!" Skip boomed. "But first you got to fuck the nigger that's in the coat!"

"Yo, split!" the Leader said.

The crew broke up, screaming. Red sneakers flew down Flatbush. The Leader ran the best.

"We just playing with you, yo!" the Leader shouted over his back.

"Now we'll never know," I wheezed.

"Skip, don't ever use that N-word in front of me," I said. "I hate it. Had fistfights with fools who used that N-word. Never! Are we clear?"

My body made me slump against then nearest parked car. Adrenaline drained out of me.

"Lemme go back inside," Skip said. "Call that donut dump again."

"Got a gun carry permit?" I asked.

"What for? Don't need it. Jesus didn't need it. C'mere, Jesus!"

He stomped back inside.

Somehow, I could not remember how many guys had been in the crew. Tunnel vision killed my memory. Calling 911 now was a waste.

Skip's voice hollered and threatened into the phone upstairs.

The same tan Ford lurched back from the Flatbush Avenue traffic and bumped into the car that was holding me up.

The driver, a gangly black man with a pair of cracked eyeglasses tilted on his face, leaned across the passenger seat, balancing a stack of donut cartons that smelled fresh and comforting.

"Donut man?" I whooped at him.

"You paying for it?" he asked. "With money?"

"Credit cards are just plastic waiting to melt, pilgrim," I said to him.

"Real money?"

I looked at the narrow jaws, stubbled with hair, and missing a few front teeth.

"Why?" I asked.

"I don't be having no troubles with them peoples upstairs there now," he said. "And their goons. Now, they know me."

That made me scrutinize him more.

"What do you mean?" I managed to say, like the ace detective that I was not.

"That's okay," he said. "I don't be involved with all that. $13.85. Watch it, the boxes don't fall."

He would not say anything else.

CHAPTER 6.

Breakfast at Last

"Everybody," Cooper said to the group. "Max and I both need breakfast now. And not just donuts, like the rest of you."

We left the office. We both avoided looking down Lincoln towards the spot where Lutz had been killed.

"There's a super diner on Nostrand Avenue," she said. "I probably don't have what you like in my kitchen. I don't cook much."

Looking at her clear eyes and skin glowing in the morning light, it seemed hard to see last night's grief. She probably wanted to put it behind her as well. Her generation hated to ask mine for help.

"Toomey's," I said.

"That's right. I keep forgetting that you had worked here. Toomey's would be where you officers went for your doughnuts, right?"

"Since about 1940."

I looked at her casual Saturday pink blouse. It reminded me of the black man in my nightmare on her floor had been wearing. I doubted that they knew about each other.

The tailored blue jeans fit her snugly, showing her strong slim thighs and calves. A man's wristwatch with a pilot's face hung on her left wrist. Her face showed no signs of makeup. She was going natural today. Maybe it was her way of baring herself to the outside and forgetting about Lutz.

We both needed to forget about Lutz.

So I spun on my heel in front of her and seized her wrist. I struck a pose and sang love song from Shakespeare:

> In delay, there lies no plenty,
> Then come kiss me,
> Sweet and twenty!

"You silly!" she grinned, trying to pull her wrist away.

"And you're looking to see if anyone is watching us," I said. "You're still a Yankee maiden from New Hampshire. This is Flatbush. We could raise a family in that bus-stop over there, and nobody would care"

It was silly. But both of us were smiling like kids, walking along the sidewalk.

The second chorus of the song escaped me. That worried me. Maybe early dementia was blocking my memory.

თ

Toomey's workers remembered me from the nights on Patrol. That warmed me. We ordered the traditional coffee and. She took a salad and I had eggs Benedict.

"You're smiling," Cooper said. "But you have a faraway look on your face. What is it?"

For once, I dropped wisecracks in favor of the truth.

"This food," I said. "And you, Cooper. You're drawing me back to Flatbush."

She formed a question with her face.

"These eggs Benedict, this coffee that could poison a whale, bring those Patrol nights all back to me," I said. "Patrol slung me into so many bizarre and bittersweet moments. After work, it felt as if my head would explode with all that I'd seen. That's why so many of us blast off in beer-gusher bars. We explode our families."

She cocked her head and smiled a flirty smile.

"Are you planning to explode me?" she asked.

My dollars paid the check, and we left.

თ

We walked onto Rogers Avenue.

"You put contact lenses in your eyes this morning," she said. "Can policeman wear them?"

"Some can. My eyes are terrible. I cheated on the eye exam for the Job. I shoot okay. But maybe I'm legally blind. Or close to it."

Walking off the breakfast, we cruised back to Flatbush along Maple Street.

"You see that house with the Grecian columns?" she said, pointing. "It has a wading pool alongside it. Every house on the block has a garage. Some have front lawns. This was an elegant place up until a certain time."

"I heard the many stories when I worked here," I said. "You can ask any old Flatbusher when the neighborhood started to crumble. They'll all tell you that it was 1958. That was when the Brooklyn Dodgers were sold and became the Los Angeles Dodgers."

"How was the crime here before 1958?"

"Good question. The NY Citizen's Crime Commission used to bore us with their stats. You should only trust murder numbers."

"Why is that?"

"Because victims get robbed, raped and burgled and never report it. Murder almost always gets accurately reported. The culture and the survivors insist on it."

"And what did the numbers say, Max?"

"Citywide, we suffered about 200 murders a year in the 1950s. 1960 changed all that. Murders started to soar. 300, 400 per year. The NYPD was untrained, loose, corrupt and non-responsive. Some were even *frotteurs*.

"But we still boasted some great cops. Gerry McQueen, the homicide genius. Sonny Grosso, the real brains behind and partner of Eddie 'Popeye' Egan of the French Connection, David Durk, Frank Serpico and Chief of Detectives Al Seedman. Ray Pierce of the Seven-Five Precinct.

"In seventies, it got worse. The number that disgusts me is that of all the bloody city murders, only forty percent were ever 'cleared' by an arrest for any crime. So, if you wanted to kill anyone, you had a sixty percent chance of getting away with it.

Middle-class blacks and whites fled Flatbush fast. Houses devalued. Schools closed. Ebbets Field became a city housing project."

"When did murders peak?"

"Crack exploded. In 1990, the murders hit 2,245."

"Now the media says that murders are way, way down," Cooper said. "What stopped it?"

Pausing on the sidewalk, I gave her my best candlepower smile as I did a folding ballet *plié*.

She giggled.

"You're taking credit for it?" she asked. "Just you?"

"Mayor Rudy Giuliani, Jack Maple, Police Commissioner Bill Bratton, John Miller and Tom Reppetto also helped me."

"I'll call them to thank them," she said. "But that group has no women in it."

She was tossing her head back and forth in that coquette's lighthearted way.

"And don't you try to be the first," I said. "Not in Flatbush. It takes training and instincts that you cannot attain in New Hampshire. For some reason, Flatbush is the only part of New York City that did not improve. It has stayed dangerous."

"Why?"

We were drawing closer to Flatbush Avenue. The houses grew smaller. Garages vanished.

"Ask the victims who live here," I said, jerking my chin at the Dutch-style gingerbread houses of tan and chocolate brown.

A group of black teenage boys hung out near the houses.

"Most of the folks in this neighborhood are good and innocent victims. Cops should protect them better."

I nodded at the teenagers.

"A cop should walk into that group and start a connection somehow. I did. And like I told you, I don't care a fig about skin color. Racists do."

"So do *frotteurs*," she said.

"Yes, *frotteurs* do. And when cops see kids like that group, those cats may be saints in training. Or they may be scoping out the next person to mug. You don't know until it is too late."

We were on Flatbush Avenue now.

"Can't the police arrest them for loitering?"

"Civilians always ask that. It reminds me of the enormous and widening gap between cops and civilians. The graybeards on the Supreme Court struck down the loitering law as unconstitutionally vague in 1967. Loud groups like the ACLU and CAPA watch cops for any civil rights violations. So cops have to walk way soft. Or lose their pensions. Where the devil are you bringing me, my dear?"

"Flatbush Secure," she said. A storefront echoed her words with the name on the glass window.

She entered the door and I followed. Six or seven black guards, in dark blue uniforms lounged in chairs, talking. None of them wore guns. A couple had old-fashioned wooden nightsticks hanging from their belts.

The uniforms reminded me of last night.

Nobody looked like they were on fire to fight crimes. Guards usually did not. These were older than my forty-eight years.

The uniforms looked like secondhand NYPD issue.

Some wore black dress shoes. Others wore black sneakers, trying to pass them off as uniform issue. In Patrol, I had done the same thing but with better quality shoes that responded to polish. But these guards made minimum wage and could not afford much.

A TV set was broadcasting a courtroom reality show with a Latina woman waving a diamond ring at a blond man about forty years older than her.

Across the room, a black woman in her twenties, rust-colored hair teased high on her head scanned Cooper and me.

"Mister Manry," she said. "Can you come out here, please? Friends of Flatbush here now."

A man emerged from the inner office. He wore a crisp gray suit against his black skin. His wide face was lively with bunched muscles easing into smile lines. His face drew me and made me want to like him. It was an actor's face, fast-changing and expressive.

He stood three inches over me and looked like a football player in peak condition. He weighed about my weight but with lean muscle instead of fat. Shoulders and arms bunched with power. He shook hands like he was pulling me into his world.

"Louis Manry," he said in a foreign accent. "Security Director of Flatbush Secure. Cooper, I am so sorry with the news about your friend. Please come with me to scoop up more guests and go to your Friends of Flatbush office. Got to pick up those weapons there and give them to the precinct."

Cooper glanced at me and nodded. Her eyes said that she did not trust her voice.

❧

Manry brought us outside the building.

We walked across Flatbush Avenue, then past a music store and a newsstand.

Manry opened a door beside a print shop and led us up the creaky steps to the Friends of Flatbush office.

There were about a dozen people in the room, a mixed black and white group. They wore tony casual clothes, the kind that wealthy people favored because they lasted forever. Their stances and their good teeth said that they had cash behind them. The new arrivals grouped around the now empty donut boxes.

"For everybody recent, this is Max Royster," Cooper announced. "Max was a Flatbush detective. And he can help us with our crime problems."

The crowd showed those teeth in approving smiles.

"Hold that thought," I said. "I was just a blue suit, pounding the beat, dragging that piece of plastic baton behind me. Never a detective."

"I didn't know that you were a cop," Brigden said. "It's so awful about Lutz. What do you propose to do about our crime problem?"

"I don't have enough information yet," I said. "If I want to talk about something without knowing anything about it, I'll go into politics."

Nobody smiled. This was going to be a tight crowd.

"Before we quiz Max here," a bulky black man in an orange African-style blouse said. "We've got to address the problem of squatters at Lefferts Historic House. Max, I'm Reuben Epps, one of the local boat-rockers."

"The situation is getting worse," Brigden said.

"I know," Manry said. "I'll take care of it."

"They're camping out. Trashing the grounds," Epps said. "Flatbush Secure guards that site. We can't let them filthy bums ruin a landmark building that's two hundred plus years old."

"I know all about that, too," Manry smiled a smile meant to reassure. "You won't see them after tomorrow."

"You going to gas them?" I asked.

Only Cooper heard me. She shot me a look.

"Everyone in this room suffered a loss," Epps said. "Lutz Charles used his own wit and humor to rally people to our cause, to have a decent Flatbush neighborhood again. I say that we as a group offer a $25,000 reward for information leading to the arrest and conviction of his killer."

"Absolutely," Brigden said.

The others voiced their approval.

"We got all these murders this year," Epps said. "Seventeen so far in this precinct. Other precincts around here got four or five. As some of you know, I put down a considerable part of my life's savings to get two houses on Midwood Street. I'm goddamned if I'm going to let fifteen-year-old thugs devalue my investment. With things playing out now as they are with this local reputation and these murders, I would be lucky to sell at the same price. When I call the precinct captain, he says that he's working on it. Chicken feathers, I say."

The others nodded.

"Things are getting safer," Manry said. "We making progress. You'll see fewer bad rascals around here next week."

"Why next week?" Brigden asked.

"You'll see," Manry smiled with that actor's face of his.

"Max, do you have any ideas to help us?" Epps asked.

"Yep."

"We'd like to hear them," Epps said.

"For your people that have a business here," I said, "buy a coffee machine, milk and sugar. Tell the local cops that you're selling it for a dime a cup to them. That makes it legal. Or free, if the cops are risk-takers. Hate to say it. But cops are cheap. They will be in and out of your business all day for that coffee. It's good protection that costs you very little. Believe me, you will see blue."

"Anything else?"

"Look at your home. And your neighbor's. Make sure the address is written on the door. It should be easy to read. We cops roll on your calls and spend our lives hunting for addresses at night, in stress and low-light. When you call us to your house, we got no magic way of finding it."

"But the police really do not work to protect us," Manry said. "You think that they do. Being a cop, you see us private security professionals are just unskilled trash labor."

"Untrue," I said. "I've known some minimum-wage guards who should be police commissioners. And I know some police commissioners who should be security guards."

"Those cops don't do anything!"

"How many of you know the cops who patrol your area by name?" I asked.

Two locals put up their hands.

"It helps to learn them," I said. "Socially speaking, cops are lonely. Pass them your card. Ask them what they need. Around the room here, I see people who made smart business investments before. Invest in your cop."

The room stirred.

"But we can fill the gaps," Manry said.

"I hope so. But within the law."

"The law is too slow," Epps said.

"Don't I know it? But in New York's history, some groups formed vigilante groups. The groups did what police could not or would not do."

"That's ridiculous," Brigden said in her wispy voice. "We would never condone vigilantes."

"No," I said. "Just law and order."

"You probably dislike yuppies like us," Brigden said. "Young urban professionals."

"Or call us 'buppies'," Epps said. "Black urban pros."

These nice people were starting to show their teeth and use me to clean them. I felt small and scared.

"I don't call you either name," I said.

"Certainly not *frotteurs*," Cooper said. For some reason, she seemed amused by this back-and-forth.

"The term 'Flipper' seems appropriate for you," I said. "Because you want to buy a house cheap in a dangerous area. You try to improve the neighborhood. If you do, you can sell the house or flip it for a profit."

"Is that wrong?" Epps asked.

"Look at your sign outside that says Flatbush / Lincoln / Ignatius / Parkville / Parkside / Empire / Rugby Road / St. Paul's Place. Put those words together and what do they spell?"

"FLIPPERS," Brigden said. "Hot spit! I never saw that before."

"Max, you have a sick sense of humor," Epps said.

"Can't you all be serious about our problems here?" a wispy black woman in a jogging suit asked.

"There is nothing evil about making a shrewd real estate investment," I said. "You bump into this dirty and dangerous hood and learn about the history here. Grow nostalgic about how it used to be in the 1950s. Maybe nostalgia is dangerous if you want to break laws to get it."

My eyes shifted to Manry. He should get this message.

"In the 1950s, guards COULD manhandle the homeless without getting in trouble," I said. "But you can't now, Manry."

"We only react in self-defense," Manry said.

"Glad to hear it. Then when Flatbush becomes safer, you can flip your home for five times what you paid for it. That makes you a happy Flipper, good sir.

"That helps Flatbush," Epps said. "If we can just stay alive while we're flipping the neighborhood."

CHAPTER 7.

Whispers from the Street

One Police Plaza loomed against the chalky gray sky.

Dressed in a dark blue secondhand suit from the Cancer Prevention Thrift Shop, smooth white shirt from the same tailor, borrowed bowtie and U.S. Navy shoes, I drew near the Plaza. I snapped my fingers a few times, from nerves.

Looking around and imitating the look of the Committed Professional, I slung my black nylon briefcase over a shoulder. Detectives and uniforms were trudging to the Plaza like their grandfathers had trudged to the mines.

Inside lurked danger, pals, routine, adventure and treachery. It was just like the mines.

Someone was practicing trumpet badly somewhere too close.

Garbage trucks whined near the Plaza. They were hauling shredded police files away. Maybe mine was in there.

The garbage smell floated in the air.

Two uniforms were bringing a stout black prisoner across the Plaza in handcuffs. One was a round and black with a triangular tiny beard under his chin, his name tag reading "Chase".

"He came up to me on the corner and told me to move," the prisoner was saying.

The uniforms looked young and bored by the prisoner's monologue.

"So I says, 'Listen up, slick. You ain't no cop, you just Security. I don't gotta move for y'all.' Then he shove me, and we get into it. Felt him grabbing me like for a weapon or some-thing. Then, more security, his homies, come jump on me. Call you all. And you find that crack on me right where his hand was. He planted it on me."

That got my head turned around.

"That's a new one," one uniform said. "I never heard that one before."

"Me, neither," said his partner. "Ever."

This client had some heft on him, weighing in at about 200 pounds on a six-two body frame. The heels of his tan shoes looked clean. They were not scuffed from long days walking or hanging on. Crack often burned up the user's fat.

This client did not look like a crackhead to me.

"Excuse me, officers," I said to the uniforms. "I'm Royster, off the Job. Can I speak to your collar for a minute?"

The taller uniform, brownish hair and tortoise-shell glasses shook his head. His name tag read "Benkert." His collar brass was "BSTF," "Brooklyn South Task Force."

"Sorry, cousin," Benkert said. "Sarge says process him im-mediately. Thinks that we're padding this collar for overtime."

"We are," his partner said.

"And proud of it," Benkert said. "You working PI or something, cuz?"

"Nothing that clear," I said. "Just got an interest in Brook-lyn. And guards who play cop. Where did this collar go down?"

"Talk to the bosses."

"I'm innocent!" the prisoner shouted. "This is just Throw-the-Darky-in-the Cell Day. Again."

"C'mon, Benkert," I said. "A collar is public information."

"Brooklyn," his partner said.

"I can read your collar brass," I said. "Brooklyn, where?"

"Corner of Flatbush and Erasmus Hall Place," Benkert said.

"Right by Erasmus Hall School. The guard was hanging there."

"The guard was from Flatbush Secure?" I asked.

Benkert's neck cords stiffened. I had guessed right.

"Who knows where a guard comes from?" his partner said. "Or cares?"

"That's it, cuz," Benkert said. "Have a nice day."

"I didn't have that crack on me!" the prisoner shouted.

The three walked away. Sixty feet later, I could still hear him giving out throat for his innocence.

∽

Then I called on Lipkin in his homicide task force cubbyhole.

"Good morning," he said in a hurried way. I could sense his paperwork was climbing to the sky on his desk. "Got your stuff on the Lutz kill. Whenever the hell I can, I'll be delighted to look into it. Bother the precinct."

"Do it in between shootings," I said. "Good idea. That way, you can make some new enemies."

I told him about yesterday's meeting.

"And you didn't speak up against this?" Lipkin asked. "Yuppies with cash using guards to push people around?"

"Nothing's happened yet," I said. "Just talk."

"And you got a possible new girlfriend for the first time this year," he said. "So you don't want to argue with her friends."

"Arguing never solves anything," I said.

"Even a bad Jew like me is taught to question all things," Lipkin said. "It's part of the Talmudic tradition."

"And it drives us Gentiles crazy," I said. "There are good reasons to do it. To be corny for a hot second, we have seen what happens when nobody questions authority."

Somehow it felt like Lipkin was lecturing me.

Saying that I was running late, I hung up, leaving him in his office with all his paperwork.

CHAPTER 8.

Not a Sock Salesman

Simon, my lawyer, met me on the eighth floor of the Plaza.

Simon stood small and dapper and neat and quick about himself. Something about him reminded me of the 19th century freewheeling lawyers who rode circuit on horseback and took whatever clients that they could.

Black curly hair crowded over a pale skin and flesh-toned eyeglasses. He weighed about 135 pounds and stood about five feet four inches, always dressed like a senator in dark suits and white shirts.

Two lawyers for the Job and a uniformed lieutenant named Gargulo ushered us into a cramped office filled with buff-colored folders, law books and paperback mysteries. Maybe they read them when work bored them.

My case was not important enough to tie up a conference room.

"Now, Mr. Royster, we've read your requests for reinstatement in the Department," the first lawyer said. He sported a bent nose, thick glasses and gray hair receding back into a pink scalp. The name on his desk read "Allan Frier."

Lux, the other lawyer coughed. He was as thin as a skeleton, with bulging blue eyes and hair the color of fresh mud.

"Your personnel record from the Department states that your first command was the Seven-One Precinct," Frier said.

"Do you remember stopping a car driven by a Morton Blake on Bedford Avenue and Martense Street?"

"Nossir, I don't."

My fingers snapped again, quietly now.

"Well, he remembers you, Mr. Royster. I'll read from the Internal Affairs file. 'Complainant stated that this white officer, later identified as P.O. Maxwell A. Royster of the Seven-One Precinct, pulled his vehicle over for no reason and asked the complainant for his license and registration.

"When the complainant said that he did not have his license on him but could go home, get it and bring it back to the officer. Whereupon, the officer gave Mr. Blake and Mrs. Selena Frazier what both describe as 'a prejudiced look'."

I shook my left arm because it was going numb.

Frier caught the move and frowned. He was old enough to know what it meant. The others were too young to understand it. Stress was building in my heart region right now. It was causing my left arm to get less blood and to go numb. That could trigger a heart attack. Rooms and talks like this one did that to me.

"Now I remember Mr. Blake," I said. "Please read the rest of the report."

Gargulo shook his head. He was a friendly looking guy with bright eyes in a dark complexion under a mop of black hair.

I wondered how many naive cops he had suckered with his open look before jamming them into charges. He worked the Legal Bureau, and that was sometimes how they operated.

"There is no need for that," the other lawyer said. "This speaks for itself."

"*Res ipsa loquitor*," I said. "Latin. 'This thing speaks for itself.' If you agree with that, please read the rest of it."

"Mr. Lux, I agree with my client," Simon said. "You can not introduce this document as evidence of any kind, read from it and then choose to censor it."

"No purpose would be served," Lux, the skinny one, said.

Ignoring my arm now, I swiveled to face him.

"Who decides that?" I asked. "Lieutenant, have you read this file?"

Gargulo did not answer.

"That's a bit vague," I said. "I think that we should drive on here without stopping."

"If needed," Simon said, "we can re-introduce this document in court. And you could explain to the judge just why you chose to stop at that paragraph."

Frier looked at Gargulo and Lux and got nothing back.

"'The complainant was asked to show what constituted 'a prejudiced look.' He attempted to do so for about five minutes. His companion Ms. Frazier also tried. To this officer's estimate, neither was able to demonstrate what 'a prejudiced look' was. Therefore, the charge of Racial Profiling was dismissed against this officer.'"

I sagged back against the chair.

"But it stays in my file forever," I said. "That's why cops get off Patrol and stay off. They do Crime Analysis, Lost Property, front desk, coordinate school crossing guards and other popular hiding places."

"You knew what the Job was like when you took it," Gargulo said.

"Nobody normal thinks about complainants trying to re-create 'a prejudiced look'," I said. "And the Department enabling them. Does your file say that the good Mr. Blake pled guilty to 512 VTL, Driving on a Suspended License? And the busted taillight for which I stopped him in the first place? That he also ran from me when I found a gravity knife on him, assaulted me and then pled to those two charges as well? Dame Frazier also kicked me and pled guilty to Obstructing Governmental Administration and Assault."

"I never had a Racial Profiling charge against me," Gargulo said. "And I worked the Two-Eight, in Harlem."

"I was a street cop," I said. "Not a sock salesman."

"What does that mean?"

"Means that the way to rise on the Job is to do as little as possible," I retorted "Don't make the clients unhappy. Or else they'll complain on you."

"Don't make yourself out a martyr," Lux said.

"Even with our citywide crime stats dropping," I said, "some neighborhoods have rising murder rates over last year. If you don't let good cops work, some vigilante groups like guards may try to do the work themselves."

"You mean like in Brooklyn?" Gargulo said.

It had just slipped out of his mouth. As soon as he said it, his amiable face closed up.

"Come on," I said, swiveling in on him directly. "What do you hear about Brooklyn? Where in Brooklyn?"

Gargulo looked away.

"Let's get back on track here," Lux said.

"You have other charges against you on paper," Gargulo said. "Your sergeant wrote you up for Careless Driving once, and it cost you three vacation days."

"That's me," I said. "I'm driving my RMP solo because my partner's out sick. A car comes in front. I remember it off the hot sheet as stolen. I put it on the air and try to wait for backup. But the driver sees me and bails out in Prospect Park. I stop the car and run after him. Then a fender hits my leg. It's an RMP. I look to see who is the idiot driving it. The seat is empty. It is my own car.

"The client starts laughing. Nice, smart guy turns out later. 'Po-lice run over hisself!'

"I had not fully engaged the parking gear. When I had jumped out the car was still in drive. It just kind of followed me.

"I jumped back in my car, jammed the brake, parked it and started again. The client was laughing so hard that he could not run. So I snagged him on foot. It was the only way that a guy my size could catch him.

"'Po-lice try kill himself!' he kept saying.

"At the precinct, he told my sergeant about the chase, such as it was. Sarge asked me if it were true. I said yes. He hit me with that charge then."

"You should have denied it," Lux said. "No witnesses."

"Lying to a sergeant can get you fired," I said. "You wouldn't last long on Patrol, Mr. Lux."

"Gentlemen," Simon said. "Officer Royster led the Seven-One Precinct for six months as top producer of arrests and summonses. Nine Excellent Police Duty Awards and twelve Meritorious Medals in just ten months. There were 378 officers assigned there at that time. He risked his life consistently to protect that community. Does that count for anything?"

"Some of his supervisors said that he was disruptive at roll call and at other times, seemed withdrawn and moody," Gargulo replied "They called him a 'birdie' and worried about psychological problems."

"So do I," I said. "Theirs."

"P.O. Masak said that when you rode Patrol with him, you mentioned having nightmares that had him in those same nightmares. So he sent a memo to your captain about your mental stability. He said that one time you smacked him on the lower back, for no reason. Is that true?"

"I have no idea," I said. "Football teammates do it after every good play. Did Masak think that suspicious? As I recall, he is a former Marine. Marines whack each other on the butt for fun. And I was never no Marine. He was. Maybe you should check out his psychological state."

"Once again," Simon said. "I have not seen any documented evidence that Officer Royster should not be rehired. Absolutely none. Please show it to me."

"He's just not suited for the NYPD," Frier said. "He's an oddball. A birdie. We can show that at a hearing."

"Many officers have refused to work with him," Gargulo said.

"How many?" Simon asked. "Who? And for what stated reasons? Did Max work them too hard?"

"This is just what I was told."

"You three gentlemen have the power to recommend re-hiring to the Civil Service Commission," Simon said. "What will it be?"

My breath sucked in. Simon might get them to fold right now.

I leaned forward and then back again in the chair.

All three shook their heads.

"We have to look at the big picture here," Lux said. "What if we re-hire you and you shoot some innocent civilian?"

I stared at him.

"What makes you ask that question?" I asked. "Do you know how many gun arrests I made already? I did nothing careless."

"It's something that we have to live with," Frier said.

"Then live with this," I said. "I'm not going to drive a limo, tend bar or work worthless security somewhere. I'm going to ignore this boy's softball team gossip and backstairs whispering and get my shield back."

"You can't," Gargulo said. 'It's finished."

The force was building up steam in my chest. My left arm still felt numb. I had to get out of that room.

"You just watch me," I said.

తో

Forty-five minutes later, I was out of my schoolboy suit and in my gym gear in Nancy's gym uptown, hammering the heavy bags with palm heel, bottom fist and elbow strikes. Usually, exercise and me were not easy friends.

But tonight I needed it, or I would fly apart trying to sleep.

CHAPTER 9.

Manry Lays Down His Law

Cooper drew me into the creaky doorway of her home and kissed me long and searchingly. My mouth moved in a smile. So did hers.

We re-aligned our lips.

I tried controlling the rush inside me.

Brooklyn dipped and spun all around me.

Nothing else mattered.

"This is kid stuff," I tried telling myself. "Don't put so much into this, Max. You'll just get hurt again."

I did not care.

Her kiss tasted of cinnamon.

My shoulder muscles scrunched as I move in closer and tighter to her. She did the same. We clutched each other.

Everything kept spinning.

Behind my closed eyes, an image formed; the wooden Flatbush house spinning on an oiled axis, skittering sideways and bouncing high into the sky. It kept climbing among the Italian-ice pastel colors of the universe.

Everything whirled around me.

Like swimming underwater, holding my breath as long as possible to keep seeing the dark edged beauty of the glide, I did not want it to end.

"What's going on?" I tried saying to myself again. "This is crazy."

"Cool it," the same voice said.

I ended the kiss as gently as I knew how.

We were still standing in her doorway.

"Wow," she breathed out.

I leaned against the doorframe and nodded, hangdog style, unable to put anything into words.

"For once, no wisecracks, Max?" she breathed.

My head wagged.

She grinned again.

"If I don't throw you out now, this kissing will go on all night," she said. "And I've got to study some for a conference tomorrow at eight."

ဢ

My feet brought me back down those steps and onto Lincoln Road again. But Flatbush looked different now. It seemed as smooth as a river of milkshakes, easing down my throat.

All of Brooklyn, with slam-hammer factories and quitting time whistles and screeching monster subway cars clashing steel against steel SCREECH! lay sprawled out like a city on a hill.

"Slow it, Max," I said aloud. "You're not in high school anymore. Show some maturity."

The houses passed me. They got smaller. Some apartment buildings changed the block. Then I was heading north, towards Prospect Park.

My feet felt as if I could walk all day. Moving slowly, I could go from one end of Flatbush at Empire Boulevard to the other end at Quentin Road in just two hours. Any way that I hoofed it, Flatbush was still a two-hour walk.

The air felt fresh and warm. Someone was baking bread and on the same block a sharp curry smell bloomed.

The thin fringe of Flippers and white adventurers and punk-rockers hugged Flatbush Avenue. They did not extend as far as Nostrand, not yet. Maybe they would next year.

Sharp by the park entrance on Flatbush Avenue, Lefferts Historic House stood, white wooden walls done in green trim. The plaque alongside it read "Constructed in 1783." Small vegetable gardens sprouted around it. A red brick smokehouse showed the daily life when the house had been built.

A group of homeless people, Latino, black and pink, sprawled on blankets and sleeping bags in the grounds around the house. Some hung their clothes on a steel spiked fence that surrounded the site.

Rap music bellowed from a passing sports car.

Sirens sounded, to the south.

"Don't you try climbing that fence!" a black homeless woman shouted at her son. "You'll fall and get stuck!"

Flipper-type joggers rolled past on the road, two hundred yards away.

Dogs roiled through the area, barking.

"Police officer, can I talk to you?" someone asked in a foreign accent.

The words stopped me.

I turned to see Manry, the Flatbush Secure boss, stride onto the grounds.

He did not see me observing him.

He flashed a gold shield in a black leather case. Manry wore a different business suit now, midnight blue with a red and black necktie, white dress shirt and black loafers.

Manry might be many things. But he was not a cop.

"Detective Charles Dumahel from Brooklyn South," Manry said in the bored way of cops.

It was a good imitation of how a detective identified himself to a dumb and hostile public. And nobody in Brooklyn South could check a foreign, easily mispronounced, name like "Duhamel". The command was just too big with cops rotating in and out constantly.

Anyone with some luck and fifty bucks could buy a police shield at a yard sale or on eBay. It just needed to look legit. Civilians never looked at shields anyway. Old-timer cops called a police shield "the panic button" because when you flashed it, civilians would blank out. They would remember nothing about the shield except its color.

He had chosen his hustle well. I admired it. Watching it would take just a minute of my time.

"The Lefferts House caretaker has asked you repeatedly to leave," Manry said. "Tried to show charity. But now a trespass ordinance has got signed and filed with the Brooklyn District Attorney. You got just five minutes to haul your butts off the premises."

"We've been all through this," a white, shaved-headed man in his thirties said. Dirt streaked his faded green T-shirt and crusted blue jeans. Most of his front teeth were gone. "We're represented by the legal clinic of Us-The-People. An injunction that we can stay here. Lemme show you a copy."

"Don't bother," Manry said. "Will you leave now, sir?"

"Drop dead," a squatter with a corncob pipe said.

"And do it today."

Manry shrugged and then stepped forward, swung his arm like a softball pitcher underhanded and grabbed Shavey's crotch. Manry twisted and stepped in close. Shavey yelped, hopped backwards and tried punching Manry. But Manry was in too close to hit.

"Let him go!" a black woman squatter shouted, waving a screwdriver.

"Police brutality!" a black grandfather type with a solid white beard said.

"Off the property," Manry said to Shavey. "Or else I will ruin you."

"Okay," Shavey said. "We find another spot."

Manry released him. Shavey punched Manry in the face. Manry stepped back and then forward. He slammed his fists into Shavey. Manry's arms moved like pistons, pounding into Shavey's guts.

Groaning, Shavey dropped.

Manry calling himself a cop was just wrong.

My hand took out my phone and punched in 911.

"911 Operator 582," a Latina woman's voice said. "Where is the emergency?"

My mind changed right then. I hesitated. Getting Manry arrested would hurt me with Cooper and her Flipper friends.

Street people like these squatters rarely followed up after they filed complaints. They would lose interest and drift away. Detectives could never find them for court.

"Never mind," I said into the phone. "I don't want to get involved."

"Involved in what? Where are you calling from, sir?"

"No victim, no crime," I recited from the Patrol years. "Nothing's going on paper. Sorry to waste your time. I meant to dial 411 and hit a nine by mistake."

The cellphone folded back into my jeans pocket.

"If you don't leave now, private security officers under my authority will use chemical spray on you," Manry said.

"I'd like to see that," the black grandfather-type said from the ground.

"You won't be able to," I said. "Your eyes will be swollen shut."

Manry lifted his arm.

An unmarked black van drove in the gate from Flatbush Avenue and slid the doors open. Some guards that I remembered from the Flatbush Secure storefront office jumped out of the van. They wore plainclothes with batons in their hands jumped out. One big bruiser wore a dark blue NYPD T-shirt. Anyone could buy that shirt. They ran towards the squatters.

"Look out!" a teenager squatter shouted.

"They'll kill us with those sticks!" the woman screeched.

"You're under arrest!" the guard in the NYPD T-shirt said. "Don't move!"

Everyone kept running.

One baton caught the woman's shoulder. She dodged the next one and ran past a guard swinging sideways. His stroke just missed her head. I winced.

"No batons!" Manry shouted. "Give them the gas!"

Two of his underlings obeyed. From where I stood. I could smell the familiar scent of OC Capsicum spray, a mixture of cayenne pepper and water.

The teenager caught some in his face as he charged a guard. He bent over and rubbed his eyes.

The license plate on the van that had brought the guards was taped over. I walked over to it like any other passerby. The chrome lettering was missing, but it looked like a Ford.

Using an old cop trick, I put my palm and fingers on the back panel. That way, my fingerprints would stay there until someone washed it. Later on, I could ID the van by using my own fingerprints.

Then I re-thought it. There was no way that I was getting involved in this mess. Spending an afternoon kissing Cooper on a throw rug was what I wanted now. My prints on the car would drag me into some cops-and-robbers game where nobody could win.

I wiped the prints off the car.

The squatters had already broken and run.

Guards holstered their sticks and clambered back into the van. The van lurched forward as the driver gunned the gears. They clashed.

The van bucked and shot down the avenue. It had been in and out of the scene in less than a minute, a quick and professional job. Probably Manry had planned it that way.

And my victims were all gone. Collecting them for court was impossible.

"That is so wrong!" a white youngster in punk black clothes shouted at Manry as he approached. She was rail-thin with a pierced lower lip and gold stud "You can't treat people like that."

Others stopped and stared at Manry. One whipped out a cellphone and tried to take a picture.

Manry did just what a cop would do. He turned and walked away. If he stayed to defend himself, he would be putting himself here.

Again, as a cop, I had learned and done exactly the same thing.

He crossed the sidewalk, coming closer to me.

The youngster trotted after Manry and circled in front of him.

"What's your name and badge number?" she spouted out.

Manry walked into her. She fell back against a parked car.

Manry kept walking.

My feet pulled me behind a tree. Manry seeing me here would complicate my life. And I did not want complications.

The youngster ran after Manry. She was no quitter, that was for sure. She squared off in front of him again.

He dodged her and kept walking.

"Leave him alone, little sister!" someone called from behind us. A group of locals stood near the park, still watching. "It ain't worth it!"

"You hurt that man!" she blurted at Manry.

"Those bums were making your park all dangerous for you," Manry said. "Who do you want there? Them or me?"

He was still walking fast.

The youngster fell behind. Her steps slowed, and she went towards the group in the park, dragging her feet and backhanding her own wet eyes.

CHAPTER 10.

TSoM

The next morning, I was waking up in my Manhattan apartment when my cellphone buzzed.

It was Lipkin calling me.

Something made me ignore the call. I could not put a name to it. Talking to Lipkin right now gave me a ticklish feeling.

My shoes turned different ways on the sidewalk until they pulled me into El Barrio Fight, Nancy's gym.

She was already open and was toweling herself off from a workout. Without the thick glasses, her eyes looked childishly naked.

"Mister Royster," she purred.

"I know," I said. "It's a lovey-dovey little surprise, at this time of day. This means that I have finally realized that I cannot live without you."

"Wow."

"You and your heavy bags. And your Ninjutsu wall charts on how to kill. Your two-burner stove in the back. It's the closest thing to a home that I know in Manhattan."

"I'm flattered," she said.

"I'll work out and talk," I said.

My hammer fists and palm heel strikes hit the rubber water bag that I liked. Nancy had others hanging like ruined fruit, stout leather bags older than I was.

Her morning incense smell still hung in the air. The sweat stench would come later when the gym filled up.

My words came out as I hit the bag. Nancy listened to all my prattle about Cooper, Flatbush, Manry and the Flippers.

"I'm happy that you've got someone in Flatbush," she said.

"Not yet I don't."

"But you will."

"Like you say back in Kansas, now we are both breathing hard," I said.

"Does it worry you that she works in finance, and therefore is supposed to care a lot about money?"

"Why is it that sometimes you talk like a lady hooligan and other times like a successful psychiatrist?" I asked.

"Dunno."

"We would need another headshrinker to learn why. Nancy, like a lot of folks with messy lives, you can see the mess clearly in the lives of others."

"Thanks. I suppose."

"Al Lipkin warned me about these Flippers. Maybe he's right. But if I raise any sand about what I saw, that may end Cooper and me. She may find someone her own age. Some *frotteur*."

"You told me all about *frotteurs*. That bothers you so much, Mr. Royster? What IS the age difference?"

"I'm not sure. She looks and acts about thirty. So that's eighteen years. It's an important number."

"Maybe to you. Maybe not to her."

My hands struck the bag again as I chewed that one over.

"You're not a cop anymore. So what could you have done with Manry?"

"Pointed him out to cops responding to 911. They will find his fake shield and lock him up for it."

"And what would he get for that alone? Since all the squatters had fled?"

"Get? Most likely, he's got a clean sheet. He'd plead guilty to a B Misdemeanor and get six months probation. The state might lift his guard license for a year. So he would have to put a straw man, his brother-in-law or some such, into the boss's chair for that period."

"Screwing up your love life to get him probation is dumb," Nancy said. "I wouldn't do it."

"Every shrewd bully knows how to choose their victims," I said. "Attack those who won't squeal to cops. That's what Manry did.

Those squatters may tell their ponytail Woodstock hippie lawyer about Manry. But they won't trust anyone else enough to tell them. And nobody can tag Manry or his minions for that attack."

"Except you."

"Even I can't do much. Without his victims, a desk sergeant will refuse to book Manry because there is no case."

"Gotcha," she said. "And you're worried that this group of Flippers has enough money to buy brute force and hurt more innocents? Turn fascist, like you say. What was that saying about fascism in America? 'It can't happen here.'"

"But it can," I said.

"Of course, it can. It is as close as Mexico. El Salvador. Haiti. Dictatorships always look good to the frightened ones with power."

"When I was on the Job, I stood up for all the cuckoos and Ritz Crackers who had been hurt by the system. Some of my partners and bosses hated me for it. They helped to force me off the Job. No pension, no Worker's Comp checks or disability cash. Just off."

My elbow and knee strikes hit the bag some more.

"Can you walk away from this Cooper right now?" Nancy asked. "Because you might lose your integrity later."

I spun and low-kicked the bag with my heel as hard as possible.

Her question backed me into a corner.

"No," I said. "I can't. Not now."

"That thing that you and I never talk about," she said. "And other men never, ever, talk about."

My neck muscles bunched and hummed. I could tell what was coming.

"I call it 'TSoM'," Nancy said. "The Softness of Men."

"Come on, Nancy," I said. "We all know that men are not soft. Parents tell us that from birth. Got it? Men are tough. Women are soft. My side has the beards, the big cigars, the

400-pound bench press, huge cars and the rest of it. So what does a man do if he starts to feel soft about a woman, and she changes him?"

"Stay who you are," she said. "Those damn fat boring classic lit books that I read in prison got me thinking. Book after book whined about women. Always men scribbling them books. "A man daydreams on a woman, and she softens him. Gide, Dostoevsky, Goethe and Maxim Gorky write about it. A writer suffering for his love all over the place.

"Yeats, the poet, said that his girlfriend 'hurt me into art.' Even rap music gripes about it."

"You don't mean men not getting it up, right?" I asked. "Midnight failings and such."

"You can get drugs for impotence, Mister Royster," Nancy purred. "That softness that I'm talking about is much more lasting. And more important."

❧

Flatbush drew me back again. Packs of kids roamed the stores. Some of them shoplifted and dared the store owner to try stopping them. I walked around, thinking.

I reached the Prospect Park carousel, just off Flatbush Avenue next to the zoo entrance. Beside it lay Lefferts House.

Margaret ran the carousel and heard every whisper in Flatbush, a red-headed Irish encyclopedia of all knowledge. She was built strongly and generously, her ample body filling out her Kelly green jogging suit. On her back, the shirt read: "Brooklyn Girls, Best in the World!"

To the east, someone fired off what sounded like a shotgun. By habit, my right hand went back to my hip. But there was no piece there anymore.

"Well, well, the guardian," Margaret said in her giggly happy voice, remembering me from my Patrol days. "Haven't seen you for a time, Max."

My eyes flicked to the painted wooden horses on the carousel. Telling Margaret would be tough.

"I've got to be up front with you, Margaret. I'm off the Job. Not my choice."

"Yeah?"

"The other cops probably told you already."

Her big head, with the red curls on its top, inclined.

"How you handling it?" she asked.

"This way," I said.

Then I started talking.

She had known Lutz and heard about his murder. But she had nothing new to give me. Gently, I probed some more.

"Security guards sometimes like hitting bums," I said. "Nothing new about that. Sometimes, guards are losers, Margaret. You know that. Give them an order, and they will walk on anyone they get near. They don't have much of a worldview. Like some cops I know."

Margaret smiled. Her delicate skin cracked around her cornflower blue eyes.

"If I hear anything, I'll let you know, Maxy," she said.

✿

At Toomey's, I sank a quick cup of coffee, quite light, and an English muffin, well-done, no butter. Christoforos, the bald fireplug of a man who ran the place and cooked the food, spoke to me in grunts and Greek words that sounded obscene. Skating around the issues with him, I learned a bit less than nothing.

Maybe I was just killing time until I knew where I had to go.

Trying to cool my nerves, I circled the block three times before going in.

After three, at shift change, I stepped into the Seven-One Precinct lobby off Empire Boulevard.

"Royster, Jesus," Sarge Mirpolo at the front desk said from behind his *New York Post*. "Only come across this threshold, you got a crime to report, pal."

Like many cops on the Job, Mirpolo showed strong feelings of some kind. But nobody could say what they were.

"Sarge," I said. A fixed smile stayed on my face, and I swore to keep it there, no matter what.

Mirpolo showed some teeth going black at the roots, a sagging belly that ballooned over his creaky gunbelt and a scarred hand where a crack whore had thrown acid on it.

"Maybe you better tell us why the surprise visit," Mirpolo went on. "Since we ain't seen you since you got Admin Transferred for the Good of the Service."

Mirpolo was playing it loud for the other blue suits on the desk. They had never met me before.

"Sarge, I didn't want to break you up emotionally by constant coming and going," I said. "Might be too much for you."

"Seeing you now is too much."

Again, the eyes fixed me without blinking. It was impossible to decipher what was going on behind them.

The others shifted, not sure which way to jump.

"Now I bet that you're back as a PI," Mirpolo said. "Just what we need. Another private eye shoveling for the insurance companies and wanting to look at our MV 104s for traffic accidents."

"No, Sarge. Just came by to kiss you on top of that shiny head."

"Royster!" Finnerty, a beefy sergeant came out of the roll call room, clapping fat hands. "Didn't these humps offer you coffee and? What's the Job coming to?"

"Finnerty, you Budweiser tribesman," I replied. "Very light, no sugar."

"Come here, you hump," Sgt. Finnerty said. His grip nearly took my hand off at the wrist. We left Mirpolo and the other happy crime fighters behind us.

"Give me a meat hook, you big mahoska."

Finery's smile looked like a kid's on Christmas morning. His blue eyes screwed backwards in the fair freckled skin. His hair was going white but remained thick and luxuriant.

"TV did a piece on your secret Hardy Boy-Nancy Drew group, the Playpen Irregulars," Finnerty said. "About how you help each other and solve crimes sometimes. Bunch of rich maniacs, right? But some good-looking women there, too. You the den daddy, Max?"

"Guess so."

"Sounds like something for kids that never grew up. Bring those women around here. Tell them that I want to join."

"You had a kill here, Sarge," I said. "Lutz, black do-gooder for the neighborhood."

"I read it at roll call," he said. "Other than that, I know nothing. Whaddya got?"

Telling him took a few minutes. I left out the part about Manry playing cop but told him how the Flippers had me worried.

"Sure, these SWIPpies —"

"What?"

"Silly White People — want to get their real estate killing into high gear right away," Finnerty said. "They figure that they don't got to wait patiently or nothing like that. Ordinary people got to wait. Surely not them. So they'll cut corners."

"They're doing it already," I said.

"They can't do much to foul up this neighborhood."

The coffee that we drank joined the earlier cup in my stomach lining. Together, they danced the rumble number from *West Side Story.*

"Can't friggin' help you on that kill." Finnerty said. "I'm still on Patrol, not Detectives. No files or anything coming my way."

"Royster, why don't you go haunt a house?" Piva asked from the doorway.

"How many rooms?"

Piva wore a slate-colored suit, wilting red tie and blue shirt. Finnerty made a face and set down his cup. Precinct gossips had probably told Finnerty about Piva slugging me. The Job loved gossip.

"Why are you here today?" Piva asked. "Just a coincidence or something else?"

"Why coincidence?" I asked.

"Because you remember that I liked OB, Obadiah, that mutt, for the killing of that Lutz guy," Piva said.

"Yep."

My bruises sang again as I said it.

"So I put it on the wire," Piva said. "Not a warrant, not a suspect. Just a person of interest. For the Uniforms. Pick him up and call me. Possible connection with a homicide. OB lives all over the place. Sisters seem to love this brother. He's a ladies man. Women everywhere."

"He's probably never soft," I said.

"Yeah, sure," Piva said. "But dudes hate him. Always giving him up for everything bad. So me and Funzio hit a couple of his haunts. Get snake eyes. Nobody knows nothing. Except that OB's packing a big gun now. Like a Desert Eagle or a custom .45 job with a ventilated rib barrel. Takes heavy slugs, go right through our vests. Royster, you remember Lott Place, off Church Avenue?"

"Yeah."

"Two rookies rolling by in an RMP spot someone they think is OB. But they're not sure. So they don't call it in."

"Uh-oh," I said.

"They give him a good lead and then pull in behind him," Piva continued. "Why the hell they got rookies working together in a precinct like this beats me. So when they pull up, they don't shout 'Police! Don't move!' They got the flyer that downtown put out. Names, nicknames, all the description.

"They shout out, 'Hey, OB!' So he knows that they want HIM. And not some other perp. So he runs. So they chase him. On foot. They never called it in."

"Brave," I muttered.

"OB goes to ground real fast in a vacant lot. They stumble into it. OB pops up and runs. But now they see that he's digging inside his pants for something big and trying to run at the same time.

"One hollers 'Gun!' when he sees OB haul a big black semi-auto pistol out of his pants. They both shoot. They shoot a lot. They do this just as OB throws the gun thirty-five feet away. Their bullets tear him up and smack him down.

"They check the vitals and OB is deader than a mackerel and gone to whatever reward was awaiting him. Then it hits them, that maybe this was not great police tactics, going after him alone.

"But they call the Precinct and the Precinct calls me. So does the captain. Because the big black gun was a Desert Eagle all right. But it was a kid's BB gun, with the orange safety barrel painted black just to scare people. OB always carried it, and it did indeed scare the bejeezus out of people. But it got him rendered very dead by our two rookies."

"Oh, hell," I said. "Don't tell me that."

I sank down on a broken chair, feeling broken by the news.

"OB had a release slip in his wallet. It was from Nassau County jail, outside the city. Seems that OB was locked up there the night Lutz got killed. They don't like him in Nassau, either.

So OB was not our killer. Our champ is still out there, living it up. And the media and Internal Affairs are going to drive the Department nuts over this shoot. The IAB rats are coming over tonight to grill me just like I had fired those shots.

Don't be around for them, Royster. Favor for me, okay? You're a civvy. You're allowed to disappear. We're not. So take off, Royster. And don't come back."

"Don't worry," I said. "I can do that. You all just watch me vanish. Right now."

CHAPTER 11.

Getting Muscled

Cooper's hair lay across my chest on the bed. I breathed in it.

She was just letting me sleep alongside her now. She wore black Chinese pajamas with white piping, and I covered my body with a joke tie-dye T-shirt that came down to my knees.

My body might look too old to her, too pouchy and hefty and defeated. The best bet was to win her mind over with friendship and whatever wisdom that I could plagiarize from adults. By the time that I won her over, I hoped that my body would not matter so much.

My phone buzzed.

It was just after ten on Saturday morning. Lipkin was calling me. With him at this hour, it would be important.

"Okay," I said into the phone. "I'll get a job tomorrow. I promise."

"I don't want to talk on the phone," Lipkin's boyish high voice came through. "Gimme a corner."

"Bedford and Maple."

"Ten minutes," he said and killed the phone.

"Hey," I said to Cooper. "Al Lipkin wants me to get out of bed. He must have heat stroke."

❧

It was a gray morning with a hint of rain in the air. One corner of Bedford and Maple had a stately old corner house with a stone lion on the front porch. I waited for Lipkin and noted the cars going past.

"Hey, you got any spare change?" a boy's voice asked me.

Turning, I saw a group of teenage boys all around me. They crowded against me. Hands were coming up near my beltline, where the wallet was.

"Not again!" I said. "Déjà vu all over again."

My legs shook. I was scared and caught flatfooted.

"Get that money, homes!" one of them shouted.

I dodged one guy and stepped onto Bedford Avenue. Another grabbed my shirt. I went with his pull, put him off balance and slammed him into his closest buddy. But there were too many of them.

Brakes squealed in front of me.

"He's driving at us, yo!" one shouted.

"Crazy man!"

Lipkin stopped his car and stood up in the open car door.

"Police!" he shouted. "Don't move!"

His right hand flew backwards to the hip holster.

The kids exploded like a bomb and ran down Maple Street, zigzagging. One yanked a nickel-plated gun from his pants and pointed it our way.

"Al! Gun!"

Lipkin had his hand on the .38, still in the holster.

"I see him," Lipkin said. "Don't sweat it."

The gunman and the group vanished down Maple Street, heading to Rogers Avenue.

Lipkin blew out a breath and took his hand from under his business suit.

"No sweat, because I knew that he couldn't hit me first," Lipkin said. "Experienced cop keeps the gun holstered until he gotta draw it. Rookies draw quick, maybe shoot too soon. Often hit the wrong guy."

"You bet your life," I said.

"This is the hood that you're trying to turn all nice and polite?" he asked me. "What's that word? Gentrify?"

"That's the word, Al."

I blew out a breath and sagged against his car.

"Takes a certain kind of dumb to run from a cop and THEN decide that you just have to wave your piece at him," Lipkin said. "Just like OB Obadiah did with those two rookies. Must be a new fad or something. Run and then draw. Silly."

"I dunno."

"Hope the fad passes without any more killings. Especially with a toy gun. The Brooklyn District Attorney and the media are screaming that OB's shooting looks like an assassination."

"It sure does," I said. "Like he wanted to assassinate himself."

"Flatbush is way uptight about it," Lipkin said. "Speeches and ultimatums."

He palmed his cellphone and called in a description of the group and the gunman to the 911 operator.

"I'll be at the Precinct in twenty to do up the report," he said into the phone. He snapped it shut.

"I don't want an RMP responding here and seeing you and me talking," he said. "So I'll keep you out of the report. You'll just be a nobody."

"That sounds truthful," I said. "Thanks for the backup, Al. They had me boxed."

He looked irritated in his dark blue suit.

"Boxed is what you're going to be if you keep playing around in this neighborhood," he said. "Remember that I danced with your friend Cooper that night at the church."

"I forgot that."

"She's beautiful, yeah. But you don't get something for nothing. She'll use what she's got to box you in is what I'm saying."

My fingers snapped. Right now, Lipkin looked old and crusty to my eyes. My nerves still clashed and jangled from the kids grabbing at me.

"That's enough of that, big brother," I said. "You're sore vexing me with that warning about Cooper."

My voice sounded like someone else's. He took me in with those same eyes that missed nothing at scenes of slaughter.

"You want back on the Job?" he asked. "This ain't the way."

"The Lutz kill, Al. Whaddya got?"

"This one is deep and dark, Max. You didn't get this from me. They're clamping down on leaks and taking things very serious at HQ."

"They always do. Give."

"Lutz was hit on the left thigh with a long stick or club of some kind. There was skin damage and bruising. It happened just before he died. The Medical Examiner can tell by the tissue damage and blood flow."

"The stick could have been a police-issue baton," I said.

"Probably was. We both agree that that chase of the mugger and Lutz's death are related. Nine RMPs responded to look for the mugger. Six guards admit driving or running around looking for him."

"Who got mugged?"

"The usual. Black female living at 74 Empire Boulevard. She was coming home way late in a gypsy cab because her daughter had been in a car accident in Rockaway.

"The mugger jumped her, smacked her down and grabbed her purse right by the construction site on Washington Avenue. Flatbush Secure guard was working that construction site. He saw the mugging, ran after the mutt and shouted it over his radio. Flatbush Secure guards started to play cop. They rolled in on jeeps. One called 911."

"And then chaos took over."

"Yup," he said. "Everyone running everywhere. I guess that the mugger skated away clean. At night, Flatbush Secure uniforms look like NYPD. If you're a drunk, how would you know?

"Someone came on Lutz, who'd been boozing it up with his friends in a gin mill on Rogers Avenue. Pretty well hammered, they said. If some running sweating security guard or cop told came galloping up to him and tried to freeze him, he was probably too drunk to obey. His BAC was .17."

"We know that .10 is the legal limit," I said. "He might have tried running. The baton goes across his thigh. BAM!"

It was a standard police tactic. Instructors taught it to me in the Academy. It is supposed to shock the common peroneal nerve in the thigh. Otherwise, cops get scared and swing for the head. If they connect, they can kill the client.

"So they wanted to shock the leg nerve so that he drops. Except this time, he fell down into a car bumper with his head first."

"The kill was for sure an accident," Lipkin said. "From what we know now. Like I said, a rookie cop or a guard moves too fast sometimes. Uses too much force. That probably happened here. Maybe somebody wrote 'OB' to shift blame on our poor dead pal OB and off himself. Nobody liked OB. Too damn violent.

"Everyone is covering up. All the cops say that they never left their cars. That sounds right. I mean, would you jump out of your RMP to foot-chase a mugger in this precinct at night? It's not worth it. You get hurt bad enough, the Job will try to throw you off without a penny, saying that you violated procedure."

"I've been all up and down that street," I said.

"We both hate to point a finger at cops. Or even security guards. I mean, some are slobs, for sure. But they do hairy, dangerous work for minimum wage and try to do the right thing. I've gotten good tips from them on cases. So I got nothing against guards."

"Me, neither. I just want to stay away from them."

Lipkin looked down Maple Street where the gunman and his group had gone and said a bad word.

"Gang like that make it so easy to be afraid of black kids," I said. "So homeowners throw money at the problem. Gated communities, card access, maybe pushing black families out of the area."

Lipkin shook his head, angled himself back in the un-marked car and headed out of the parking space towards the Precinct.

"If I'm lucky," I chanted to myself, "I will get right back to where I was, in bed with Cooper."

And I did.

❧

Wrapped up in Cooper's scent and feeling of her body against mine, my heart slowed down after the kids had grabbed me. Patiently, I waited for my body to unkink.

"Why is your heart beating so fast?" Cooper murmured.

"Doctors call heart attacks 'the policeman's disease'," I said. "That's because we cops leap from sitting in a car to racing up six flights of stairs on a regular basis. The ballistic vest, Sam Browne belt, backup gun and Department clodhopper shoes weigh us all down. And most cops, like your humble servant here, weigh too much. The average American man dies at seventy-four years of age. At fifty-nine, the average U.S. cop goes to his reward. "

"That's frightening," Cooper said.

"Might be the bean counter strategy to reduce pension costs."

"Somebody should do something."

"You are. For me."

With these lighthearted thoughts, my body sank deeper into the pool that was Cooper.

Another cellphone buzzed.

Cooper sat up, slipped away from me and snagged her mother-of-pearl cellphone case and slid the phone out. The sleeping teenage beauty changed into Today's Woman Executive.

"That could be a crank call," I mumbled, still groggy.

"Hush."

"Or a telemarketer."

"Swenson," she said, snapping out her last name like a Marine command in the war against poverty. "Uh-huh. Go ahead."

"I spend half my life listening to other people's phone calls," I mumbled into the pillow.

"Yes, he's right here," she said.

"Who, me?"

She waved her free hand.

"You got another man stashed around here in some broom closet somewhere?" I asked. "I'm the only one that I see."

"Yes, we'll be right there," she said and snapped the phone shut.

"That must be the editorial 'we'," I grumbled. "I'm not planning to be right there anywhere."

"That was Brigden."

"Breathless Brigden."

"There's an emergency meeting of the group in a half hour," she said. "They specifically asked for you to be there."

"Really? I'm flattered. But maybe I could specifically ask to spend more time lolling with you here in bed."

"Plenty of time to rest when you're old and decrepit, Max."

The world "old" got me to my feet.

That age thing should not be an issue between us.

For a second, I thought about the softness of men. Nancy's face and TSoM floated before me.

I rolled to my feet and acted jolly about it because I wanted Cooper to owe me later on today. Maybe we could become lovers.

ひと

Twenty minutes and some brisk walking later, we came across the triangle formed by Flatbush and Washington Avenues. A blue-and-white city sign read "Lloyd Sealey Square".

"Hey, I know that name," I said. "Never noticed the sign before. Sealey was a boss on the Job. One of the first black cops to promote to high rank when the Job started growing up. Fought for black cops to promote. He must have lived here."

Check-cash places, fried chicken joints and liquor stores reminded me that the neighborhood was struggling against odds. Boarded-up storefronts indicated shops that had gone under. Between Prospect Park here and Brooklyn College, four miles away, no bookstore existed. If the Flippers got what they wanted in improving the area, one might open soon.

ひと

In their office, the Flippers had gathered around the snack table.

Standing in a corner, Breathless Brigden stretched her slim and full-breasted frame into yoga poses while the men tried not to get caught ogling her.

Skip was dominating the room.

"You and I need to speak a bit before this meeting," Skip said. "Let's grab us some privacy, shall we? Over here?"

These were not questions. Skip was used to obedience.

We put twelve feet between us and the nearest Flipper.

"I've managed to get some properties in this neighborhood," he said. "I'm a crazy damn baseball nut, you might say. As a kid in Harlem, I always wanted to see Ebbets Field where Jackie Robinson and the Brooklyn Dodgers first cracked the color line in 1947."

"Here comes more of that Flatbush nostalgia," I said.

"How true, baby. But we all suffer from it. We know that this hood is a forgotten paradise. Used to be white and crime-free. And I be a stone hustler. Out for ME! So I dig on that old nostalgia, enjoy it and try to pass some on to the next newcomer."

"Someone like me."

"When I first waddled myself here, I figured to see plaques put up by the Government. Should be dozens of National Historic Landmark houses protected here. Only three. Ebbets Field oughta have a museum for it, like the baseball Hall of Fame in Cooperstown, New York. And not just baseball.

"Look at the celebrities from this neighborhood. Barbra Streisand, Rudy Giuliani, Neil Diamond, Eli Wallach and Neil Sedaka. New Jersey Governor Christine Todd Whitman grew up down the block at 109 Maple Street. But no plaques nowhere. Ain't no neighborhood pride.

"And I don't hate us black people who are living here now. We all God's children. But they can't like living here either. 'cause it slid into a high-crime, dirty and dangerous neighborhood. With not one swinging dick walking these streets after dark except the crack gangs. Why I need your help."

"Uh-oh," I said, trying to break up his rhythm. "But I ain't got no MONEY."

"That's okay," he said. "I have."

"That's okay for you."

"Want to give some to you," he said.

"You have my full attention, sir."

"Among other things, I own Flatbush Secure Guard and Patrol Service. You've met my Director of Security, Louis Manry."

"Yessir. And seen him in action."

"Louis got some damn family crisis in Haiti. He's leaving tonight. I did some checking and I want you as my Acting Director of Security until he returns in a few months."

Shock stepped me back.

Skip looked sane and serious but he might be neither.

He had command presence. His way of talking made me think that it was real life calling.

"No, thanks," I said.

"Why not?"

"Because private security does nothing. Guards are minimum wage losers. Everything they touch turns to cowflop."

"We do something, Max baby. Fixed and mobile patrols, on foot and in vans. Radios that go right to your 911 system. Seven of our forty-four men got gun carry permits. Eighteen more are pending."

"It's just not for me, Skip."

"I repeating myself but you sure impress the group. Flippers, like you say. So I ran a quick check on you. Everything says that you could use the money."

"Pal, that's as plain as the dick on a moose," I said.

"I'm a hard man to work for, I know. Raise all kinds of sand and cuss and run around calling on Jesus for help. Help me now, Jesus! What did you like about being a cop?"

"Putting my body out there to help innocents," I said. "Changing lives by locking up wife-beaters who had been bullying the world for years. Excuse the cleesh, but I liked doing good."

"You can do good with us. Join our team."

"I'm trying to shoehorn my way back into the NYPD."

"Cool, baby, cool. If they call you, go. And we part as mother-trucking good friends."

"If your guards baton the wrong guy, that guy will sue your company and me personally," I said. "That will gack up what's remaining of my life."

"We've got mammy-jumping solid lawyers behind us, Max. Including me. Sixteen years in the guard business and nobody has collected a shiny dime from us. You are pro-tected."

"Your guards got a rep for being heavy-handed," I said. I was feeling my way. I wondered what Skip was thinking. "How did Manry deal with that?"

"Got no idea. But if you take this job, they won't be 'your guards' anymore. They will be Max Royster's men. Discipline them mammy-jammer fools the way that you think is best."

Skip walked to the bathroom door and tore it open.

"Hey, Louie Manry!" Skip wailed. "Don't go, Louie! Come back, Louie! Max ain't sure."

The bathroom yawned empty.

"Attention, everybody!" Brigden said. "Mr. Epps just called to say that he's running late. Traffic on the Belt Parkway. The meeting is postponed until five. Go get coffee or something and return here at five, please."

"There's your half-time intermission," Skip said. "Go rap it over with your girlfriend. And we'll have to pay you something, a police expert like you."

"I'm only an expert in getting beaten up."

"I'll pay three times your police salary, Max. Want you to think long and hard about how that money can help you."

Cooper looked askance at me when I asked her to walk with me.

⌘

We drew ourselves towards Prospect Park as I told her about Skip's offer.

"Ohhh, Max, take it," she breathed. "Before he changes his mind."

Excitement pushed more color into her face. Her changing expressions always fascinated me.

"I'm no timekeeper for loudmouth loser guards enforcing company policy."

"What are you doing with your life right now, Max?"

"Enjoying our walk."

"And where do you see yourself in five years? What are your long-range career goals?"

"Rob a bank," I said, "and run away with you to Brazil. No extradition treaty there."

"Max, be serious."

"Didn't I tell you?"

We were entering Prospect Park by the Carousel now. Margaret was taking tickets and placing kids on the painted wooden horses. She waved to me. I brought Cooper over, introduced her and left them to talk while I called Simon on the phone.

He always had time to speak with clients. That was rare for a New York lawyer.

When he heard about my job offer, he spoke his mind.

"If you take this job," he said, "it will make things so much easier to get you back into the Department. You'll show stability. Responsibility. Someone trusting you. A state license for security. All their question marks about you will dry up and wither away. Take this job, Max. You can't afford not to."

"Thanks for your time, Counselor. I'll let you know."

Margaret and Cooper were enjoying their chat, but Cooper grabbed my arm and pulled me with her.

We walked past the Lefferts House, where Manry had slugged the guy.

Some homeless folks still lay on the grass. They must have returned after the fracas.

Cooper's face exhilarated me again.

"Max, you say that guards are losers. But they probably had loser bosses. You could teach them, lead from the front and change their lives."

"Do you know what security guards need to have in New York?" I asked.

"A lot of training?"

"Forty hours worth. No felony convictions. That's all. You can boast twenty misdemeanors for beating others up or carrying knives and still become a guard. Guards have absolutely no power beyond a regular citizen's ability to arrest for a crime done in their presence."

"Max, everyone knows that Flatbush is a hard and dangerous place to live for anyone, white or black. But we are starting a food co-op next month. Already a literacy program, a community vegetable garden to get the locals away from sugar and lard. Still, people are afraid to walk to anywhere after dark. You and your guards could help Flatbush to where the streets were safer. Think about what you could do with that idea."

She put her body against mine.

"Working together for that common goal would bring us closer together," she whispered. "That is the kind of bond that only gets stronger with time. You know that I'm renting, but I want to buy. Can't you join me in this adventure?"

CHAPTER 12.

Off-the-Wall Free Hand

"Skip, if I take this job, I need a free hand," I told him. "I run the agency my way. My system. If someone is helping us, he gets a better deal because of it. If he is hurting us, he gets a chance to improve. If not, he goes. Okay?"

"Just what I want to hear!" Skip roared. His actor's voice climbed. "We got Ted doing payroll and assignments. I'll run around cussing like crazy. Calling on Jesus to help us. You just keep the flipping things running."

"No," I said.

Skip's eyes flicked over me.

"I'll keep things improving," I said. "It won't be like it was under Manry. We'll all do better."

"Then it's a deal," Skip said.

We shook hands on it like Lewis and Clark agreeing to explore the Louisiana Purchase.

He passed me keys and a cellphone. It struck me that he must have figured that I would accept it.

"All the guards are black or Latino, right?" I asked.

"Yep."

"Somehow, I don't want to look like the white overseer on the plantation," I said. "The politics are all wrong on that. I'll try interesting some whitey-type guys in part-time jobs with us."

"A white guard will have a tough row to hoe on some of our sites."

"Oh, yeah?" I asked. "Aren't we going to try gentrifying Flatbush?"

Back in the meeting, Cooper hugged me. Her breasts and her twisty-muscled arms thrust against my thicker frame.

"Max is now running the guards!" Cooper announced to her Flipper friends. "Watch him make Flatbush safe!"

The other Flippers clapped in a restrained kind of way. They did not know what they were getting into.

Neither did I.

ↄ

That night, Cooper and I celebrated in the Lincoln Road Tavern off Flatbush Avenue. It was the hangout for the slim, tattooed white adventurers who were renting here. They were too young to buy or to care much about it. They walked a dangerous, shaky gangplank through this neighborhood.

"It's like the Old West," I said over shrimp scampi and mussels and white wine.

"We're pioneers," said Cooper.

"You're settlers. Pioneers are the guys with arrows in their backs. And each of you settlers pushes a little bit farther into the wilderness than the one who came before him."

"And you think that we are crazy for doing it?" Cooper asked.

"In those same days, some settlers came by boat from Europe and never lived more than three miles from where their boat docked. My own family didn't move far. Others explored the frontier of upstate New York or Pennsylvania. That was their unknown then."

"And Flatbush is the unknown now?" she asked.

"To these twenty-two-year olds waiting tables or working as bike messengers, yes. They gamble their lives for cheap rent because the safe neighborhoods cost too much now."

"You and I are going to make things safe," she said.

That night, we held onto each other and kissed. It felt like high school, when the kisses had seemed to go on forever and ever. My blood pounded. It felt like hers did, too. We clutched each other until our bodies cooled.

Nancy would probably say something about The Softness of Men.

ↄ

The next morning, Cooper woke me with kisses and her espresso and pancakes. She seemed captivated by her own morning routine.

Dressed in a root beer-colored pantsuit, she was quickly out the door and churning towards her office in Manhattan.

I had different values. I went back to bed.

My cellphone buzzed.

"Baby, Maxy!" Skip's voice cracked in my ear. "The DMV called me about that baby that you left in their waiting room yesterday. They know it's your baby, because they showed the baby to all them New York driver's licenses and that baby picked out yours! And I don't know how you got that little baby, 'cause he got nappy hair!"

My hand closed the phone.

The phone buzzed again. My ear went to it.

"He got nappy hair!" Skip roared.

❧

By eight-thirty, I was up and shaving.

Skip had left me another voicemail. This one was serious. Maybe an adult was listening.

"Max, can you get into our office around noon?" Skip asked. "I'll be there, preparing them for their new boss."

So I rolled over to Toomey's. In the kitchen, Christoforos, singing Greek songs to himself, flipped skillets.

"Good morning, Tabitha," I said to the waitress. "A ham steak, two fried eggs, biscuits and gravy and keep the coffee coming."

Gently nuzzling for information about the Lutz kill, I got nothing new. They had heard street talk about it and that was all.

❧

Flatbush Secure had about nine sites within walking distance of Toomey's.

My clothes that day were an old blue denim work shirt with white snap buttons and older jeans and suede desert boots.

Manry had always worn a suit. But he was black, and I was white. It was bad enough for me to have pink skin and red hair and green eyes. The guards should not see me as another

– 92 –

empty suit sucking up to the power structure. So I would dress rough, like they dressed. One of Manry's suits was a month's salary for a guard.

Flatbush Secure should know that there was a new sheriff in town now.

∾

Skip walked me around the other Flatbush Secure sites.

We first stopped at the Maple Street Academy near Prospect Park. Our guard was a round black man with a lisp who kept sucking on a cold briar pipe.

The next site was the famous Erasmus Hall School on Flatbush Avenue. Skip introduced me as the new boss.

The guard was a full-bodied Latina woman in her forties in the dark blue Flatbush Secure uniform.

I noted that she carried a baton in a leather holder on her belt, next to a tear gas canister. So she had probably been working security for a long time to acquire those toys.

Even in a school, she might need to swing on somebody. Abusive boyfriends or husbands often showed up at schools to snatch children or beat up a mother.

She even wore the eight-point police hat on top of her curls. It was the identical issue to the NYPD uniform hat. But this one had the same square flat badge as the one on her chest. The badge read "Flatbush Secure" with a three-digit number.

"It is time to go badge-shopping," I told Skip. "We at Flatbush Secure need better badges. I'm going to inspire us."

With Skip clucking disapproval, we drove to a police supply store near Atlantic Avenue. I ordered a handful of six-pointed gold star badges, three inches across. They shone like jewelry.

While Skip chatted on his cell-phone, an idea hit me, and I ordered special design lettering for the badges and had them shipped to our office. They might take a while.

These badges would surprise Skip.

∾

Skip left me and rolled back towards the office.

My next site was the Food Castle on Church Avenue. Inside the store, the guard was a skinny black guy who did not look twenty-one years old, the minimum age required for a guard job. But he was old enough to be unshaven, with a three-day beard growth under the toothpick he was rolling in his yap. He did not wear a Sam Browne belt, just a thin, dark cheapie one to hold up his pants. No equipment hung on it. He was new fish. Judging by his uniform and beard, he was just along for the ride.

"Excuse me, sir," I said to him. "Do you know what time the market closes?"

He looked at me, sniffed and walked away.

Then I went to a construction site on Winthrop Street and New York Avenue. This was one of the tougher blocks and I scanned the corners and saw knots of kids hanging out, eye-balling everybody who passed by.

"Hey, mister," one voice asked from behind me. "You got any spare change?"

Sweat sponged me. I kept walking.

Sneakers flopped closer.

I stepped fast to my left, spun around with both hands ready and legs bent.

"No," I said. "No change."

Three kids stopped and looked me over. My stomach turned upside down.

They turned away, back to their pals on the corner.

"These are times that try men's souls," I said aloud. "Pardon the cleesh."

But they were too far away to hear. And they were too young to have heard that expression before.

Six or seven workers were digging out a large square hole at the construction site. A squat yellow tractor lay perched above the hole. Water and mud lay mixed in the bottom of the pit. God only knew what they were trying to build here. Maybe it was a slam hammer factory.

There was no guard here. I scanned the site and the street and checked my printed list. The address was right. There were no other construction sites nearby.

So I sauntered across the street to a rundown superette. They had only candy and soda and other junk.

A black teenage girl sat at the register, reading a hardcover book. Bulletproof glass protected her in a wide sheet.

"Do you see anything that you want?" she asked.

"It's a bit pricey here," I said. "Three dollars for that soda? I'm a poor man."

She sighed and put down the book. Fat softened her face and her body in her red dress. Her hair was pulled back in a severe style, highlighting her arched eyebrows.

Her book was entitled David Hume's Philosophy.

"My uncle's store," she said. A city accent flavored her words. She spoke primly, just the same.

"Like a lot of places in the hood, he can't get insurance of any kind. Too many holdups, suspicious fires. Around here, owners insure their stores to the max and then torch them for the money. They call it 'Jewish lightning.'"

"Not refined, my dear," I said. "What would David Hume say about that anti-Jewish expression?"

"David Hume never encountered anything like these damn fools running around here, robbing stores for twenty dollars and all the beer they can run with. Prices gotta be high. Wholesalers don't wanna be dealing with us. Gotta buy our merchandise at the supermarket on Rogers and then sling the crap on our shelves at a markup price. The only way that we can break even."

❧

Back across the street, I sipped on the overpriced Yoo Hoo soda and scanned the street for the Flatbush Secure guard. Workers kept digging in the pit and shouting back and forth.

After twenty-odd minutes, a guard came back with a paper sack of fast food. He was a black guy with a crown of hair standing up three inches above his forehead. His uniform hat dangled on the wooden baton on his belt. Muscles ran from his neck and down onto his thick arms in the short-sleeve uniform shirt. A trim moustache hung above the proud mouth.

"Good morning, sir," I said. "Do you work for Flatbush Secure?"

He ignored me and walked onto the construction site, easing under the safety rope.

"Let's try again," I said. "Sir, do you work for that Flatbush Secure guard agency?"

He opened up the food sack. A smell of hot grease turned me hungry.

"Listen, partner," I said. "If I want someone to ignore me, I'll get married."

He took out a handful of French fries and started chewing them. I felt like I was in a three-reeler comedy film from the Golden Age of Hollywood.

"Are you working here?" I asked. "Or you just stopped by to see if they switched chefs?"

"Man, I don't be playing with you," he said in a Caribbean accent. "Leave me alone."

This was liable to be a thorny employer-employee discussion. So I struggled for the high ground.

"Sir, your uniform says 'Flatbush Secure'," I said. "My name is Max Royster, and I am the new Director of Security at Flatbush Secure. What is your name?"

He asked me to perform an acrobatic act.

"I couldn't find you here for a while," I said. "Did you have a medical emergency of some kind?"

"Man, I was right here."

"Did you tell Flatbush Secure that you would be off the site for a while and needed a replacement?"

"Why, man? I never left!"

This game was fast running into sudden-death overtime. His face was closing up and squinting at me.

I sighed and stepped away from him. Nerves made my fingers play pianos in the air. The phone number to the Flatbush Secure office was busy. There was no tape message.

"Name-plates for every guard," I said aloud. "And a phone message tape. Our hero has things to do."

᠀

It was close to noon as I walked along Nostrand Avenue.

Flatbush Secure finally answered the phone. I introduced myself, made some requests and kept watching the streets and alleyways as I walked.

My phone heated in my hand as I called Nancy and a few others, asking for white guys and women who might need to work as guards. Nobody seemed to be jumping at the chance.

Nostrand had more closed-up storefronts than Flatbush Avenue. It felt like the area had given up. Small restaurants hung on next to churches for the Haitian refugees. They had French names like Église de Dieu or Jesus, Notre Seigneur. More packs of kids hung out on street corners.

Skip was standing outside the office, puffing on a thick cigar.

"We've got our work cut out for ourselves securing Flatbush," I said. "I just walked around Nostrand. It looks worse than when I was worked Patrol here."

"Recessions, big and small, keep smacking us in our shorts here," he said. "That's why I cuss so much. Call on Jesus to help us. C'mere, Jesus!"

"Skip, I'm jumpy sometimes. It's easy to fear every black kid that approaches me."

"The Flatbush revitalization area starts on this corner," he said. "Flatbush Avenue and Lincoln Road. New cafes and businesses. Kids starting them, white and black. But the further you walk from this intersection, the more dangerous and lonely the streets get."

"No pink boys walking those streets near Nostrand," I said. "They know that some muggers will jump them because of skin color. The old reliable."

"Just thieves."

"Just thieves who had their fathers, grandfathers and uncles jumped because they were black," I said. "That's the thing on the street about payback. The man always comes around."

"My Lord, Max, but you talk damn funny for a cop."

Skip brought me inside the office again. A paunchy black man with sideburns going into a moustache sat behind a desk. Half-moon glasses rested on his pug nose. A gold tooth winked into a smile of cautious greeting.

He wore a loose, light green polo shirt and khaki pants.

"This is Ted, our timekeeper and office manager," Skip said.

"Mr. Royster," Ted said in a deep voice that came up from his beer belly.

"Just 'Max' is fine, Ted," I said.

"I do it for the respect, sir," Ted said.

"Thank you for that, Ted. But we'll deal with respect later. Right now, we've still got plenty of other things to do. Like get this company into better shape. Who was that guard at the construction site who was absent and would not give me his name?"

"Alvin Cobb."

"Thanks. What's your policy on breaks?"

"Cobb ain't supposed to leave that funky old site. From six a.m. to three p.m., he just gotta be there. Supposed to bring his own lunch and use the Porta-Potty just like the construction guys. It's too far for us to send a replacement on foot for his lunch."

"Thanks, Ted. Going to change that, please. Starting tomorrow, have one of our vans bring a relief there at the same time that the construction cats knock off for lunch."

"Why do you want to do that?" Ted asked.

"Well, Ted, what do you think? Aren't nine hours kind of a long time to be stuck on a sixty-foot construction site for five days a week? Might the guard get a little antsy and want to jump the fence?"

"He can't."

"But he did."

"We'll lose money," Ted said.

"I can feel it happening."

A few guards sat in their office chairs, listening to this. Some of them had been with Manry chasing the squatters at Lefferts House.

It was time to bring that up before my nerve left me. Hopefully, my voice would not crack during my speech.

"Good morning, everybody," I said.

Nobody saluted. Nobody cheered.

"Like you all know, my name is Max Royster and I'm the acting boss here. I'm going to get you better uniforms, better equipment and more pay for staying with the company longer."

Skip looked up at that. This surprised him.

"You officers do a dangerous and difficult job in this neighborhood," I went on. "And you deserve better than you've been getting. Every month, you will sit down in complete privacy with a psychologist, Dr. Sunick, and talk with her about your troubles."

"Max," Skip said.

"She's doing it *pro bono* and will not charge us a penny," I said. "And these interviews are not voluntary. They are mandatory. Under New York State law, they will be completely confidential. It is the best and cheapest way that I know to head off trouble in a job like this. Have any of you ever sat down with a psychologist or psychiatrist before?"

"In the Army," a grizzled big-chested guard said.

"Thanks. What's your name?"

"Lynn Martin, boss."

"The name is Max. Thanks, Lynn. That experience with the headshrinker, did it kill you?"

Martin shook his head.

"Right, Lynn. And neither will Dr. Sunick. She's a good listener. You'll enjoy talking with her. I promise you."

"We'll have to talk about this, Max," Skip said.

"Sure. Dr. Sunick will make general recommendations to me about what we can do to make us all happier. Since it is required of everyone, nobody can point a finger at you. Nobody will lose their reputation sitting down with the doc. You need to do it to keep your jobs."

"There are legal problems with that, Max," Skip said.

"Not if everyone agrees to try it. Hey, do you guys like women?"

A few nodded. One smiled.

"So you get a free session with a nice lady who listens to your troubles and is trained to help you. Does that hurt you? Usually, the way I look, I have to pay a barmaid-type woman heavy bread for her to listen to my troubles. And leave a tip. This way is cheaper."

Nobody laughed. But their uniformed bodies relaxed a bit.

"Let's call my time here 'The New Deal', like President Roosevelt's program in the Depression. In my New Deal, nobody breaks the law anymore. Not one single law. No pushing anyone off a street corner."

Their bodies tensed.

"Because the other day, I was at that old Lefferts House in the park," I went on.

The room turned dead quiet.

"I saw something that I did not like to see. My memory for faces is pretty good. Any day now, I could start remembering who was there, so let us leave yesterday alone. Tomorrow is what matters now. We don't search anyone unless we have them on a citizen's arrest. We don't use teargas or our batons unless it is self defense."

"Man," a gangly young man in the back row said. "This is just so much whiteman bullcrap."

"You tired of working here, Rindall?" Ted asked. "Is that it?"

"Hold that cleesh, Ted," I said. "I'm here to learn today."

"From him?" Ted asked.

Skip growled. Ted noticed it and flinched.

I turned to Rindall and pitched my voice low so it would not shake. Because I felt like a fool.

"This is my first day in school, sir," I said. "So can you break that down for me?"

"We black and making minimum wage here in Flat-bush," he said, twisting to face me. "We got no schooling and no skills and nothing going on. Most of us got some light-weight record keeping us out of good jobs. And I'm tired of this job anyway. Degrading, man. Boss tell us to do something, we got to do it or get fired. Boss don't want to hear about no laws. Boss just say, 'Do it.'"

The guards nodded.

"Can you give me an example?" I asked.

"Manry, he got his orders from those whitebreads in that citizen's group," he said. He had a long head, lantern jaw and prominent Adam's apple, just above the open uniform shirt collar. Like Skip, he had a good face, made for a comedian. He looked like someone who enjoyed laughing. But he was not laughing now.

"They don't care about us," he said. "And they don't care about us black fools growed up in this hood. They just move in, buy a home cheap and want to sell it for more money. And they tell us not to let brothers or sisters hang on their block corner. Search them for drugs or weapons. Gas or hit them with the stick, they give us some lip. Or get near they kids or their precious cars. You the first one talking about laws and stuff. Manry, he just say, 'Do it. I the boss.'"

"Good that you brought that up," I said. "I don't really care what Manry told you to do. You're lucky that nobody complained on you to the cops. Guards can't move people off a public street or search them. And, Rindall, I want you to stick around and try this job my way. Following the laws. You may like it more. Like yourself more."

"Man, I like myself just fine. Got my food catering thing going on, hitting parties and bars on the weekends. I don't need this jive-time job."

"Yes, you do," I said. "Medical and dental benefits after ninety days. You don't get that as a caterer. But I can give you some really strong reasons to obey the laws so long as you work here."

"I don't care."

"Okay. But you brave enough to listen to the reasons? You got the stones for that?"

He nodded and sat back in his chair.

"Thanks," I said. Today was fast turning into a soup sandwich. It was not what I had expected. "One, obey the laws because if you don't, the cops might arrest you."

"Again?" he said. And he cracked a wide happy smile, like a rascally little kid.

Some of the others smiled as well. He was the class clown.

"If they arrest you, they may slam you down into Riker's Island jail for a few months," I said. "I was a cop. And I know that Riker's is not where you want to be, locked down with crazies who set their mothers on fire and rapists who want to teach you a new kind of sex you never before considered.

"Two, the person whose rights you violated may sue. Don't need to be smart or well-read to do it. Lawyers hang out in courtrooms just to find people like that. They get a judgment against you, they can attach your salary for the next seven years. So you pay them instead of you getting paid.

"Three, obey the law because if I find you breaking it, I will fire you. To protect myself and the company, I gotta do it. Otherwise, Flatbush Secure gets sued and has to shut down. If that happens, I will find you, serve papers on you and sue you myself for breaking our rules and causing me all this grief. How do you like those reasons?"

The guards just sat there, taking it in.

Skip looked very unhappy. I might have the shortest career in the history of private security.

"Ted, you want to see me?" someone asked from the doorway.

It was the same guard from the construction site, the one who had left the site open and then lied to me about it.

Ted motioned towards me with his thumb.

"Cobb, this is Mr. Royster, our new boss," Ted said. "Mr. Royster, Alvin Cobb."

"Ted, man, why you tell me, come in here?" Cobb asked. "Send that fat tub of crap Morgan to replace me today! Embarrass me in front of everybody at the site."

"Mr. Royster's orders, Cobb," Ted said.

"You Royster, man?" Cobb asked me.

"Yup."

BAAM! The back of my head hit. It hurt.

I was on the office floor. Cobb had slugged me. He came back in. He punched downwards.

It caught my mouth. I fell back again.

"Cobb! Knock it off!" someone shouted.

Maybe Cobb thought that he meant my head. Because he tried to knock that off. Another punch hit me.

I threw a jab from the floor. My foot kicked out at his leg. He toppled down on top of me. He weighed a lot. And it was solid muscle. He probably lifted whenever life confused him. Maybe that was daily.

We collided with a desk. It barked my spine. The nerves screamed. I was learning about my new office on my first day.

Cobb grabbed my throat and cocked his other hand. I grabbed his wrist and elbow, locked them and spun him into the wall. The noise hurt my back more. The wall shook. A plaque from the Citizen's Group came down onto his head.

The plaque hurt him more than my jab had. He jumped up, shouting in a thick Island patois. The words came too fast for me to understand them but then he was back out the door and running helter-skelter down Flatbush Avenue, with his heels kicking up high behind his still shouting mouth.

Skip, Ted and the guards looked at me lying bloody-mouthed from his punches on the floor of my new career.

"If I can stand up," I said, "I'm taking a long lunch at home. In a nice hot bath-tub. Because today is my first day in school, where I learned about the golden opportunities in my new career in private security."

CHAPTER 13.

Bathing

The bathroom had dark brown wood trim along the walls and sink and a floor of square white tiles. A wide mirror above the sink reflected us, mistress and man.

Cooper's hands cupped warm water and pooled it onto my bruises.

"Between Brother Piva and Alvin Cobb, I'm becoming a walking and breathing bruise," I said.

More warm water caressed my body. We were inside her bathroom and for some reason whispering like children.

"This is the first time that I've been inside my lady's private bath," I said. "It is an honor."

"Seven rooms and two bathrooms on this floor indicate that a wealthy Flatbush family owned this house," she said.

"More Flipper talk."

"I mean, isn't this a bargain, compared to what you get in Manhattan?" she asked.

"My little Flipper, can't you just admire," I paused for effect as the warm water coined and dribbled over my flanks, "the Body?"

"Oh, but I do," she cooed. "You look much bigger stripped than you do wearing clothes."

Faure's "Pavane" played from her dining room stereo.

The bathtub was generously built, with metal claw feet, deeper than any that I'd ever been in. Scents of perfumed soap hung in the air. Cooper wore a rose-colored bathrobe that I had not seen before.

"And you're real natural, Max. I said 'strip', and you just stripped and fell into the tub, looking more dead than alive. A lot of men would have been too shy or put on shorts. But I like that in you. 'Strip,' I said, and you stripped."

"Like a manly love slave who fears his beauteous mistress's wrath," I whispered.

The music spun as the water eddied and lapped.

"Brigden called me," she said. "Some squatters went on camera to say that the police violated a restraining order and threw them out of that old house in Prospect Park."

My soapy head came up. The shoulder fell back against the tub, stinging my wounds.

"The police deny it. Isn't that just like them?" she asked.

"Not necessarily."

"The police went on camera to deny it," she said. "But they're lying. You can tell by their faces, Brigden says."

If I spoke up about Manry and his guards, I could clear the cops. But Brigden and Cooper and all the other immediate-police-experts would think that I was lying to protect my old partners in the Seven-One, buddies like Police Officer Piva.

"You Flippers wanted them out of that place," I said.

"But not this way. We wanted them to leave peacefully, of their own accord, once they saw that they had to."

"They couldn't do that, Cooper. They're squatters. They've been reasonable and peaceful in other places. That's how they wind up on the street."

"Now they can go into a shelter."

That shut me up. Nobody was going to believe that I had seen Manry run them off and then sat on the story for days.

"Penny for your thoughts?" she said.

"You would talk money. I never took a job for it before."

"And you have not done so now. You took this job to change lives."

"At a cheerful salary," I said. "I look into the eyes of so many well-dressed and educated New Yorkers who have sold themselves for a good salary. And they are screaming in their sleep."

"Oh, hush, Max. Instead of going to Haiti or Nicaragua to rescue poor people, you're doing it right here in your birth city. And facing much more danger. It takes a special kind of man to do that, Max. My special kind of man."

"You, my sweet, are a harsh Yankee mistress. Not for nothing do they call New Hampshire 'the Granite State'. These bruises are my poisoned blood turning black under skin tissues done dead by trauma."

"That's not exactly medically true," she intoned.

"But it feels medically true. How many other contusions and abrasions do you count, my Yankee taskmistress, and may we well recall who inveigled me into this painful line of employment?"

"There are others, it's true. But the good news is that I can't tell if they are new marks from today or from when that policeman manhandled you. So, that's a good thing, isn't it?"

"It means that since I started with you on this Flatbush adventure, stalwart muscular warriors of our police and security forces deem it fitting to beat me on a regular basis. This likes me not a whit, to quote the Bard."

"What bar are you talking about, Max?"

"Bard. B-A-R-D. Shakespeare. The wordsmith of our mother tongue. But I don't think that there is room for him and me in this bathtub at the same time."

"I used to think that I had ugly hands," she said. "Made for sports and rock-climbing and stuff like that and not much else. I did all those yuppie sports. But look at the mitts on you."

Perfumed soap creamed along my flanks. My thighs braced against the tub wall. Water thrashed.

"Yes," she said. "Sweet."

Then it was full dark. We lay naked in her bed. We made love.

"Max," she kept whispering. "My Max."

⌖

Daylight streaked the sky outside her window.

I felt like a happy teenager again. My bruises ground against her immaculate sheets.

We thrashed against each other again.

⌖

Then I was floating along the Flatbush sidewalks towards my second day in the new job. Trees waved overhead on the morning breeze, making me remember other love affairs that had started on mornings like this.

Maybe Cooper was using all this to bring me into her idea that I should be the Great White Daddy, teaching poor black guards how to climb society's ladder as Flatbush enriched all who touched it.

It was also possible that I should start thinking like a teenage lover again and not like a fired street cop.

Pink joggers passed. Cooper jogged every day.

White Flippers were noticeable on the sidewalks, heading to the subway station on Lincoln Road. Skip had been right. Lincoln Road and Flatbush Avenue was the center of the new adventurers here. It was Flipper Central.

Ted looked up when I entered the Flatbush Secure office. His face indicated that down through the years, he had seen do-gooders and idea-men come and go. Ted and I were probably going to lock horns pretty soon.

A black woman with stylish red hair and a strict look gazed at me as I came in.

"Mr. Royster, this is Chantal," Ted said, pointing to the woman. "She will be temping with us for a bit here."

"Welcome aboard, Chantal," I said. "It's only my second day, so we're both new fish here."

Chantal did not smile. Her grip was brief and hard. Maybe she saw me as a white taskmaster riding horseback high up on the plantation.

But neither of them was going to dent my morning's feeling.

Four guards were in the office on standby. That meant they could relieve guards on meal or handle the sites for whoever called in sick. Business was looking up.

"Alright, where do I take over here?" a voice said from the doorway. "Where's the Man-with-the-Plan?"

Six feet two inches and 260 pounds of pale white man filled the doorway. Thick glasses, one end taped together, bobbled dangerously around innocent and injured baby blues. He always looked unjustly accused. His mouth hung halfway open, showing a fat pink tongue lying upon bright white teeth. His thin arms and beer belly showed the notoriously beery body of Irish New Yorkers, the ones I called the Budweiser Tribe.

"Who are you, man?" Ted asked from his desk. His hand cradled a tear gas canister on the desk.

"Captain Murray here!" the white man bellowed like he was shouting down a football field.

"You from the precinct?"

"Me? Naw! The real Job! TBTA!"

"What is TBTA?"

"The cops are New York's Finest," he sputtered, store-teeth wobbling, "the firefighters are New York's Bravest, Corrections Boldest, Sanitation Strongest and the TBTA is New York's Feistiest."

"I'm not sure that 'feistiest' is a real word," I said. "Chantal and Ted, meet Captain Patso Murray of the NYC Triborough Bridge and Tunnel Authority or TBTA."

Chantal's frown sharpened, if that were possible. Ted made pop eyes of surprise.

"And," Patso went on without taking a breath, "the Taxi and Limousine Commission Inspectors are New York's Yellowest, the Park Rangers are New York's Greenest and the District Attorney Investigators are the Loneliest. Because nobody knows who the Investigators are."

"Man, who ARE you?" Ted said.

"Are you quite through there, Captain?" I asked. "Because we've got a business to run. Ted, throw this, uh, character an application and two fingerprint cards, please."

"He's going to work HERE?" Ted asked.

"Why not?" Patso asked. "Don't you hire honkies?"

Chantal whipped her swivel chair around and faced the wall. Then she went into our unisex bathroom. Ted looked after her and tapped a finger against his skull three times.

Patso looked at the bathroom door.

"Is it me?" he asked. "Did I say something wrong?"

"Naw," I said. "She's just a cool one. Very dry. Maybe after work tonight, she will go home, pound down a quart of whiskey and bounce off the walls screaming."

"Like to see that," Patso said.

"How can you work here and still be a captain in whatever the hell that bridge and tunnel thing is?" Ted asked.

"I'm retired off on three-quarters pay from a back injury," Patso said.

My eyes popped.

"Don't make that face at me," Patso snapped. "It's a legitimate LOD —"

"What?" Ted asked.

"— Line-of-Duty injury."

"Ted, that same week of the back injury Patso went upstate to see a back specialist in Albany. And he lost all his luggage on the railway."

"How did that happen?" Ted asked.

"The cork came out of the bottle," I said.

"Go ahead," Patso said. "Make jokes. But I'm here to work!"

"Sure you are," I said. "All you ever wanted was an honest week's pay for an honest day's work."

"You got any recent references?" Ted asked.

Patso screwed up his face as if the question were an insult.

"From the Police Commissioner, His Honor the Mayor, Brooklyn Borough President and then down from there," he said.

"Don't you guys on the bridges and things just take money and fares for the bridges and tunnels and crap?" Ted asked.

Pat's barstool face flamed. He stamped to his feet and opened his green-and-red Hawaiian print shirt. His enormous stomach, covered with orange wisps growing like coir, the fiber on coconut hulls, boasted a wide belly button and knife scars. A chrome revolver with a six-inch barrel and mother-of-pearl grips was jammed crosswise into a suede holster in the waistband of his bluejeans. A gold shield reading "Captain – TBTA" was clipped to his belt.

"We are peace officers under New York State law," Patso said. "With the same authority and power as FBI agents."

"Bet the FBI doesn't know that," I said.

"We protect America's bridges and tunnels against another terrorist attack," Patso said. "You know how easy it is to shut down Manhattan's exits and entrances by bombs? We enforce all laws there. Sergeants and above carry guns. We have shotguns, assault rifles, SWAT teams, K-9 and everything else that we need. 1,545 of our officers make about 8,000 arrests a year. Pal, I could tell you stories."

"And he's going to," I said. "Over an adult beverage or two."

"Now, wait a minute," Patso said. He sounded wronged. "You're giving me the old razz."

"On second thought, fingerprint him later, Ted," I said. "Right now, I want some training time with my officers. In my office."

Four guards, three in their forties and one looking about twenty-six, sat on folding chairs in my afterthought of an office. Patso caught my nod to sit in the middle of their group.

My new office held a desk, phone, laptop computer and six walkie-talkies in a green-lit charger. The bookshelf was empty except for a few old Brooklyn Yellow Pages and some Chinese restaurant menus. That was going to change.

But the office was big enough for me to pace comfortably.

"Like you all saw," I said, "Patso here is going to join us as a guard. I asked him to. He brings some experience in policing to the table. But he is a guard, just like you. In this outfit, we all help each other and learn from each other."

Nobody stood up and cheered.

"I don't know names yet," I said. "I'm ordering nameplates for each officer. Can you tell me your names now?"

Nobody moved. This might be tough. The biggest guard, black union-plan eyeglasses, a double chin and hands like shovels, nodded.

"I'm Jacky Hart," he said. "But everyone calls me Mugsy."

"Thanks, Mugsy," I said.

Nobody else spoke.

It was time to let that one go.

"Today I'll be talking about the laws of arrest and civil rights," I said. "Who can tell me what the power of arrest means to security guards like us?"

Nobody reacted.

I had to bridge another gap.

"We got none," I said. "We can only make a citizen's arrest. And if we are wrong, watch out. We can go to state prison for Unlawful Restraint. And get sued. So we need to learn this stuff."

A few minutes later, as I was still teaching, the youngest guard wearing ripped black shoes, yawned and stretched.

"This is some dry stuff," he said, like one of the trouble-makers in a classroom. "And those people paying us don't care what we do."

"Thanks for sharing that," I said, like a California hot-tub guru. "Can you give us an example?"

"Man over at that new restaurant, Porto DiSicilia, says to keep the panhandlers away from his customers," he said. "Doesn't care how we do it. So I move them off Flatbush Ave and have them keep walking."

Patso scowled.

"You can't do that," I said. "It's a public street."

"Me and my man grab a panhandler, and I put a choke-hold on him," the guard said. "If he moves wrong, I can snap his windpipe. My man sometimes finds crack on these fools. So we can make a citizen's arrest. One less fool on Flatbush. And then the restaurant feeds us for free in their kitchen."

Blood gushed to my head. I tried to speak slowly.

"Even NYPD cops cannot use a chokehold," I said. "It's forbidden. Because it is too easy to kill someone by accident. And what is your probable cause for that search? You can't arrest him until you find it. Knock that off before you get in a real jam."

"I don't care. That wop food is good."

"Hey, Mr. Royster?" another guard asked. "I know we are getting paid because we on standby and all. But could you teach us something else? This stuff is boring."

The others nodded.

This was mutiny time.

CHAPTER 14.

Beating and Streeting

It was time for Our Hero to take a deep breath and re-think things.

"SOOO. Okay?" I raised my voice to street level. The guards shut up. "You're bored with law. Sounds logical to me. Who is a fighter here?"

They looked at me and then at each other. Patso smirked. He knew the routine.

"You serious, man?" Mugsy asked me.

Speech patterns were starting to change around me. Most of the black men that I knew now, no matter what their spot in life, seemed to use the term "man" a lot.

White men who used the term were either youngsters or trying to sound that way. Or else they were holding down jobs like musician or bartender that demanded a certain amount of cool. They could chew that term all day, and it fit.

"I'm serious as road-kill," I said. "Some of you carry batons on your posts. Some'll even get gun permits for some sites. But fighting can save your life. You all know that. So who here is good with their hands or feet when the flop hits the fan?"

"Why do we got to be good fighters?" another guard asked. Gold glasses winked over full cheeks on his face. He was starting a moustache. I stopped. My hands played piano in the air again.

"Man, this is boring."

"If I bore anyone today, chalk it up to my second day here. You all heard what happened to me here on my first day."

Mugsy did not smile.

They were forgetting that I was the boss. My face felt hot. The small mirror nailed to my wall showed my face as red. Today was making me go cold and hot.

Patso sat in his chair against the wall and watched. He was in one of his quiet periods. I knew those periods well. But they never lasted long.

"Why do you come off like that?" the young guard asked.

"I boxed a lot without a headguard as a kid," I said. "Maybe took too many shots to the brain. What's your name, partner?"

"Root. Tommy Root."

"Tommy, can you show us any fighting stuff?"

"Nope. I just know, use everything that you got."

"Who has been in a lot of fights?" I asked.

Another guard raised his hand. He had sharp chin over a skinny neck, and his skin had a reddish tinge.

"It come to me," he said. "My parents kind of fell apart from each other, and I got state-raised in different places. Check it out. Show up, one of the homeboys going to try you out, take your stuff and try to punk you. Check it out."

"Down South?" I asked.

He shook his head.

"Rochester, New York," he said. "Up by the Canadian border."

"Boss man, whoever, your questions are all jacked," Root said. "Makes me ask you one. You think that we're all from the plantation down South? What a bore, what a bore. How many black people do you know? And don't count the ones that you worked with or the sisters that you see-duced. Just black folks that you made a decision, hang with them, apart from sex or work. Give me a number?"

Nothing moved in my office.

Nancy's words about The Softness of Men came back to me.

"Okay, okay," I said. "For the purpose of today's class, I admit that I have a lot to learn. And guess who is going to teach me? And who has the responsibility for what I learn?"

They looked at each other.

"Congratulations," I said. "You thought that you were brothers. But now you are all the fathers of a 220-pound baby son. Of the white skin variety. You and I are now security guards. We don't get respect. We are in about the same position that cops were a hundred years ago. They were supposed to be dumb illiterate losers with sticks and guns."

"But we got no guns!"

"New Yorkers needed cops," I said, "but did not trust, respect or like them.

"Bachelor Number One from Rochester, what do they call you?"

"Andy Gentry," the man with the sharp chin said.

"Okay, Andy," I said. "Can you show us what you learned fighting?"

Gentry stood up. He was lanky but muscled through the chest and arms. He looked to be about forty-five and fast in the clinches.

Someone was watching TV news in the office outside. Cigarette smoke flowed into my office..

"You got power in close," he said. "So do this only when you are right up against the dude. Put your arm hard against your own rib cage. Check it out. Elbow points down. Make a tight fist. Keep your arm against your ribs. You move, your arm stays locked against your side."

"Why do you do it like that?" Root asked.

"For power. If y'all moves the arm away, you lose power," Gentry said.

"Then it is arm punching," Mugsy said. "No power in arm punching, bro."

This was getting better. They were learning from each other. Maybe we could all form a team.

"Your fist hangs tight at the top of your shoulder," Gentry went on. "You see your target. Can be the head, ribs or belly. Then you spin your whole upper body towards it."

"Is that where you get that power?" Mugsy asked. "Right on. Dig, you do not move that fist off your shoulder any more than you gotta. Your body twists to give y'all that power. Twist as much as you can. That's more punching power. Stand up and try it on someone's shoulder."

"Or use this instead," I said and took an old Yellow Pages from the shelf. "I don't have to tell you."

"No, you don't," Root said. "That's cool. We know enough not to hit each other's head thisaway."

Gentry demonstrated on Mugsy, who held the Yellow Pages at jaw level. His fist stayed at the top of his shoulder. He spun his body towards the phonebook.

His fist smacked the Yellow Pages. My bruises felt it. Mugsy stepped back two paces from the blow.

"They call that 'the shovel hook'," Gentry said. "Use your whole upper body to push that fist at your bad rascal that you want to put down. Takes practice."

"But do it hit hard?" Mugsy asked.

"You guys ever figure out many fights you been in?" I asked again.

"Me," Gentry said. "State picked me up at six years old. Moved me to different homes. It was like riding on the boxing circuit. So figure two or three fights a week."

"Until when?"

"Until I got out on my own."

"I mean, how old were you?"

"Eighteen."

"Me, I don't play that," Root said. "I just box at the PAL sometimes. Do three or four sparring deals."

"How often for you, Root?" I asked.

"Like I said, three or four times a month."

"I never get in no fights," the unknown guard said. His face was slack, with jowls, over a strong chin and a bull neck. His hair was almost gone and forgotten. "No arguments, neither. Because it takes two fools to have an argument. I just tend my patch."

"Wise man," I said. "What's your name, wise man?"

"Mark Piker. Nothing bothers me unless it's in my face."

"I had fights in high school," Mugsy said. "But no real ones since. It's too dangerous. You don't know what these fools are carrying these days."

"Right on time with that," Root said. "Hey, boss man, you going to give your friend here all the good guard jobs? The ones where you can sit and read the paper and don't have to stand up all the time? What a bore, what a bore."

Root's words shocked me. I could not react.

Patso just shook his head and smiled. He seemed content to sit and watch.

"Everyone works the same here," I managed to say. "Whether he's my friend or not. Who do you think that I am, anyway?"

"Mister Charley on the plantation," Root said. He laughed. So did the others. "Whiteman up there on the horse, making good money, watching us poor fools working on our feet in the hot sun."

CHAPTER 15.

Time to Call a Man
Who Knows a Man
Who Knows a Man

In the middle of the night, I woke up in Cooper's arms, felt her smooth legs with the soles of my feet and kicked back, half dreaming and half remembering from the Patrol years.

The dream wafted over me.

Ↄↄ

We first saw the car together, on Flatbush and Empire Boulevard. It was a green Toyota Prius.

"Hot one," Santo Randino said. He bounced inside the NYPD blue uniform. "Gotta be stolen."

I was driving.

My driving was terrible. I did not want to chase a car.

"Check it," I said.

He read the plate over the air.

"Negative, Seven-One David," the radio said. "10-17, not reported stolen."

"Oh, yeah?" Randino said. His lion-colored mane of hair seemed to stand up whenever he got mad. "That Brooklyn South dispatcher, she trying to get my gonads twisted or what, the way she talks?"

Then he thumbed the siren control.

The siren growled.

The Prius bucked forward.

"Jackpot!" Randino shouted.

The Prius straightened out and zoomed down Empire. I cussed and tried to follow. The old RMP cop car shimmied whenever I pushed it over thirty-five miles an hour.

It shook like crazy now.

But we could not stop.

"The owner didn't report it stolen!" Randino shouted. "Or else, they're hauling crack or guns in it right now. They won't stop for us!"

They did not.

I felt like throwing up. We coursed up and down quiet Flatbush streets. The Prius kept pulling ahead of me. Randino got on the radio.

The Prius ripped through Flatbush. It reached the train tracks in East New York. Then the engine quit.

Randino jumped out of our car. He pulled out his Glock. I was still braking. Randino reached through the driver's side window and yanked the client out. The client's ankles barked the window frame on the way out.

Randino slung him down, dropped his knee on his face and holstered. I ran up and cuffed him. So far, okay.

A train whistle blew.

"Get that car off the tracks," I said. "Or we'll cause a train wreck."

Randino stuffed the client in our RMP. I tried starting the Prius. No deal. Randino ran back and tried pushing it. I helped.

The train whistle blew closer.

Both of us pushed harder. The Prius stayed on the tracks.

Sgt. Wynn's RMP flashed over from the street. He was a screamer.

"What's the matter with you?" Wynn wailed. "That car gets hurt, I'm suspending you both!"

He parked and screamed some more. We kept pushing.

The train's headlight showed.

The Prius moved a bit. Then a few inches.

"Don't stop now!" Randino shouted. "You do, I'll bite your skull! I'll rip your lungs out!"

We pushed the Prius to safety.

The train whistle screamed past.

"How could you be so goddamn dumb stopping him?" Sgt. Wynn said.

"Hey, Sarge –"

"Shut up, fool," Wynn said. "You talk when I'm through talking. What do you have between your ears? Bacon fat? I never saw anything so stupid in my life. You two characters are in a lot of trouble."

The train hit the emergency brakes. It rocked. Metal squealed. It slid to a stop and smacked Wynn's RMP.

Wynn screamed like a ruptured platypus.

He stood right next to us. The train pushed his RMP aside. The RMP's grille buckled.

"Sarge, you parked on the tracks!" Randino said. "We tried to tell you!"

"You tried to jam me up!" Wynn shouted. "I'm telling the captain and Internal Affairs that you told me to park there! I hate this funky black Flatbush hood and all you funky cops here! I want Kew Gardens, Queens! I'll get you fired, Royster! You, too, Randino! Get me out of Flatbush!"

☙

Waking that Saturday morning, the same feeling bruised me.

"Get me out of Flatbush!" Sgt. Wynn had screamed.

January would come and end my chances.

Even looking at Cooper, still lovely and twisted in sleep, did not distract me.

My cellphone was cold in my hand as I punched in a number.

"I know it's early," I said into the phone. "It's time for you to call a man who knows a man who knows a man who knows a man. Tell him that I'm ready for a sit-down."

Thinking about the ambiance of the Flatbush Secure office, I dressed in a dark blue lightweight shirt, blue jeans and ripple-soled running shoes.

That day was Saturday and Cooper stayed asleep for a change. On a workday, she would blast out of bed to exercise, shower, dress and kiss slumbering old me. Then she would whip together her breakfast of pancakes and espresso. After that, she jogged.

Pressing a kiss on her cheek, I was cheered to see her smile in her half-sleep, knowing that it was Max.

Then she opened her eyes, saw me and smiled again.

"Remember what we talked about last night," she murmured. "I want you to move in with me."

I swallowed hard.

"I remember," I said. "It is very fast for that kind of decision."

"Maybe," she mumbled. "But I conduct my private life by my rules. Not those of some clueless relationship counselor."

∽

Flatbush looked innocent and clean this morning. The trees met over my head. It had rained during the night, and a floating carpet of twigs crusted Lincoln Road. Feeling light-hearted, I still scanned the street corners for clients and crossed Lloyd Sealey Square. Metal gates covered the line of stores that were still closed for the night. A reggae shop sold flame-colored shirts with the Ethiopian Lion of Judah design. Music flowed out of speakers. The song made me want to dance.

Skip was inside the Flatbush Secure storefront. Ted was plowing through *The New York Post*. Patso, my White Man rep, was just going out for his breakfast. He nodded at me. Drinkers like Patso often woke up crumbled and quiet from the night before.

"For an owner, you are working too hard at being here all the time," I said to Skip.

"Good morning," he said. "Did anyone mention a dress code to you?"

"They better not."

"When you were a detective, what did you say when the Department enforced their regulations?"

"Told them to go sandpaper a monkey."

"Are you going through life that way?" he asked.

"So far."

"Has that been easy for you?"

"Not yet," I said. "But the other way is impossible."

Ted kept farming the newspapers with his eyes, wetting a thumb to the page corners.

"Remember that I never made detective," I said. "Just another Budweiser tribesman struggling through life in the blue."

"Ted is Management, Max," Skip said. "So we can surely speak in front of him."

Ted just kept reading.

"These promises that you make to the men —"

"We have women working here, too."

Skip took off his wire-rim glasses and spun them in his hands.

"Max, baby, anyone ever rap that you can be exasperating?" he asked.

"Three times a day. After meals."

"Max. Come here, Jesus! Walk with me!" Skip waved a fat hand. "Max, do you want this job?"

"Only if I can improve conditions and the guards' lives. Sure, I need the job. But I'll keep my word. I'm corny that way. If you want an empty suit or horseholder to agree to everything that you say, I can give you some names. Lots of them."

Ted kept checking *The Post* for typos.

"We can't run no cotton-picking replacements for when guards take them their foods," Skip said. "Gas alone would ruin us."

"Can we think about them taking the bus, then?" I asked. "There must be some way. If you stick a guard on post for nine hours, you'll have him playing hooky like my good friend Alvin Cobb did. Uniforms are too costly to change right now. I agree with you.

"Badges — I am doing something about. Training, too. This may be a dead-end job for most but I want our guards to feel proud about working here. That starts with us treating them better than the other guard companies treat their workers."

"You stone crazy. You need Jesus to help you get straight. Like I wrote in that essay for my Bible class. Come back, Louie! But your idea about visiting that Thorazine-shufflin' shrink is just so wiggy nuts."

"Is it? Do big corporations have Employee Assistance Counselors to keep their workers happy and productive? The two go hand-in-hand. You think that those companies do that just to be nice?"

"No," he said. "They does it to stop burnout."

"And the depression that follows burnout," I said. "And low morale. Tossing down the beers more than you used to. Arguments. Toxic relationships. Reduced productivity. And then they worry when their lowest-level employee shows up at the Christmas party to show off his brand-new deer rifle and then demonstrates how it works, blasting holes in upper management livers."

"Guard work be so different, Max."

"Don't agree. If I ever get to be a police chief somewhere, which this morning seems highly unlikely, I'll order the same therapy. Each employee confers with the wizard once a month. Problems will require more talk or referrals to other pros. Wouldn't you want to be the first security agency to take that step?"

"Wackenhut, Pinkerton, Allied-Barton and the other guard services might laugh at us, Max."

"They would be after me with a net."

"And a pay increase? I am the damn money tree?" He wiggled his hands like branches. "Just come and pluck me."

"Guard agencies don't want to pay a penny more than they have to," I said. "So they keep repeating the same problems for decades. The cycle continues. You challenged me to break that cycle."

"I did?"

"Maybe I challenged me. Anyway, the challenge is there. Maybe someday, we can have a Flatbush Secure Family Day over by the Prospect Park Carousel. Hot dogs, ice cream and balloons. We will get to know our workers better that way. Because, whether we want to or not, we better learn about them."

"We'll have to see about that," Skip said. "Know what will cost us? Louie! Max is making me crazy! Lordy, lordy!"

"Sure. These are new ideas in security," I said. "Ted, what do you think?"

Ted looked up from his paper, breathed out and leaned back.

"It's all bullshit," he said.

Patso returned with a huge take-out bag of food.

"That uniform does something for you, Patso," I said. "Gives you stature. Command presence."

"I better not try commanding nobody around here," he whispered. His baby blues rolled. "You and I are the minority around here."

"It's sure going to be fun watching you adapt to black America."

"You, too."

∽

That day only two guards came in to pick up their paychecks. Feeling looser, I ran through a quick class on the law-of-arrest and avoided any sticky topics like whites and blacks.

"I'm going down to the library and check some law books," I told Skip and Ted. "Be back soon."

"I'm going at three myself," Skip said. "Like you said, I be working around here too much. Just wanted to kind of get your pink butt launched."

"I'm launched," I said. "At something."

∽

I had lied to Skip. There was no library in my plans.

Instead I took the #4 train to the Brooklyn Borough Hall Courthouse.

I scanned the crowds around the public squares. The area was packed and hot.

My own nerves steamed my body under the shirt. What I was doing now could wreck my life.

CHAPTER 16.

When The Man Comes Around

Modern surveillance could track someone through a crowded street.

So I went through the criminals and their counselors, the beaten-down government employees, the hopeful applications twice. I zigzagged to the gray stone Municipal Building. Then walked down six flights of stairs. The hand-rubbed wooden railings felt sweaty in the heat.

On the seventh flight down, I tapped on a fire door. A round-faced oldish man with a pate of cream-colored hair opened it. Well-dressed for today's Brooklyn, he wore a three-piece charcoal gray suit. Across his lay a gold chain with the ring of a secret society. The tang of cheap aftershave wafted from him.

"Nice of you to come by," he said. His voice was whispery, perhaps from a childhood illness. To me, it sounded pitched for backstairs conspiracy gossip. "You can just call me 'Buddy'," he said. "Everyone does."

He was keeping his own name out of it.

He led me down a gray-painted hallway and into a cubbyhole office, stale with the aroma of dead air. A gray file cabinet leaned against a beaverboard wall. An ashtray humped with prohibited cigarette butts lay on the desk. Buddy switched on an all news radio station and turned up the volume. Sometimes the old World War Two spy tricks still worked best.

Even today, that radio noise would foul most electronic bugging devices. My senses were screaming SETUP! SETUP! My feet dragged on the floor like a boxer's. I was poised to strike and run. The Job had tried to jam me into a mental hospital before. If anyone tried moving on me today, I would take them down.

"Please have a seat, sir. What may I call you?"

"Buddy, my friends call me 'Sport'," I said. It was no lie. Some friends did. They were in their eighties and whiskey-and-baseball cronies of my grandfather. He was the original Sport.

Giving a nickname also gave me some legal protection. It was not technically an alias. But no paper existed to tie me to "Sport". Being cagey did not come naturally to me.

"I understand that you have a friend who wants to get a city job," he half-whispered in that voice of his.

My new pal Buddy was being cagey, too.

"You mean, 'Doctor, I have a friend who thinks that she is pregnant.'"

"Come again?"

"Sorry," I said.

Maybe if someone were taping me for court, they would let me slide if I were too crazy to prosecute.

"Yes, that is correct."

Buddy said nothing.

My friend was playing cute.

I would have to speak the next words. These would be the criminal words. They could send me to prison. Nightmares of prison turned me awake and nauseous in the middle of the night.

"My friend," I said, "is very anxious to apply for this city job. He is ready to try twenty times to obtain this job."

That meant that I could throw twenty grand at him for getting me back onto the Job. It was all the cash that I could scrape together from my IRA and loans and bank accounts.

My new pal, Buddy, had been a political worker, a judge's clerk and a lawyer for the Civil Service Commission. That much I had heard from our go-between.

His wrinkled gnome face frowned.

"Your friend doesn't sound serious enough about this job," he said. "Tell him that he should be prepared to try a hundred times for this job. Not just twenty."

I felt as if someone had just slugged my left arm. It went numb. That was my physical heart reacting to his words.

His response meant that he wanted a hundred grand for putting me back in the Job. He did not want just twenty thousand. He wanted five times that. One hundred thousand round iron men.

"Try a hundred times," I said. "That sounds like too many times to try for just one job."

Something hammered inside me as I said that.

"As I said," he said, "your friend should try harder. If he gets this city job and retires, what will his pension check read for one year? Just one year."

"About 30K," I said.

"That is correct. For something that rewarding, he should keep trying until he obtains that job. It doesn't seem to be that a hundred attempts is too many to ask for."

100K was out of the question right now. But Cooper was asking me to move in with her. With my Flatbush Secure gig and illegally subletting my Manhattan place, I might have 100K by Christmas.

"Now, your friend needs to make a decision today," my friend said. "He must say yes or no. Because these things can grow quite complex rapidly."

"Today?" I asked.

"Today. Because wheels have to be put in motion. In order to process your friend for this year, we need to move today. Or else, it will be too late."

Something cracked in my back as I leaned forward. Throwing up felt like a good idea.

This was unexpected. Nobody had prepped me for this. Maybe my new pal was running his own hustle here that nobody knew about.

"Let me go into the hall for a minute and call my friend," I said. Keeping up the fiction about the friend seemed vital now.

The hallway yawned.

No federal agents jumped out in dark blue windbreakers with pump shotguns to arrest me. Not yet. They could come by morning. Or they could choose their own time.

The Government now could case me for Attempted Bribery. They could put me and Buddy before a Grand Jury and see if they could get an indictment. My existence would become a runaway tragedy, fast going downhill.

The smart thing today was to agree to set it rolling and then back down. That way, nobody got hurt.

After enough time, I stepped back into Buddy's office.

"My friend is still interested," I said. "He said that he wants to keep applying. Anything that we can do would be greatly appreciated."

"Fine," he said. "But we'll require a show of good faith at this point. To make this move."

"What would that be?"

"That number stays in my head somehow," he said.

Twenty, I realized. He wanted twenty to start things. And if I did not get the rest of it to him, he would keep the twenty thousand.

"Can we meet again in the fall to discuss this?" I said.

"Absolutely not. This has to be ironed out soon. I'm scheduled for heart surgery next month. And I may not survive the operation."

That rocked me on my heels.

"I'm sorry to hear that," I managed to say.

"Don't be. I lived on steak and Scotch and cigars, worked too hard and took the job too much to heart. Seems silly now. But I have to get all these affairs in order before that operation."

"I'll do what I can."

"So let us meet a week from today," he said. "Right here at the same time. And I'll let you know if we made any progress."

That meant that next week, he would take twenty thousand in cash off me. There would be no checks in a deal like this. Nobody wanted a paper trail.

As he got up from the desk, he rubbed the desktop with his fingertips. That was to erase any accidental fingerprints. This was damn sure not his office. It was an open one, with nothing to tie him to it.

"I certainly hope that I'm still around at the holiday season to help your friend," he said. "But I just don't know."

CHAPTER 17.

Playpen Irregulars Hit the Streets

Nancy and her squeeze, Santiago, both sporting athletic gear and toting nutrition bars in free sample cases, met me inside Dino's on Flatbush Avenue. The wide, wood-paneled dining room, with its purple crushed velvet booth cushions and red-and-white checkered tablecloths, was filled with customers waiting for or already consuming their morning espresso and cannoli.

Saturday morning bloomed with promise outside the sparkling windows. Nobody looked like a gangster on the sidewalk. As a rule, gangsters usually slept late. Chicory coffee aroma mixed with the fragrance of warming bread and prosciutto.

In a corner booth, Tisa from Ecuador and Ivan from Far Rockaway cooed like two turtledoves.

"Some jokers see things," I said to "But they won't call the blue suits with what they saw. That's street law. I hear stuff from Lefferts House. So we have to draw it from them."

"How?" Santiago asked.

"By acting differently than most governments act," I said. "It's a favorite topic of mine. So I harp on it all the time and drive normals mad with my routine."

"I still don't see how," he said.

"From the first word you say, let your sources know that their life has gotten better because of you."

"How?"

"By being different," I said. "Different from anything that they have known before. Not being petty or cheap or in a hurry. You want to listen to them."

"Damn, man, that ain't nothing, slick. Salesmen can do that."

"Sure. But can a salesman clear a murder?"

"Say that you manage to find out who aced this fool Lutz," Santiago said. Prison weightlifting had strengthened him, with a chest that looked like he was always inhaling. Gray already spread through his charcoal hair. A gold canine tooth winked. Nancy saw everything good in him, but dealing with him always made me want to wash. "What do you get out of it?"

"Just feeling good," I said.

"I don't know about all that," he said. "I got root-canal bills for my ex-wife's kids, cable bill, my own college loan, lawyer fees. Feeling good? I'll feel good when I pay them."

"I got those same bills," Leo, the janitor with missing fingers, said as he joined us. He smelled of laundry soap, a fresh leather belt and the aroma of Kahlua that flowered from his coffee cup.

"Me, too," Cooper said. "Except for the kids and the root canal."

"We meet back here at six for the best Italian food that you ever ate," I said. "With wine. And I'm paying for it. I'm the wine buyer for this case."

"What's that mean?"

"You'll see," I said. "You'll like it."

Buzz Edwards bounced into the café like the jaunty Corrections Officer that he used to be. His scarred and lumpy black face opened when he saw the other Irregulars.

"Free food, good friends and wild women!" Buzz shouted. "Yessir, buddy!"

"Hard pavement-pounding first, Buzz," I said.

"These sidewalks do look hard," Buzz said. "Broke brothers be walking them."

Nancy hustled Santiago into a booth near Tisa and Ivan.

"Were any of these Irregulars cops?" Cooper whispered. "I would imagine that you all become pretty intimate with each other."

My breath ducked in. My left wrist shook, from the quick pain down my arm from the heart. Wisecracking seemed like my best escape.

"I would imagine-" she repeated.

"Imagine away," I said. "That's a two-part question. Which part would you like answered first?"

"Don't bother," she said. I had not heard that tone of voice before from her. "Can you and I do this kind of Irregular work together?"

"Not today. Because I have to work Flatbush Secure now. And you live here. It's dangerous for you, even under-cover like the others are doing. If you get anything good, you may have to testify in open court."

"What about you testifying?"

"I'm scared about it. But if someone wants to kill me, I'm also professionally quite annoying. Never do what I'm supposed to do."

Something sparked in Cooper's blue eyes. Her nostrils flared.

"You are expecting me to jog home and clean the house?" she asked. "While you, the little boy, runs around with his se-cret society of other kids who never matured? That's your im-age of our future together?"

Oxygen gave blood its bright red color. Mine felt de-pleted, dark right now. It ran sick and diseased from Cooper's words. In the bar mirror, I could see my own neck pulse beat faster. I felt it, too.

"It will pass," I told myself. 'She's just acting up. Like I do sometimes. It means nothing."

The grin that I pasted on my face felt fake from the in-side, too. All at once, I felt the crawly feeling that all of us lov-ers, Cooper and I, Nancy and Santiago, Tisa and Ivan, were just little kids running through our time and playing at love like six-year-olds. No matter which way we turned, some edge would cut us.

Cooper turned and left.

"*Gringa* women," Tisa said from Ivan's shoulder. "They worry too much."

"You think?" I asked, fighting to sound cool.

"Too much education," Tisa announced.

Dino opened the front door himself. He was a wizened pine-knot character with a heavy walrus moustache.

Sgt. Finnerty followed, dressed in plainclothes. His face flushed as he took in everyone. His seersucker jacket, blue Oxford shirt and red striped tie told me that he was dressing to hunt women today.

Usually his gold wedding ring sparkled on his left hand. Today, the skin of his ring finger looked pale and naked.

"Finnerty, me boyo," I whispered in an Irish brogue. "Be ye going a-sweethearting this fine day?"

"These ladies are some Irregulars?" he asked.

"You might ask them," I told him.

"Hellfire," he said, staring at Tisa with Ivan and Nancy with Santiago.

They looked away.

"These two look attached to their men," he whispered, an act that required some doing on his part.

"Joyously."

"Then why am I here?"

"Truth and justice?"

"Just wanted to see, you know? See if it was a real secret-handshake society," Finnerty said. "But you know how the Job slams us for working with outsiders. I could get burned."

"Curiosity killed the cop," I said.

"That's the real deal, Babe," Finnerty said. "Got some things to do today. I'll holler at you later."

He and his seersucker jacket went back out Dino's door.

"What did HE want?" Tisa asked.

"Adultery," I said.

"Men!" she giggled. "They are just pets. You gotta feed them, wash them, run them tired, supply them with their favorite toys, keep them from mounting strange bitches and finally put them to bed."

Ivan nodded. His glasses bobbled.

"Irregulars," I said. "Remember that we have to talk these witnesses, schmooze them, like they say in Yiddish."

"I'm going to get my hair done as close as I can to the murder scene," Tisa said. "On a Saturday morning, beauty parlor ladies know everything about neighborhood gossip."

"Amen," I said. "Nancy, you and Santiago set up your health food stand near Lefferts House. Patso, where will you be?"

Patso bent his head nearer to talk low.

"I think that I know some bartenders around here," Patso said.

"What a surprise," I said. "Go, get 'em, boy. Squeeze that talk out of them."

"Hey, hey," Santiago said. "I got to stand up sweating in the hot sun and selling health food, and Patso gets to cool it in a bar all day?"

"He prepared for the job very young," I said.

"That's bull crap," Santiago said. "I mean, it's just not fair."

"I don't know about you," I said. "But I tossed that phrase 'It's just not fair' out of my vocabulary years ago. Many things aren't fair. I don't need to remind myself about it on any kind of a regular basis."

The other Irregulars seemed to study the floor. Santiago and his mutiny pulled me away from Cooper's words, which were still hammering me.

"My Irregulars," I said. "This is the kind of hissy-fit cat fight that blocks progress. We're here to farm gossip to clear a murder. That's more important than anyone's comfort. What's our watchword?"

Some picked up their heads now.

"Schmooze!" they cried.

"Then, get out there and go schmooze," I said.

CHAPTER 18.

Daddy Max Meets Daddy Fix

That afternoon, I picked up new business cards at my office. A little after six, I met Skip outside Dino's.

"Why the hell did you schedule this meeting on my date night?" Skip griped.

Nancy and her squeeze, Santiago, both sporting athletic gear and toting nutrition bars in free sample cases, met me inside Dino's on Flatbush Avenue.

"All us Irregulars get hungry at sundown," I said. "That's why we set this Wine Buyer dinner now."

"You just drag me along because I'm a fat black man," Skip snorted. He stumped inside Dino's.

Being a scaredy-cat made me always scan everyone for weapons. Skip's left pants leg hung slightly askew just above his Gucci loafer, well concealing an ankle holster weighed down by a gun.

The smell of cream sauce filled the restaurant.

Dino had opened up a private back room for our dinner. The space had ignored decades of dramatic changes churning the neighborhood outside. Oil paintings of Italian peasants in golden fields hung on the walls. Brass knickknacks looked down from shelves upon solid wooden tables. High-backed chairs hinted at the lost elegance of a century ago.

Skip blew a kiss at Dino.

"Oldies music night, okay?" Dino asked.

I nodded, and he put on "Spinning Wheel" by Blood, Sweat and Tears.

Brass horns mixed with the singer's voice.

"It's on shuffle," said Dino as he exited, "Let me know if you want to change the mix. I'll send someone in to take the drinks order as soon as your people start drifting in.

"You know I love to eat," Skip said. "But tell me what this Wine Buyer's dinner is,"

"You won't be staying for dinner," I said. "I'm sure that you have better joints to hit on Saturday night."

"True that. But why can't I stay?"

"Only Irregulars can eat at a Wine Buyer dinner," I said. "Rules."

Skip rolled his eyes.

"Just who started this Playpen Irregulars gang?" he asked. "You?"

"Guilty," I said. "Cops and civilians seldom talk to each other. Rarely do they understand each other.

Civvies live in the city. Cops hump together on Long Island or upstate. In housing developments that look like fortresses. Surrounded by other cops.

So we Irregulars go where they can't go and come back with info that clears crimes. Along the way, we help and support each other, with laughs, hugs, meals, liquor and mental health getaway days."

"I just bet you do, player," Skip wheezed. "And you the Big Daddy Max, feeding all his children."

"Jealous?" I asked.

"You naive, baby," Skip said. "Think the world be a holy temple. But I'm realistic. You may be Daddy Max. But I be Daddy Fix."

He heaved himself up and out through the door, favoring his ankle-holstered leg.

The song kept massaging my nerves as the Irregulars started coming inside.

A few minutes later, Patso arrived, smelling of the liquor absorbed during his bar-crawling.

"Shrimp scampi appetizers," I said. "Rhine wines by the glass. Dino has a special on Lobster Newburg tonight. Order whatever you want."

"I know," Santiago said. "You're the Wine Buyer. Means what?"

"We eat and drink the best as we pool information," I said. "Brainstorming at the same time. Putting together tiny bits of data. Mapping out plans. You'd be surprised how well it works."

"Especially if you get all slap-ass drunk."

"Pounding down wine helps," I said. "It lets the wild animal inside us break loose. And we talk more. Talking breaks cases."

"No, it don't," Santiago said. "The Man keeps finding me with that crack and taking me down. Ain't no talking involved."

"Well, maybe you're doing it all wrong," Nancy smirked as she leaned on his arm. "My little angel."

"And how you pay for all this?" he asked.

"I sacrifice," I said. "Suffer in silence. But it's worth it. So eat this Veal à la Milanese. Broiled seafood platter. New potatoes, creamed spinach, risotto, bruschetta and crème brûlée for dessert.

"Daddy Max, the Wine Buyer, sees his family eat and is happy," I said.

☙

Everyone talked about everything. Then I took over.

"Who got anyone talking about the Lutz kill today?" I asked.

"Lutz, d/o/b 04-13-66 in Kings County Hospital, lived at 522 Lincoln Road," Tisa said, checking her notebook.

Her black trusses, plumed high, reminded me of coins showing the head of Atahualpa, the Inca chief. She rolled a thick lit cigar from one side of her mouth to the other. Smoking in restaurants was now illegal. Tisa did not care.

"St. Francis School, Midwood High School, Medgar Evers College. Three arrests for disorderly conduct and unlawful assembly. All dismissed. Taught school at Lenox Road Academy, did stand-up comedy all over Brooklyn. Member,

Flatbush Friends of the Neighborhood, Citizens Against Police Abuses and a dozen others. Mother living at 615 Flatbush, third floor. Ex-wife working at Hair Care on Church Avenue and Nostrand. Three kids living with her."

"How do you get all this?" Santiago asked.

She fluffed her hands through her luxuriant hair.

"I got it done while we talked. Beauty parlor ladies know everything."

Wine flowed. We Irregulars rested our feet and ate.

Dino entered, nose wrinkling as he smelled Tisa's cigar smoke. When Tisa lowered her head and glared at him, he grimaced like a suffering martyr and gracefully backed out of the room.

"Some guard hit an old homeless couple near Erasmus Hall School last week because they wouldn't get off the public entrance," Tisa said. "That's all. No names or witnesses."

"Good work, Tisa," I said.

"Heard that same story from a big guy in the park," Nancy said. "But he didn't have time to talk much. Just walked off from me."

"Even better," I said. "Verifying the first story."

"Lutz had a car," Patso said. "Orange Kia."

"He sold it," Nancy said. "To his ex-wife's brother."

"I heard that it was the cousin," Ivan said.

"Just listen to all that street gossip," I said. "I love it!"

Outside Dino's windows, family groups thinned out. Clumps of youths, some spiffed up for Saturday, some spiffed down, increased.

"I know that look," Tisa said to me. "You're suspicious of those kids. Remember that not every kid walking, down the street – white, black or Latino – is a mugger."

"You're right," I said. "Sometimes I think that the street has infected me."

"Better watch that, pussycat. Don't get cynical."

More wine flowed.

"Today, everyone worked hard and made Big Daddy Max happy," I told the Irregulars. "We got some good background. It all helps."

"It still amazes me," Ivan said. He dandled crème brûlée on his spoon. "We got no authority, reputation or guns. But somehow, witnesses gab to us."

"About everything," Buzz said. His brown eyes lit up. "Don't seem possible."

"Ace detectives still get amazed by what they learn just by asking citizens," I said, getting up to stretch.

The Irregulars debated over where Lutz's two sisters worked.

"Man, I can't do this kind of work," Santiago said.

I spun on my heel. Even the peasants in the oil paintings seemed surprised.

"Excuse me extremely?" I asked.

"Can't do all this for free!" Santiago said. "Kiddy crap stuff. I'm out of your Irregulars or Regulars or whatever the hell. And Nancy goes with me. I keep a close eye on my woman, player."

My hand put the brandy glass down hard on the bar. It hurt my knuckles.

Santiago led Nancy out of the room, through the restaurant and onto the street. Nancy looked past me and shrugged. Music from the CD player kept sweetening the air. It mixed with Tisa's cigar smoke.

The Irregulars looked at me.

"He's not wrong, you know," Buzz said. "We could all get busted."

"Or sued and lose our houses," Tisa said. "City doesn't like groups like us Irregulars. We don't ask no permission, nice and polite, from them. We not like those Auxiliary Police or nothing. They maybe got it in for us."

Bringing up my head cost me something. The dinner roiled my gut.

"I may leave us Irregulars," Ivan said. "But I'll do it after we find who killed Lutz. Not before."

"Me, too," Buzz said. "When we catch him."

Tisa and I looked at each other.

"Irregulars!" Tisa and I shouted.

"Irregulars!" the others chorused. "Playpen Irregulars!"

CHAPTER 19.

Chasin' Jason

Sunday morning, at a fast-food window on Flatbush, I ordered a Jamaican Spicy Beef Pattie on a paper plate.

"What do you have to wash this spicy stuff down?" I asked the senior citizen behind the counter. He wore a blue baseball hat with a white eagle crest on it reading "CIA," lime polyester pants and red shorts that showed knife scars on both thighs.

"Coke, Sprite or Acassan," he said in a French accent, scratching his scarred legs.

"What is Acassan?"

"You will like it, my friend. Try it."

"Sure," I said, pressing some cash on the counter.

He poured out a thick, light-colored liquid from a pitcher into a glass and handed it to me. Feeling like a foreign visitor in my birth city, I drank it.

It tasted like poured honey mixed with gold. It flowered in my mouth.

"That is great," I told the man. His face split open in delight. Boyish lines grooved around the mouth.

"Yes," he crowed. "I knew that you would like it so much."

"What is it?"

"We make it in my country, Haiti. Corn syrup, milk, cane sugar and other things."

"I may never drink anything else."

Doing what I was planning to do required a full stomach and a cheery heart.

Empire Boulevard yawned ahead of me.

Ebbets Field Houses stood like a block against the green of Prospect Park nearby. This was where I had wrestled a PCP abuser three years ago.

That night's memory swam up again, the chemical smell of the drug sweating out of the user mixed with my new gun leather scent. Emotions spiraled and crashed in my bodily fluids again.

Just looking at the Houses brought all this back to me. Fear had been the syrup sticking to me no matter what I did.

The same small stone plaque lay on the grass in front of the building. Years ago, when the wild client on PCP had jumped me and grabbed my gun, beating his gun hand against this plaque had saved my life.

A wide black woman stood outside the lobby door. She wore a blue windbreaker with butter-colored letters, "Tenant Housing Patrol," on the back. Makeup and mascara crusted at the corners of her wise eyes.

"I'm trying to give a man a job," I said. "His name is Jason Rouse and he lives around here."

"This don't sound right. He black?"

"Yup."

"'course he is. Just a few white fools trying to live around here."

"How long have you been living here, ma'am?" I asked.

"I was coming up here for the ballgames at Ebbets Field. Whole neighborhood was Irish, Italian and Jewish. No black folks yet. So that makes me older than I care to say. What kind of job you got for that man?"

"Security officer."

"Shoot, that ain't no job."

"I hear you," I said. "But it can grow into one."

"Like to know how. It's just minimum wage and dirt-dumb doing that."

I took in my gut, trying again not to sound naive.

"I'm going to make it different," I said. "Better kind of outfit."

"Why you want to hire this man?"

"Because he saved my life."

"That's kind of cheesy, Mister Man. You think that you rewarding him so much with a guard job? Your life worth that little?"

"It's all that I've got," I said.

"Then poor you."

"I tried to find Jason before. But he moved away."

"Maybe he's not interested in your guard job. I know I wouldn't be."

"Here's my card."

I handed her my Flatbush Secure card.

"I'm Max Royster, the Director of Security, like it says on the back. He can call me. Does anyone named Rouse live in this place?"

"Not that I know of. Come around Monday and ask at the Housing Office."

ↄ

The day went on like that. Strings of talkers unrolled along Flatbush. Each string led somewhere. Their words made me follow each strand.

"Yeah, I know Jason," said a chain-smoking man, wearing a captain's yachting hat and leaning on a station wagon outside Food Castle, said. "Haven't hollered at him in a while. He had some trouble with a gangsta. Give me your card. I'll talk it up, see where he's hanging."

Martense Street, Sullivan Place and Montgomery Street pounded back up through my shoe soles. Acassan sugar propped me up for another half hour.

Tiredness came, and I slumped on a park bench near the Prospect Park Carousel. Margaret was putting kids up on the wooden horses, her cellphone tucked under her chin.

After all my far-ranging investigating skills, no Jason Rouse showed up. That was just as well. Cooper's scent and touch were still on me. After just a few hours, I missed her. Briefly thinking about The Softness of Men, I turned my shoes back towards the bed that we now shared.

ↄ

That night, Cooper and I slept wrapped up in each other's arms.

Tumbling over half-seas asleep, I dreamed that we were slow-slide swimming over the bluish waters above the ocean's Continental Shelf.

Awaking the next morning, the dream's afterglow still lingered. Cooper had left hours earlier, as usual. Maybe she had jogged through Flatbush first.

❧

Still feeling light and floating, I entered the Flatbush Secure office and greeted the guards. They were in their usual hard plastic chairs, watching a basketball game on TV. Ted sat behind his desk, checking off guard assignments on a metal board. Today, he wore a yellow polo shirt, loose bluejeans and his usual smug expression.

He had the ability to look distinguished and handsome when he was not cutting the fool with me. Everyone suffered complexities. There was no reason that I could see why Ted wanted a war with me. Maybe offices did that to people.

"Good morning, Ted," I said, sounding as hearty as I knew how. "How are you?"

Ted did not answer.

The guards stopped talking and watched.

My fingers snapped from nerves. I stopped halfway across the waiting room.

"Ted," I said. "How are you today? Did you get over your cold?"

"I'm okay," he said, forcing it out and not smiling.

"That's good," I said. Somehow I managed to get this out. "Because I was worried."

This effort cost me. Putting on a bold front, I got to my office, unlocked the door and nearly fell onto my small desk.

"Ted's wearing me out," I muttered. "He's planning my first heart attack."

Taking in a deep breath, I went back into the reception room to show that I was strong and in charge.

The guards were still watching their basketball game.

"You look way different," a black man said from the doorway.

"Compared to what?" I asked.

"Couple of years back," he said. He was compact, with a slim face on a corded neck. He wore a black T-shirt with a yellow duck's head on the chest, khaki shorts and tan socks jammed into strong brown leather sandals like monks wore. I recognized Jason.

"Jason," I said. "You've lost weight."

"Yeah," he said.

Ted and the guards watched us.

"Have you had coffee yet?" I asked Jason.

He looked ten years older than I remembered him. A small shock roiled me.

"I'll buy you a cup. You name the spot. It's your neighborhood. I'm just a carpetbagger."

Nobody reacted to this.

Ted came out and stood so Jason could not hear him. My heart hammered.

"What cold are you talking about, dude?" Ted asked.

"The cold that you're going to get when I get tired of your silent routine and have to let you go," I said. My voice cracked. Playing boss hurt. "And that will feel like a windy cold day to you. Ted, I need you working with me. No more silent routine, please. Thank you, Ted."

Ted formed an unhappy face.

Jason did not seem to hear this

⁂

Jason and I headed south, into the tougher section of Flatbush Avenue.

Walking with him after those few years, I felt an attack of shyness and tried talking through it.

"The ADA had only an old address on you," I said. "316 Rutland Road, if I remember right."

Jason had a direct way of looking at me and everyone else.

"I peeled out of that nut-house," he said. "Some gangstas was after me but good. Got me so mad I swore that I'd feed them to the cops."

His face fit snugly over flat ears and a high forehead. Everything about him seemed disciplined and controlled. He was the kind of athlete who could spin deftly and move faster than his teammates. He stood about seven inches under my six feet but swaggered as if he were much bigger. It was a cocky rooster kind of swagger. His biceps and forearms still showed traces of muscles from serious weightlifting. But he was down low on weight, and I wondered if he were on crack. Crack often speeded up the user's metabolism and burned off their fat.

"I hear that you've got some kind of job for me," he said.

His hearing would save me a trip to the Housing Authority Office on Monday.

☙

We found a luncheonette with four tiny tables and sat at one of them. Reggae filled the air.

"Have whatever you want," I said. "This is a business power brunch. I can deduct it off my taxes."

He squinted at the dishes offered and nodded to the big-boned waitress. She was reading a Jamaican newspaper, *The Daily Gleaner,* at the counter. The place smelled of fry grease.

"Steak-and-egg sandwich, fries and black coffee," he said. "You?"

"Coffee light, English muffin, very well done, please, and no butter," I said to her.

Jason's hands still held the square and muscled look they had before.

"You're making me feel stupid," I said. "Lady Luck threw me in charge of a security agency."

"And you need a manager?"

"I guess that you could call me the manager," I said. "There's an Operations Boss, named Ted, and the owner, Skip. There are not a lot of middle management slots yet."

"Do you feel like you're paying off a debt?"

"I'm not sure. Where did your thirty pounds of muscle go?"

"Into the past," he said. "I had some hard traveling and couldn't get to the gym. Gangstas be watching for me there."

"How do you stay off the street?"

"Who says that I do?"

"Where do you sleep?"

"Friends."

"Then you need any kind of gig," I said. "Come in with us. Union and medical benefits after ninety days."

"At parties now, I'm doing disc jockey stuff," he said. "Write my own songs and sing them. Hip hop and rap and even some soul. Flatbush is starting to know me. This used to be a swinging cool hood."

"Not many brothers praise the old Flatbush," I said.

"Because they do not know about it. But let's stay in the present. Putting me in a monkey suit for minimum wage is a big step down in image."

"Think of it as insurance," I said. "A foundation that lets you take chances with your music jobs. You can hold out for bigger and better parties if you're not always scuffling for that next fifty dollars."

"This some kind of undercover front for the cops?" he asked. "How come you quit the cops?"

"It's a long story."

"I mean, it ain't not normal, boss man. You want me to be some kind of flunky for you because I stepped in for you a few years ago?"

"You won't be a flunky, Jason. The job and the image are lousy right now. We both agree. But security is the fastest-growing business in America. Mister and Missus Square John Property Owner want someone watching their turf because they are scared to lose it. They are not going to sit out front with a stick and a radio themselves."

The waitress set down our food and coffee and eased back to her newspaper. We drank and ate. Jason ripped into his sandwich.

"You can't hire me," he said. "The law won't let you."

That stopped me. The waitress was still farming the fashion section of the paper and nodding to herself. She was too far away to hear us.

"You've picked up a record?" I asked.

"Burglary in the Second," he said. "I thought that the house was abandoned, and I needed a place to sleep. Broke a window by accident getting in. Big pit bull took a chunk out of my leg, and I bled so much that I passed out."

"They should have offered you Criminal Trespass and not Burglary. Who the devil was your lawyer?"

Jason's voice dropped. He looked like this was tough for him to go through.

"Actually, the pit bull owner came out with a baseball bat when I got bit. Had to put him down or he might have taken me out permanent-like. The D.A. dropped the Felony Assault Charge and offered me Burg Two, with a promise of just thirteen months upstate."

"And if you wanted a trial?"

"Conviction could be seven to fifteen years. I had some misdemeanor priors like fighting and carrying a gravity knife. So my Legal Aid joker told me to take the deal. I did the thirteen months and then made the street. But with a felony conviction."

There must be some way to hustle around this.

"Jason, you could be valuable to my outfit. So fill out the application. Tell the real deal. Let it all hang out. I'll worry about the rest."

"Why you going to all this trouble?"

"Because you've got qualities that I need in this outfit, Jason. Don't think that I'm doing this for you. I'm doing this for me."

CHAPTER 20.

Good Morning, My Soft

Cooper breathed under my ear, still half-asleep.

Her sound system played sweet classical music in the bedroom that I now called ours. As gently as possible, I disengaged myself from her clutch and rolled onto my back.

"Feel that music, Cooper?" I murmured.

"Awesome," she said.

She spoke as if the morning were too fragile to break by loud talk.

"'Symphonie Fantastique' by Berlioz. I took music appreciation at Skidmore, and this piece is about how romantic longing cripples the composer."

"Shoot who?"

"So many of the great classical composers were sexually frustrated, pining for a love that they'd never seen. 18th and 19th century European life was very controlled."

"You mean that there wasn't a swinging singles scene in 1830s Dresden?" I asked. For some reason, her tone made me puckish. "Nobody getting no hank."

"None whatsoever." She shifted her body and squeezed it against me. "'Whatever 'getting no hank' means. Perhaps I don't want to know. You have some odd expressions.

"Anyway, the composers channeled all that romanticism and sex drive into their music. Psychology calls that 'sublimation'."

"Cooper, how can you lecture like this, with your eyes closed and before coffee?"

"These composers were all men. Name me a woman composer."

"There aren't any," I said. "They were all guys. And they are all dead. That's why I don't call them classical composers, the way that you do."

"What do you call them, Max?"

"I call them 'the dead guys'."

"Because they are all guys and they are all dead," she said. "Got it. Hector Berlioz here composes dangerous fantasies about a mythical woman. Tchaikovsky, being gay, with his *frotteur* parents arranging a marriage to save his reputation. Edvard Grieg, crippled by shyness about Norway having no great national music yet and eaten up by self-doubt."

"You sound like a book," I said.

"Well, I should, Max. I plagiarized all those lines for my final course paper."

"Plagiarism is wrong."

"No doubt. You should see the college loans that I'm still paying back. Then we'll talk about wrong. But the course stressed that 19th century men were supposed to be dominant. Most men worked with their hands. Not like now, old man. Carpenter, bricklayer, wagon master. Or a barrel maker, a cooper. That's where my name comes from."

"Real men," I said.

"Dragoons, cavalrymen, dashing generals with medals. Men were not supposed to shut themselves away in a garret and compose music about romantic love. Only softies did that."

For some reason, she wanted me to hear all this. I wondered why.

The word "softie" killed my smile. My left leg twitched. Something in her tone was scaring me.

"Why are you telling me this?" I asked her.

"Why do you think?"

Rolling back down onto her ribcage, I hugged her again. My shoulder muscles clenched. Perhaps I was hurting her. Maybe I was no softie.

Being sensitive, I wondered again how I had lasted three years as a cop. Then I wondered how I had lasted forty-eight years as a man.

She arranged her legs around my hips and squeezed.

We dove back into sleep.

❧

My cellphone buzzed. The number calling was one that I had memorized.

"Hello," I said.

"I'd like to see you about what we talked about," a whispery voice, tailor made for conspiracies, said. It was my new friend who called himself Buddy. He was going to ease me back into the Job.

"We should meet at the United Nations cafeteria in one hour," I said. "I will have everything required."

"The U.N. cafeteria? Do they still have one? It's been years since I've eaten there."

"They still have one."

"I'm afraid that I can't," he said.

"I'm afraid that you can," I said. "Or else, our negotiations go no further."

Silence hung on the line.

He would not want to lose the 20K when he was this close to it.

If the Government wanted to stake out the luncheonette to snag me, they could never set up surveillance in one hour. The U.N. was international territory.

"Why do we have to meet there?" he asked.

"They just switched chefs. He needs the business."

My hands pushed me off the bed and off Cooper and onto my feet. My bruised body protested. Inside her bathroom, I opened my shaving kit. A tube of glue lay inside the kit. The glue spread over my fingertips and dried as I waved my hands around. Nobody would notice the glue now.

"I have to go," I told Cooper. "Be right back."

"Is it another woman?"

We laughed at that and fell back on the bed together until I got up again.

&

The subway barreled me from the station and along the track underneath Prospect Park. Under my shirt, I wore a nylon money belt that I used during my travels. Everything that I could scrape together from bank accounts and friends lay inside the belt. It came to just $18,000. That was two grand shy of what my pal Buddy wanted. It was time to schmooze him about the missing cash. He would not be pleased.

The subway dropped me at Grand Central Station, and I walked east towards the U.N. building. My feet chose the street where pedestrians walked against the car traffic flow. That would make car surveillance harder for the Opposition.

The armed guard at the First Avenue gate wore a crisp uniform of French blue, black polished Sam Browne belt and a clean peaked eight-point hat. A Glock rode on his right hip. He was very smooth and direct. A foreign accent, maybe African, flavored his words. He stood like an alert warrior, a trunk of muscle bulging his uniform. His hands looked strong enough to catch a kangaroo and teach it to curtsy.

We could use him at Flatbush Secure.

He checked me through a metal detector and then ran a wand over me. I emptied my pockets on the table.

"Identification, please," he said.

As a street cop, I always picked up things. I showed him a Michigan driver's license for a Samuel D. Hestand, and he entered the information on a keypad. That did not worry me. The photo looked like me. Samuel had been a customer in a Flatbush massage parlor. A beautiful Trinidadian masseuse named Cheryl had rolled him for everything.

"This license was reported stolen, sir," the guard said.

This could blow my deal today.

My chin tucked down.

"You're damn right that it was," I said. "Every time that I come to your city, someone steals my stuff. Last year, it was a camera. Your computer list should have that license as recovered and not stolen anymore."

"Sir, I have to call my captain."

"Call whomever you wish, Officer. But here is a copy of the police report where I recovered my license and other goods. Official NYPD seal and signature. They told me to carry it for just such problems as this."

He scanned it.

"I can barely read the officer's name," he said. "Who is P.O. Maxwell A. Royster?'"

"No relative of mine," I said.

It was the truth, come to think of it.

He typed out an entry on the computer screen and handed me back the license and the copy of the report.

"I put on the system that it is recovered, sir," he said. "You should not have any more trouble with it. I'm surprised that you kept that letter in your wallet for three years."

"The police told me to," I said. "Thank you very much, Officer."

Other tourists swirled around me as they walked across the plaza. Sunlight winked off the East River against the famous glass-box building. Guards in French blue uniforms walked or rode scooters through the different squares.

Governments had formed the United Nations right after World War II. They had hoped to debate things first and prevent war.

By now, people called the United Nations a failed concept. Meaningless wars still tore innocents apart.

The luncheonette was nothing to scream about. Government gray walls, tired linoleum floors and a menu guaranteed to send American bad eating habits around the world.

I settled into a seat where I could watch both entrances. I ordered a cup of hot mud and a Buffalo Bill Burger on toasted pita bread. I also asked for a knife and fork. If they gave me a steak knife, it would be a good weapon to have for handling trouble. A teenaged tour group speaking French cavalcaded over the floor. They squealed with Gallic enthusiasm as they unfolded the four-page menu.

The luncheonette windows faced the General Assembly Building. The U.N. had probably consulted security engineers, who told them that they could prevent sniper attacks by keeping the luncheonette windows small and facing the General Assembly Building. That way, no sniper on the river or the city streets behind the luncheonette could get a clear line of fire.

Any noise made my head turn now. If my old new pal Buddy wanted to have me arrested, he would do it today when money changed hands.

No surveillance team showed up yet. Nobody in a trenchcoat was standing on a corner, reading a newspaper, or skulking in a doorway on this hot day.

Buddy came through the doorway of the luncheonette as my Buffalo Bill Burger arrived. He wore a different suit, this one lightweight tan cotton. He also carried a black leather briefcase.

"Nice to see you," he said, coming to my table, an iced tea in hand. "But somewhere else would have been more convenient."

"Of course," I said.

"How is your friend coming along with his city job application?"

"Making progress," I said. "I'm sure that he won't embarrass anyone."

"Of course. But I imagine that he should be getting some good news soon."

Electronic bugging thoughts strained our talk. Both of us were trying to sound open and honest in case the government taped this talk and played it for some Grand Jury of the Future.

Let that Grand Jury of the Future listen to me chewing on my Buffalo Bill Burger, I decided.

Lightweight clothes had one drawback. Bulges showed through the material. Before I turned to law enforcement, I had gone through life in a daze. As a cop, I had to train myself to scan everyone. That awareness had saved me more than a few times. I scanned Buddy now.

His left pants leg bulged a bit above the ankle. He was taking today seriously. The bulge was probably a gun in an ankle holster. He looked like a .380 caliber man, something light and compact, on his gun permit. Maybe he was worried about someone ripping him off once he got my cash.

He set the briefcase on the empty chair next to me.

My eyes flicked around the room. The French tourists and the white-shirted staff were still dog-paddling through their worlds.

If the FBI jumped me now and sent me to prison, I would be desperately seeking The Softness of Men in Danbury Federal Correctional Institute.

My blue jeans legs twitched under the table. I had to make the move now or something else might turn squirrely on me. My feet drummed the floor.

Getting up felt like I had a boulder on my back.

"Excuse me a minute," I said, taking the briefcase from the chair.

His briefcase felt light in my hand. That was because he wanted me to fill it up.

Threading my way to the bathroom, I kept glancing around at everyone. Everything looked dully normal.

Inside the bathroom, I went inside the toilet and opened the briefcase. I kneaded the entire case to check for any built-in cameras or recording devices. My glue-tipped fingers would foil any fingerprint experts. I unzipped my money belt and slid the bills went into the briefcase. They formed a thick clump of cactus-colored paper.

I tried not to think about my life savings going down in-to this briefcase from the Underworld. But the thoughts loomed even larger. Breath whistled in my teeth.

If my Flatbush Secure job folded, I would be living in a doorway next month.

The briefcase felt much heavier now. So did I.

Buddy was finishing his iced tea when I got back outside.

I slid the briefcase back onto the same chair where Buddy had placed it. He drained the last of his tea.

"It's been seeing you again," he said. "Let's stay in touch."

"Let me pick up your iced tea," I said. "It's the least that I can do."

He formed a pleasant face.

We shook. I kept my grip loose so that he could not feel the glue on my fingertips.

After he left, I forced myself to sit at the table and polish off the ripe green pickle that came with the Buffalo Bill Burger. It crunched against my back teeth.

Feeling drawn and exhausted, I left the luncheonette and went to a different gate and a different guard. He checked my name on his computer list and wrote the time that I was leaving.

❧

Everything looked normal on First Avenue, so I walked to the corner and waited for the light to change.

"Fantastic building," a lean stork of a bald-headed man said to me in a country accent. He was looking back at the United Nations.

"Yeah," I said. "And it's unique."

He looked at me questioningly.

"It's all international territory," I said. "Just like an embassy. People can commit crimes there, and the American police have no authority inside that gate. The only authority is those guards. And they can only arrest people for crimes that they see in front of them."

CHAPTER 21.

I'm into Something Good,
or Strawboss Max

The next morning, I was looking over activity reports in the Flatbush Secure office. Ted smoldered at his desk, still holding his grudge.

No guards were in on standby duty yet. The TV set was on. A local reporter was interviewing New Yorkers about dog turds in the streets.

"Ted, are you watching this?" I asked.

I was ready for some more of the Silent Treatment but he surprised me.

"Not really. Change it if you want."

I inhaled. This was really breaking new ground in the private security world.

"Ted, I got some magazines for you and the men," I said. "*Newsweek, Time, Field and Stream, National Football.* You want some?"

"Okay," he said. He breathed in and out. "Thanks."

He opened a football magazine.

Magazines and I normally usually kept a cordial distance. They were what I read in doctor's waiting rooms. These I had bought in Manhattan and imported to Flatbush. No store in the hood carried any of them.

Giving Ted time, I went back into my office and scanned more reports. Then I came back out.

"Ted, how many kids do you have?"

"Man, mine are grown. One is thirty-three."

"Grandchildren, then."

"Eight of them."

"Would you want them watching TV or reading?"

"Everyone knows that TV is junk food for the mind."

"So, we agree," I said. Relief slowed my words. "Let's you and I try something revolutionary this morning. We're going to take the village green and fire on the redcoats. Okay?"

"What crud you talking?"

"Just this," I said. My fingers switched off the TV show about loose doggies, disconnected the set and hoisted it into my arms. It felt like I was trying to tote a Cadillac.

"Can we let them read instead?" I asked. The strain of lifting creaked my voice. "Headshrinkers say that watching TV makes you passive. Because everything is laid out for you. No choices. But reading, reading anything, makes you active."

"Some of our guards, you don't want them too active," Ted said. A rare smile creased his jowls. "Dude, I can't wait to see their faces when there is no TV and you hand them a Time magazine."

Like most people, Ted reacted to how he was approached. The idea of surprising our guards appealed to him.

The TV set eased down onto my floor. We would keep it here in case of national emergencies.

"Max, you in here?" a sniffly voice asked from the door.

"Who you, dude?" Ted asked.

"Ivan," the man said. It was Ivan, my Playpen Irregular. His voice sounded mild and scholarly. It was the voice of someone wanting to learn, flavored with a city accent.

His bulk filled the doorway. Curly brown hair burst over chunky plastic eyeglasses. Behind the lenses, his eyes darted around the room.

"Max, there you are," Ivan said. "Is my car okay out there? I mean, like I parked it and locked it and everything."

"There's a lot of black folks out there, if that's what you mean," Ted said.

Ivan's big doggy head came up.

"I didn't mean that," Ivan said. His glasses bobbled. "It was just like an automotive-type question."

"Yeah, it's fine, Ivan," I said. "Nobody ever messes with my car here."

"You don't have a car," Ted said.

"That's the best way," I said. "Ted, shake hands with Ivan Kammerman."

"You here to do our tax books, man?" Ted asked.

"Hey, hey!" Ivan crowed. "That's a good one. Because I'm a Jew? Is it that obvious? Like Woody Allen would look like me if he pumped some iron."

"Whatever," Ted said.

"No," Ivan said. "I'm not here to do the books. I want to work as a guard."

"Where?" Ted asked.

"Here."

"Shouldn't you be guarding a temple somewhere or something?" Ted asked. "Maybe a pawnshop."

"You got a temple still standing in this neighborhood, he'll be glad to guard it," I said. "But I think that they have been vacated. White flight. The scourge of Brooklyn."

"So, let me fill out your paperwork," Ivan said. "And we'll see what happens."

Ted turned towards me, looking older than ever before.

"This your idea?" Ted asked. "This integration?"

"Ivan is one of my Playpen Irregulars," I said. "We always help each other out, no questions asked."

"Where did you drive in from?" Ted asked. "The Catskills?"

Ivan beamed. The glasses rode up on his big face.

"I drive through here all the time. Lot of beautiful women here," Ivan said. His voice drifted off as it always did when he discussed women.

Ted handed him our two-sheet application. Ivan folded it, shook hands and went back outside.

A souped-up car engine caught.

Skip stopped the mailman outside our office and took bundles from him.

Ted glared at me. Anything that broke his routine threatened him.

"What comes next?" he asked.

"Animal acts," I said. "Do you see yourself as a dancing bear?"

"Here, I am, coming through your door again," Skip gleefully called out. That day, he wore a lightweight black suit, white shirt, red hand-painted necktie and shiny ankle boots. He carried cardboard packages. "With the mail. Baby, I love playing mother-trucking Santa Claus."

Skip split open the first package – a new dark blue uniform shirt. A golden six-point star badge, a bit smaller than my palm, was pinned to the breast pocket. It read "Flatbush Secure." The same star formed the shoulder patch.

Other gold badges winked.

"Who ordered these mammy-jamming damn badges?" Skip asked.

"I did," I said. "Remember at the store? We agreed that we need a better uniform look."

"These badges look expensive."

"They are," I said. "Way too costly. But we need them to attract better accounts. We'll get the cash back ten times this way."

Skip considered this. Nobody moved.

"Well, now, I agree, baby," Skip said. "Since Jesus gave me the smarts to hire you, our absenteeism done dropped eighty percent. Our damn guards be going where they are supposed to go. Fewer calling in sick with some fairy tale. Ain't nobody quit this month. That's a first. Until I find out different, I throw you credit for this."

I could feel my mouth stretching in a smile.

Ted switched his back and forth, watching us. He relaxed. Ted was the kind of person that when the boss was happy, Ted was happy.

"Until you find out different, I'll take it," I said.

"And that younger guard, Tommy Root, the one they call 'Wild Root', was working at Food Castle yesterday. Spied the manager put about 150 bucks worth of steak in his personal car. Root says that he remembered your lectures about integrity and a work ethic and what-not."

"Stuff you never think about," I observed.

"He called an assistant manager as a witness," Skip continued, "flagged down a cop car and signed a complaint against the manager and had the cops find the meat and bust the manager. The Food Castle Manager was way impressed and happy. They are throwing us more business and recommending us to other food chains."

"'The business of America is business,'" I quoted.

"Usually, I don't take chances. Lost my paddle years ago, so I don't go upstream any more. If Root had screwed up or accused some innocent fool, we might have lost that account. Gone the way of Jesus. So I'll try the new uniform idea now."

"Holding me personally responsible if my ideas fail," I said. "And if my good friend Alvin Cobb returns to lead an uprising against the White Power Structure and uses *schmaltz* and kitchen matches to torch our office."

"Yessir."

"Alvin might need someone to show him how to use a kitchen match," I said.

"I'm not sure that I do know what that word *schmaltz* means," Ted said.

"Old Flatbushers would. It's Yiddish for 'chicken fat'."

"It's all bullshit," Ted contributed.

"How many new uniform shirts did you buy?" I asked.

"Only twelve."

"Like the apostles," I said. "How were you planning to distribute them?"

"By seniority, of course. Whichever guard has been here the longest."

"If I may suggest. Rewarding seniority smells like an old-fashioned idea. That is way outmoded. That old style never improves the product or the delivery of it."

Ted sat back and burped, to draw attention to himself.

"Consider giving them to the guards who got the best attendance record. Not the ones who call you up on Saturday night at seven with a sudden case of chilblains."

"More b.s., Max. Why?"

I moved around the office like I used to train my boxers to square off the ring.

"Shows consistency with the 'why' of why you are issuing new shirts. Reward those who made it possible. Guards who have been here for none years or more probably are not going to change."

"I wouldn't," Ted said.

"We know," I said.

The phone rang. Ted picked it up before I could. Maybe he was showing Skip what a hard worker he was.

"Guard bosses don't usually think that way," Skip said.

"I'll agree with the first part of that sentence," I said. "That's why your industry is always running behind and unable to catch up."

"Now, it be your swinging industry, too."

"From what I see," I said, "we charge the account about fifty dollars an hour for an unarmed guard. The guard carries just a stick. No piece and no tear gas.

And we pay that guard the federal minimum wage. We use our profit to run the office, pay for medical coverage and us administrators' salaries. That guard sometimes stands post in horrible weather.

Stands a chance of some burglar shooting him and nobody much caring. Who cares about a guard? They are poor, unskilled and un-educated. Not charming. Usually they are not what you see on TV, the pretty pink people with tucked-in tummies."

"Any other ideas?" Skip asked. He was trying to be a regular fellow and not the boss. His eyes glinted something wicked.

"Plenty of them," I said. "They may make you throw up."

"Whoo, Jesus! Try me."

"We call our guards by the title 'Special Agent'," I said.

"Can't do that!" objected Skip. "That's federal."

"My law training says no. Insurance companies and credit card agencies use that term. But we keep the title Security Agent for some. The new badges will have those words. The ones who reach Special Agent rank must make it through the academy."

"What academy?"

The rascal in me enjoyed watching Skip's face break up in surprise.

"The academy that I am going to start," I said.

"What are you telling me, Royster?"

"Oh, boy," I said. "Last names now? Executive hardball."

"We can't have no mother-kissing academy! Doooo, Je-sus!"

"We need one. The industry needs one. Some security outfits have them."

"Damn few," he said. "The agencies just want their guys to get the mandatory eight-hour class. Nothing more. It would kill our profits."

"Think about attracting more and better clients," I said. "And guards. Show these guys that this is a profession and not just an excuse."

"We can't do it, Max. It's insane!"

"I could work up lessons with videos and law books," I said. "It would only cost us time. Nothing more."

"Impossible now, Max."

"Maybe later?"

He scanned me from head to toe and sighed.

"Maybe later," he said. "Maybe. After I write that essay for my Bible class on the donkey that Jesus rode into Jerusalem."

That was okay. I had gotten what I wanted.

Ted was busy "yes sirring" into the phone and scribbling on his clipboard.

Written on the clipboard in purple Magic Marker were the words:

Flatbush Secure
Touch this and I kick your ass

He kowtowed some more on the phone, thanked the person on the other end and hung up.

"That was Metcalfe Car Rental," he said. "They heard about Root with Food Castle. They want us protecting their outlets."

Skip and I ate each other with our eyes. His face bulged. He showed his teeth in a fierce little-boy grin.

"How many outlets?"

"Seventeen in the Greater New York area," Ted said. "And I quoted him our highest rate, with an armed guard, and he said, 'Fine.'"

"Well, mother, pin a rose on me," I said. "Ted, was he calling from a bar?"

"Doesn't matter if he was," Skip said. "We're getting that contract. Come here, Jesus! We'll be dancing to the bank! Nice going, Max."

My body sprawled in the chair. The boss liked me.

For now.

CHAPTER 22.

Church Talk

That day, four more applicants scribbled out forms in Flatbush Secure's front room.

"I heard that you treat your people real good," one of them said. "Classes and training. I can put that on my resume."

His resume needed it.

Still feeling light and good, I strolled along Flatbush Avenue at noon. The rush about Root had taken away any hunger. But I knew me. By late afternoon, I could eat an orangutan.

Ten minutes south of Lincoln Road and Flatbush, the middle class, white or black, disappeared. Now the poor and the working poor scuttled along the cracked gray sidewalks. Street kids eyed me. When I fixed my eyes on theirs, they kept staring back at me. One sucked his teeth and spat near my feet. They failed to feel my benevolence.

On Martense Street, I stepped into a doorway marked "Dr. E.K. Breslin, M.D." My good feeling dried up.

A full reception room of black patients stared at me. The receptionist made me wait a bit.

My head sank back. Cooper's body swam back from my memory.

"Mr. Royster?" Breslin said. He was reedy, with heavy eyeglasses under a perfect oval of pale scalp skin surrounded by black hair. A city accent slurred his words.

The exam room door closed behind me. Fear cork-screwed me more.

"Based on our tests," he said, "we see some memory loss. This can be rare in a man your age. Sometimes. But, drugs like Razadyne and Cognex are doing a lot now to offset these problems."

"Cognex," I said. "Powerful name."

"I'll write you a prescription and see you back here next month," he said. "I think that the receptionist wanted to speak with you about billing."

"I'll bet she did," I said.

"Start that medication today, Mr. Royster."

❧

Feeling like one of the doomed, I trudged along Flatbush. African stores exploded with sales of kente cloth, dashikis and ebony wood carvings. One dealer sold books and incense from a sidewalk stand.

My cellphone jangled with a voicemail.

"This is Buzz," the message began. "I gonna get my New York State guard card renewed and show up at your joint tomorrow. I'm easy to please. Gimme a post without no pit bulls or rain coming down on me and everything will be cool. The Irregulars ride again!"

The drugstore on Flatbush Avenue had small cramped aisles and a sharp-looking black pharmacist behind the counter.

My breath eased a bit. This was where I would solve my memory problems right away.

"I have a prescription for Cognex here," I said. "From Dr. Breslin."

He frowned. His expressive mobile face belonged on an actor, not a pill-roller in Flatbush.

"Cognex?" he said in a crisp voice. "Cognex has been discontinued in the U.S. Nobody stocks it anymore."

"But Dr. Breslin just prescribed it for me," I pleaded.

All my panic came back.

"Call him and have him prescribe something else, sir. Try Razadyne instead."

"He's a doctor and pushed me to take it," I said. "Maybe he forgot that it's been discontinued."

The doc and I played phone hopscotch until he called in a prescription for Razadyne. Pacing sidewalks outside the drugstore failed to cheer me.

"This drug has side effects," the pharmacist said. "Like appetite loss, nausea and dizziness. Okay?"

"I can hardly wait," I said.

Too much of my cash went into the store cash register.

Flatbush Secure did not cover enough in prescription drugs. The NYPD health plan was much better. It made me thirst again to get back on the Job.

The pharmacist had no tap water available. He sold me a bottle of water to wash down my first Razadyne pill. That turned me more blue, if possible.

෴

I subwayed back down to Court Street to pick up more guard application forms from the Brooklyn Municipal Building.

Along Joralemon Street, a brown brick church stood on a corner. Whatever kind of church it was, I had no idea.

Maybe my bad memory was ambushing me again.

Cooper would not like hearing my news. She might see herself having to nurse me next year if I forgot where I lived. Nobody wanted that. She might dump me to protect herself. Telling her now would be dumb.

The doors hung open and someone was preaching inside.

Breaking my pattern, I stepped inside the church to sit for a minute and wonder about the imponderables.

An athlete about thirty, blond hair and clear blue eyes, wearing an oxblood suit, virgin white shirt and tie, put out his arm to block me.

"Excuse me, sir," he said.

"Cover charge?"

"Excuse me?"

"Do I have to pay you money to get in and hear the Word of God? Or something."

He tightened his face a bit. His hand gripped my arm. My breath choked.

"No, sir," he said. "But the sermon is going on now. We just ask that you wait until the sermon is over before taking your seat. It shows respect."

I whipped my head around to stare at him.

"Who is 'we'?" I asked. "That means you and I? I did not decide anything. Nobody asked me. I want to sit down. Now."

His smile slipped somewhere far away.

"Sir," he said. "It is just to show respect."

We looked at each other.

"I go to church whenever I'm confused," I said. "That means often. Nobody ever stops me from sitting down."

"Sir, I'm Security here. You're being disruptive. Leave or I will call the police."

"Okay," I said. "I'm leaving. You win. Your side always does. But this was how you wind up beating the losers with sticks."

"What are you talking about?" he asked.

My snappish temper made me feel guilty. He was too young to understand my rant.

"Respect, son," I said. "Sadly, tragically, some people, show their respect by just going along and saying nothing."

That dazed him.

"You're not making sense," he said, forgetting the "sir" this time.

"I didn't expect you to understand," I said. "You'll figure it out when you're older."

CHAPTER 23.

Street Piping

"Tonight, I'm doing a surprise inspection tour of our sites," I told Ted as the office was closing. "Don't tell anyone. Just give me a Sam Browne belt."

"And a baton," Ted said.

"Not yet," I said. "Nobody's trained me or issued me a card for the baton yet. Even ex-cops need that training card."

"Nobody checks those things."

"Naw, Ted. Carrying it without the training is illegal. Even ex-cops need the approved training. Cop can jail me for it. Not worth it. I'll take the next class with our people at John Jay College. Okay?"

"You're going to walk around in uniform with no weapon?" Ted asked. "I wouldn't."

After Ted closed up, I read our past incident reports for a while. At dark, I set the alarm and locked up the office.

ε⌒Ɔ

Walking the Flatbush streets in my uniform made me feel like I was acting in a grammar school play back at Saint Blaise's. But this surprise inspection tour was my own idea.

The pants were too tight in the hips and legs. The polyester fabric scratched my skin. Somebody, probably Skip, had saved cash with cheap pants. This tight feeling made me want to climb

– 166 –

out of them. Tonight my pale city skin would itch. That was nothing to look forward to.

Under my left uniform leg, on the calf, I wore an elastic surgical brace. Eight inches of lead pipe fit against the brace, making the pants bulge. But at night, nobody would care to look at a guard's leg. The get-up made me limp.

Street hoods had taught me this leg brace trick. The brace would hold a flat semi-auto gun or a dagger or anything else. Packages of crack, money or a handcuff key would go there snugly and never come loose.

The eight-point uniform hat fit me all right. The new shirt rode a bit loosely but that was good. I wanted the freedom.

An ambulance roared up Flatbush Avenue with lights and sirens working. An RMP followed the white cops inside looking bored. They were on their way to another Flatbush shooting or knifing.

Other guards were at their posts that I passed. Some sites had burst water pipes with scummy water lying flat on the dirt. The Flatbush Secure uniform stood over it like a scarecrow that was not too bright.

Keeping my distance from the sites, I saw that none of the guards noticed me. That was good. If they recognized me, they would warn each other to stay awake and active.

That would defeat my plan.

More gangsta rap blasted from cars rocketing past on Flatbush. The noise never seemed to stop.

Some streets had broken streetlamps.

Experts said that darkness increased street crimes.

They had other ideas, too.

A cloud of garbage smell wafted over Flatbush.

Four gangsta-outfitted kids with fade haircuts dangled on Flatbush and Maple Street. They were slopping down bottles of beer, popping open fresh ones with curses and streams of foam, then pouring a few swallows on the concrete in memory of dead compatriots.

Stepping into a doorway, I watched them for a few minutes. The smallest one, a wiry jokester with red-rimmed eyeglasses in big heart shapes, kept touching his belt underneath the loose orange T-shirt. Thugs carrying guns did that all the time. They wanted to make sure that the gun was still there and not visibly bulging out.

Big heart-shaped glasses on a gunman made me smile. If I were writing up a UF-61, a crime report, about this crew, I would focus on him and nickname him "Big Heart."

Staying in the shadows, I used my cellphone to call 911. The 911 operator did not sound impressed about either the beer or my suspicions on the gun.

To get it on tape, I asked for her number twice. She answered me in a voice that I could use to slice ham. Civil servants hated to identify themselves. I'd been the same way. But now, I was a freewheeling civilian.

Minutes pulled themselves past, like someone dragging a full burlap sack over a junkyard.

Lloyd Sealey Square stood empty. Few locals wanted to walk here at night. Garbage trucks cawed in the distance. Gypsy cabs ferried passengers along Flatbush Avenue.

When the cops arrived, they were careless in approaching the group.

One RMP car came down Flatbush and stopped twenty feet from the group. The cops approached from the front. They should have approached the group from the rear. That was safer in case anyone was carrying.

Big Heart twitched. To me, that meant that he would run.

"Okay," said the passenger cop, a wide, pale woman with scraggly blonde hair and a high-pitched city accent. "Put the beers down and put your hands on your heads."

Her partner was a stretched bony shape in the blue bag, big Adam's apple bobbing and quick nervous moves. If people were animals, he would be a rawboned dog, an experienced hunter. Heavy eyebrows furred his face. The same current of hair showed in his open collar and the forearms. His fingers touched the handle of his holstered Glock.

"Hey, aw, whazzup?" Big Heart asked. "We ain't doing nothing! This is all good, homey"

"Come on," the hairy cop said. "We got a call. You guys –"

"Don't mean –" Big Heart said. He lunged away.

Hairy Man tried to grab him. His fingers clutched empty air.

Big Heart dodged and spun. He sped up, running right towards me. The others whooped and ran.

From what I had seen before, I was poised and ready. But nerves usually made me fumble actions like this. Fear wet me now. But the trick was not to think too much. Big Heart was coming closer to me. Excitement tightened my body. Street Patrol happies came back to me.

I could not miss.

But I could do what had stopped Lutz. As Big Heart got near, I stepped out of the doorway, planted my left foot with the toe going away from my body, stiffened my right leg and swung it like a stick. My right leg stayed straight. It moved like a baseball bat against Big Heart's left thigh.

My leg hit the peroneal nerve. Big Heart went down as if I had chopped his legs off. He flopped hard. As he hit, I grabbed his belt where he had been touching himself. My fingers hit metal. I yanked the metal out of his belt. It was an old-fashioned Peacemaker .45, a cowboy's gun. It had blued steel and a stag handle of white and brown.

Guns like this sometimes went off by accident. More than one cop had been shot handling a client's piece when it suddenly fired. So I jammed this one in the uniform pant's wide back pockets, barrel pointed down.

Big Heart rolled on the ground. He swung a fist at my groin. I sidestepped. His hand hit my thigh. It stung, but I shook it off. Adrenaline shielded me now.

"That ain't the way, partner," I said. "Lie still or you won't believe what happens next."

His buddies had vanished down the street.

Wide Lady got to me first. Her Glock was out of the holster. Hairy Man stepped behind her.

"Who you, pal?" Wide Lady asked. "Comic book avenger or something?"

"Max Royster, off the Job," I said. "Boss of Flatbush Secure. I took his piece off him. What do you want me to do?"

"Nothing," said Hairy Man. "Don't move. I'll take the piece."

"Lie still there, homes," Wide Lady told Hearty Shapes. She bent closer. Handcuffs flashed nickel in her mitts.

"I'm the complainant," I said. "Told 911 about the gun."

"Yeah, they told us," Hairy Man said. "For once, they did it right. But don't try taking a gun guy down yourself again. Could blow you up with a piece like this. It's a big one."

He made it sound like he would punish me for getting killed.

"Yeah, right," Wide Lady said. "Don't you know that? What are you, some kind of caped crusader vigilante-type?"

"That ain't mine!" Big Heart said. "You put it that there on me!"

CHAPTER 24.

Broken Windows

"I'm no crusader," I said. "Just a guard boss."

"In this precinct, we lock up guards all the time for doing crimes their own selves," Wide Lady said.

"And you're a real riot," Hairy Man said. "Because look at this gun."

He held the Peacemaker out and snapped the trigger. Training made me cringe. The hammer fell. It clicked.

"Gun is a goddamn toy," Hairy Man said. "Nothing but that. We can only charge him with Possession of an Imitation Pistol. Not a big deal."

"I'll bet he's on probation," I said. "He has the air of a rogue about him."

"What about it, Cutie-Pie?" Wide Lady asked Big Heart, still lying on the ground. "Are you on probation?"

Big Heart asked me to perform a violent act upon myself.

"No," I said. "I don't think that I'd like to do that. I think that would hurt."

Big Heart continued on in this vein.

"And I ain't never been arrested," he wound up.

"Well, you can't say that anymore now, can you?" Wide Lady said.

"Tell me something," I said. "What did they say you did, when you weren't arrested, to get you into all that trouble?"

"They SAID that I stole this fool's car," he said.

"That's not fair," I said. "Putting you in trouble for saying something. But you only got probation. You know what that means?"

"No getting busted," he said. "No staying out late, no getting drunk or high in public, work, go to school. Or else your Probation dude arrest you."

"No," I said. "That will never happen. All that probation means is that you cannot move to Rumania or drive a pink car on Tuesdays."

"Get yourself up and in the car," Wide Lady said to him. "Before you try my patience."

Big Heart sputtered a few more sparkling idioms from the boulevards. He got to his feet without using his cuffed hands. Muscles tensed and bunched as he did it. My kick had been lucky, toppling him.

Turning his back, he opened the RMP door with his handcuffed mitts. He settled inside the back seat like I would settle down onto my bed.

"Why do you call 911 and bust our shoes over mutts like him drinking beer?" Hairy Man said. "We've got real crime in this precinct."

"I agree," I said. "I walked Sector Eddy right out of the Academy and left the middle class forever."

"Then, why?"

"Some Harvard professor jokers with hay in their hair call it The Broken Windows Theory," I said. "So let me spout it a bit. You see a broken window in a city building in your hood. You make note, tell your boss and send a memo to the city. Nothing happens.

"Months go by. You notice the window is still broken. So do your locals, white or black, on that block. They may even ask you to write the city about it."

"I tell him that I already did," Wide Lady said. "Hate it when those types, those letter writers, bother me when I'm on foot."

"Right," I said. "And when the city still doesn't fix that little window, what are they telling us in this hood?"

"That we don't count for much," Wide Lady said.

"You guys got this theory down," I said. "You don't need me."

"They read it to us at roll-call," Hairy Man said. "Useless."

"No," I said. "I got to disagree with you on that, partner. Nobody fixes that window. So the locals start drinking beer on the street near it. Because nobody cares about the broken window, right?

"So what's a little beer, after that? Then some enterprising youngster figures that since you cops haven't done anything about the busted window OR the beer-drinkers, that's the right place to sell a little grass."

A couple heading home passed us, staring at Big Heart in the back seat.

"It don't go that easy," Wide Lady said.

"I think that it does. Grass sales. Maybe some PCP. Then crack. I mean, it's a prime location, right? Then you got a territory dispute between these salesmen. These salesmen do not lawyer up. They grab their nines and start shooting. Bullet goes wild. Kills a kid in her cradle. Then everybody wants to know how this street got so dangerous."

"You got a big mouth for a flat-badge security guard," Hairy Man said. "We're just killing time listening to you."

"Enough touchy-feely ideas already," Wide Lady said.

"Then listen to this," I said. "Don't be like I was. And most cops. We get mad at the wrong things. What do you think that this client was doing with a fake gun? Rape? Robbery?"

"You don't know that."

"You think that he was carrying it to protect the neighborhood?" I asked, giving them two of my new business cards. "My office has free coffee and doughnuts for any cops. We can argue more over a cup. Spread the word."

They grunted and got back into their RMP.

"That's so old school," Hairy Man said out the window. "You think that you can buy us for free coffee and doughnuts?"

"No," I said.

Hairy Man gunned the gas and the car tore away, fishtailing.

"Just rent you a bit," I said.

&

Walking along Flatbush Avenue, I passed by more Dutch style buildings – sharp wooden eaves on the roof and light yellow walls with dark brown trim. The colors reminded me of cream on gingerbread. Brooklyn still had buildings that reminded me the city had been Dutch for the first forty years.

Cooper would still be up working this late. When I called her, she answered on the first ring.

"Are you tomcatting out on the streets?" she asked me.

Flatbush Avenue looked dead and locked up for the night right now.

"Absolutely," I said.

"Not wanting to sound suspicious, what are you doing at 11:15 at night?"

"Making some money so that you will be proud of me."

"Really."

"Speechifying about crime prevention to real cops."

"They must have loved that," she said.

"They managed to keep their love under control," I said.

"Now, what's your plan?" she asked. "I miss you. The bed is too wide without you"

That stopped me. I tapped my free right hand against my thigh. That was the hand that I would use to caress her tonight. I ached to go back there now and crawl under the blankets next to her.

"After all that loose talk, I need to wash my tongue in some hot coffee. It might take a bit more walking to find a spot. There's a Dunkin' Donuts on Church Avenue."

"You're walking? I thought that you were in a car. You'd be safer driving."

"Driving, you miss too many things," I said. "That's one of the problems with modern police patrol. I need to see all the problems on foot."

"Oh, really?"

"Of course, some of the problems may see me first. But don't worry about me. Cooper, I'm in uniform. Nobody ever mugs a guard for his paycheck."

We cooed into the phone some more and then I closed out our talk.

It still felt ridiculous about walking around in a guard's uniform when I was old enough to suffer the beginnings of dementia.

Flatbush had steel gates down in front of the display windows. Churches, clothing stores and superettes stayed behind the metal. Because of crime, these merchants could not get worthwhile insurance. They ate the loss of any merchandise.

Fear of getting mugged and hurt still fluttered through me. Other bloody victims' faces and hospital gurneys flashed through my memory.

Three different construction sites had three Flatbush Secure guards posted, awake and alert. That brought a smile to me.

ভ

Then I walked to the construction site where Wild Tommy Root was now posted. He was pacing and looking down into the ditch.

"You want coffee, Mister Max?" Root offered. "Got some in the thermos here. Nothing open around here tonight. What a bore, what a bore."

"Thanks."

Is that today's paper there?" I asked.

"Been there a month," he said. He horse-laughed. "It's *The Jamaican Daily Gleaner* anyway. White people don't read that rag. Y'all too smart, yo."

"Who says we're that smart, Tommy?" I asked. "For years, I been saying that white people are for entertainment purposes only."

Root snorted and kept looking around the construction site ditch for thieves or vandals or maybe just because he was bored.

"Let me have the paper anyway, Tommy. Might be useful later on".

ভ

Hogan Gardens Apartments on Flatbush Avenue south of Parkside Avenue was the next post.

The complex consisted of six modern apartment buildings jammed together, trying to attract professionals to live there. The idea was not working out. Professionals who worked in Manhattan preferred to live in the safer, whiter and richer Park Slope.

We were supposed to have a guard here all night, armed with a .38 revolver. But there was nobody here. No blue uniform was hanging out anywhere. I felt angry and scared at the same time. Once again, Flatbush Secure had let me down.

Five men and a few women, all in their twenties, hung out in the broad courtyard just inside the gate leading to Flatbush Avenue. Legit locals stayed off Flatbush at night. Crowds like this crowd were the reason why.

"The-Reasons-Why" would be a good name for this crew, I decided.

My phone camera recorded some still photos and videos of them under the lights. These would be useful for my guards or the cops later on. Nobody saw me film them.

In a doorway across Flatbush, I took out my lead pipe and put it inside the newspaper in my back pocket. Then I entered the courtyard.

"Hey, hey!" one of The-Reasons-Why shouted. He was fat and slow-moving but his wrists and forearms showed solid in the shirtsleeves of his party shirt. "You the new security guard?"

"The old one, we run him off," a beautiful teenaged Reason Why said, smiling a dazzling smile. Full breasts jutted over a flat tummy, thrusting against her bunny-pink jogging suit.

"I'll just bet you did," I said.

One man had "trust no bitch" tattooed on his forearm.

Another had "Greenhaven" on his leg below his cut-offs. Greenhaven was a state prison. The men had the sullen and violent look of prison inmates. They were way too much for me to handle.

Marijuana smell hung in the air. One girl staggered. They would be cocky.

They thought that they had me.

"Okay," I said. "Let's have a game. Who lives here? If you don't live here, then you must leave."

Nobody answered.

Then they exploded, laughing.

"Aw, you guys are beautiful," I said. "Locals lock themselves in here at night. And you are The-Reasons-Why. Do you like that name?"

One of the men exploded with a laugh. He sounded like Ivan.

"That's a good name for us," he said. His heavy face sparked a grin and then settled under the big Afro hair and gold neck chains. "Things go bad here in the hood and we are The-Reasons-Why," he said. He dropped the street accent and spoke clearly. "You put us here, homey. I read books. Slavery, no good jobs, CIA selling us crack."

Moving slowly so nobody would shoot me, I took out my cellphone and punched in 911. The Book Reader spat.

"Operator 836, where is the emergency?" the 911 operator asked.

"619 Flatbush Avenue," I said. "Hogan Gardens Apartments. Disorderly group trespassing. I'm the security guard here. Request an NYPD car here forthwith. Because they look dangerous to me, and I think that they have weapons. I am scared. My name is Max Royster, Director of Security for Flatbush Secure."

"Any weapons seen?"

"Negative," I said. "But the night is young."

"Yo! Yo!" said the loudest one. He sounded like a waste of time. I would call him "Wastrel". He was also the smallest, slim and snakelike and hard to corner. A brief moustache overscored his shouting rascally mouth. His eyes said that he was enjoying this. "Was there anyone on that phone, or you just shucking us?"

"Ask them when they get here," I said. "Gentlemen, a smart man knows when to settle down and when to move on. I'm asking you to move on."

"Man, we already got you! And we got your phone!"

"You're trespassing," I said. "Please leave now."

"Dude, why do you think that we are staying here with you?"

"Why?" I asked. "So that you can play some more Pin-The-Tail-on-the-Honky. But if you don't leave, I'll have to take action."

"You better not try moving or nothing," Wastrel said.

Wastrel shoved me into Book Reader with the Afro. My body felt the shock, like football scrimmage. Book Reader formed a fist.

I got balanced. He threw the punch. My gut was already moving away. His fist grazed me. They were just having fun. If they wanted to, they could have stomped me into chuck steak.

My sweats told me how scared I was. I already knew that. But they were just warming up. The man with the Greenhaven tattoo swung at me. He missed.

Again, not wanting to move too quickly, I pretended to be hurt by the non-punch and leaned against the building wall. My hands went to my Sam Browne belt and pressed my gut in.

"Easy there, guys," I wheezed. "Respect the Older Generation."

They watched to see if I would try running. If I did, they would jump and stomp me.

This had to be timed just right. A siren started up about ten blocks away. It had taken me years to gauge the distances with sirens.

Trying to look casual, I let my hand drop to the rolled-up *Daily Gleaner* in my back pocket. My fingers felt the pipe inside the paper and got tight.

The Precinct was probably getting tired of my calls and wanted to shut down tonight's crusade. The-Reasons-Why were all bunched in front of me now.

Straining now and feeling my body pound, I took the paper from my pocket.

It was time to move.

The paper snapped up. I caught Greenhaven in the throat.

"Sneaky Pete!" Greenhaven choked out. "He pipin' us!"

Everyone jumped back. Some ran.

My pipe swung backhand. It caught Book Reader across his face. He fell backwards.

My legs shook. But they took a long stride towards Wastrel. The rolled newspaper tapped his shoulder. He folded to his knees. I touched the paper to his ribs.

"Awwww!" he shouted.

Wastrel tried grabbing me. The pipe tapped his head. His teeth clicked together. He dropped, cursing.

Two RMPs blasted their way up Flatbush Avenue. Headlights hit the group. Some scattered. One jogger-type cop, wire-rim glasses reflecting the red roof lights, tried to snag the Teen-aged Beauty. She kicked the cop and ran away with her girlfriends.

I opened up *The Daily Gleaner* and let the lead pipe slide onto the street. It clanged. But the sirens and cops shouting covered the pipe's noise. I kicked the pipe towards the corner sewer. It rattled and went down.

Detective Johnny Broderick of the NYPD Broadway Squad used to hide a lead pipe inside a rolled-up newspaper. While others watched, he would tap a hoodlum's body with the paper. The hoodlum would drop, just like these Reasons-Why did. Nobody saw the pipe.

"I called 911," I said. My voice shook and broke. My thumb pointed at Wastrel and Book Reader. "Those go for Assault on me and Menacing. I'll sign the 61."

"Crap, Mister Security Guard," the jogger-type cop said. "Assault don't mean nothing."

"Now, I'm requesting an ambulance," I said. "They hurt me. That should solidify your assault case on them. Once I go to the hospital, this Assault means something."

"Aw, come on," the jogger-type cop said. "Is this really worth it?"

"It is, to me," I said. "Once I get to be permanent Director of Flatbush Secure, I'll score lots of cash somewhere down the line."

CHAPTER 25.

Pillow Talk

Cooper and I lay back in bed, panting.

Like a boat loosed from its moorings, I drifted towards sleep on my back.

Then she was talking.

I did not understand her words.

She spoke some more. It was all jumbled.

"Sure," I said. "Friday. If I can get the car."

"Stop it," Cooper said. "Do you call that an intelligent response?"

"Pretty good. Considering that I didn't hear the question. Need to sleep."

My eyes shuttered.

Everything felt buttery and smooth.

Then she was touching my arm again.

"I mean, what is your answer to this question?" she asked.

"I didn't hear it. How about some sleep? Then we can wake up refreshed and have a good talk."

"You don't want to talk. You are just humoring me."

"Without much success," I said.

Her dark hair hung over the etched face. Looking at her still thrilled me. Her eyes crackled with secret fires.

"The question is," she said, "'Why do some of my friends in the group think that you look down on them?'"

"What group?"

"The Flippers, as you call them."

Something cold iced my body right then. I shook my left arm to ward off any tension there.

"You and I both call them that," I said.

"Then, maybe I will stop. Maybe it is disrespectful."

"Do you have to worry about what everyone thinks?"

"That's better than not caring about what anybody thinks."

"How true," I said. "Let's talk about this some more when I'm rested. Or else I'll have nightmares."

"Are these your cop tricks in how to handle hysterical women and verbal disputes?"

"Are you hysterical? Or planning to be?"

"I don't like police tricks used on me. I don't think that's respectful."

I blew out a breath. The bedroom, with evening light coming through the windows, was starting to spin around. Cooper's blonde wood furniture and the modern prints on the walls started to spin.

It felt so much like the old whiskey river days of before that I slipped my foot onto the floor. Years ago, that foot used to stabilize me when the wicked wall-spins had begun. But today's struggle was different. Cooper was after something, and I seemed to be It.

"Do you consider my friends to be *frotteurs?*" she asked. "Or you just hint that all they care about is their property?"

"Did they form this group to help the neighborhood or themselves?" I asked. "If they lived upstate in the white-folks-and-Green-Mountains country, do you think that they would give a tinker's damn what happens to black Flatbush?"

"They are protecting their life's investment," she said. "And their children's futures. Why do you slam them for that?"

"Because they want to bend the law and use it for their purposes," I said. "That is how fascism starts."

It sounded silly to use the word "fascism" again. It belonged in the history books. But Nancy's words about fascism stayed in my head.

"You call them fascists?" Cooper asked. "Are you as nuts as the Department says you are? Most of them vote Democrat."

"They call my guards when somebody stands on their corner and passes out handbills," I said. "Ted the Smoothie tries explaining that the law allows everyone to stand on the street. Even Ted understands that."

"Well, they do pay you to patrol their streets and make them safer," she said.

"Not by breaking the law."

"Why can't they stand on the next corner and not this corner?" she asked.

"That's what everyone wants to know."

"This job title, Director of Security, is going to your head," she said.

"I'm trying to direct something." I said. "Security guards shouldn't patrol streets. Ain't trained for that. Believe me, it takes years to learn how to do that well. Trouble starts when they start thinking that they are cops."

"What would you have them do, then, after my friends pay your company?"

"Guards should observe and report, my dear," I said. Somehow, that cliché about observing and reporting slowed my racing heart. Cooper's talk was crashing into my body defenses.

"Prop them up in front of a store entrance or a school. If anything heavy goes down, they should call the cops. Or some other adult."

"You keep talking about guards as if they were children."

"I've been working with them two months, and some of them act like it. And so do I. Bright new shiny badges and other toys."

"Weren't you going to change all that by training and example?" she asked.

"I'm staying up late trying. But it may never work. Whenever we try explaining to the Flippers that we can't move undesirables off a public street, they all say the same thing. That is, 'Mr. Manry used to always move them for us, without any arguments.' I believe them."

"Is that so wrong?"

"I've seen Friend Manry in action," I said. "I wonder why no lawyer has sued Manry into oblivion for violating some homeless jamoke's civil rights. It was going to happen soon."

"Max, you worry about things too much."

"If I unleash a bunch of club-swinging robots on innocents, I can get sent to prison or sued. Or both. That tends to worry me, yeah."

"You call them fascists," she said. "But have you ever taken a course in repressive governments? Or finished a book about them? I invite you to learn about them and define your terms better that way."

"Any cop whoever finished a hardcover book without pictures in it knows about fascism," I came back. "We see how easily policing can slide into it."

"Did they teach you anything about fascism in your Police Academy?"

"The word 'fascism' makes the bosses too nervous to teach a course in it. They worry about the ACLU raiding the classroom if there's anything controversial in the lesson plan."

"So that gives you the right to sling that word around?"

"This seems a strange debate for two naked lovers to have," I said. My fingers played on her taut upper arm.

"No, it isn't," she said.

My gut sucked in. Everything inside me chilled.

"What?" I asked.

"Don't touch me. I don't feel like making love now."

CHAPTER 26.

The Pour Is Always with Us

"Ted," I said. "All posts are filled?"

"Nobody banged in sick," Ted said.

He switched off our free coffeepot, the cop lure. It was already working, and two uniforms stood outside, drinking their free coffees. Buzz, the Playpen Irregular, was smoking and joking with them in his new Flatbush Secure outfit.

"I don't know why everyone is coming to work," Ted said. "That can't last."

"They miss you, Ted," I said. "You're the father figure."

"It's all bullshit."

"So I'll see you tomorrow," I said. "Call me if we have any catastrophe."

Ted nodded.

The routine of leaving had me feeling good in a settled kind of way. There was a whole world of work apart from Cooper.

☙

A cool wind blew down Flatbush Avenue. Pounding the pavement, I tried not to remember Cooper turning me away. Time spent doing nothing might heal this open wound. Staying out of Cooper's apartment as long as possible would help.

So there were things for me to do today.

Lloyd Sealey Square and the gas station at Washington Avenue and Flatbush Avenue looked different somehow today. I could not figure out why.

That was something else for me to work on.

The Food Castle parking lot held a fringe of street people hanging out, not pushing shopping carts or doing anything else. A few sipped from brown paper bags.

A silver Flatbush Secure van driven by Mugsy Hart bounced into the parking lot. He wore his blue uniform and his hat on for effect, along with a mean expression.

The hangers-on snapped alert. A few put down their paper bags and moved away.

Mugsy stopped the van and bolted outside, baton in hand.

"Here comes that head breaker," a pudgy man with a full beard said. A thick gold neck chain clinked as he made an angry face. "Same fool they always send."

Mugsy swung the stick at the paper bag. Glass broke inside the bag. I felt like hiding myself.

"Hey, you," Mugsy told Pudgy. "Pick up your bag and get rid of it."

"Ain't mine, man."

"Pick it up, or you be sorry, right now," Mugsy said.

To underline it, he swung the baton at another bag. A beer can went THWOCK! Beer sprayed upward, and foam gushed over the bag.

To my ear, it sounded like Mugsy was playacting the role of tough cop.

"You ain't no cop," Pudgy said. "And I don't have to mind your silly butt. I'm going now."

Mugsy banged his baton on the concrete. The noise hurt my ears.

"Can't they leave us alone?" a gnarled woman in a New York Yankees hat and matching T-shirt said.

I shrugged. I did not know what else to do.

"Food Castle pays them just to mess with us," Pudgy said.

"They worse than the cops," Yankee Fan said. She stepped along the gray curb. She turned to go inside Food Castle. "Cops, at least, you can conversate with."

One of the managers, black and bald and fierce-looking, was standing at the door. He shook his head and jerked a thumb towards Empire Boulevard.

Yankee Fan nodded and walked away.

The manager waved to Mugsy and gave him the same thumb pointing straight up. Mugsy grinned back and jumped back inside the van. A bored stock boy, who looked Middle Eastern, came outside. As he cleaned up the wet paper bags, his mustached head bobbed up and down in time to the music he was listening to on his headset.

Stepping into the parking lot, I waved to Mugsy to slow down.

The street people watched as they walked away.

Mugsy stopped the van near me.

"How's it going, Mugsy?" I asked him through the window.

On the radio, Ted's voice squawked at Root.

"They see me, they take off," he said, looking relaxed. "Came by yesterday and told them that I would pour out a couple of their wine bottles, they still here."

I hated to feel like a boss and have my words dent the smile on his face. But nobody else was going to do it for him.

"Mugsy, when you were a kid, could cops pour out your bottle when you're street drinking?" I asked.

"They did it all the time."

"New administration," I said. "You're talking about when you were a youngster, right? When was the last time that you saw a pour-out like that?"

He nodded. The uniform hat bobbed.

This was going to be delicate. I moved my hand downwards in a settling motion. His eyes followed me.

"Cops don't do it anymore," I said. "Not in New York. Someone tapes them and there's a big hullabaloo about the wine-drinker's civil rights. CAPA screams.

"Who?"

"Citizens Against Police Abuse," I said.

"Jacked-up name," he said.

"Cops get written up and lose vacation days that way. I never did it when I rode this same street as a cop."

It felt like everyone in Brooklyn was watching us. The manager still stood in the doorway. He did not look happy. Maybe he could guess the way that our talk was going.

The drinkers and street people were still roving along Empire Boulevard, watching us.

"Okay," I said, taking a deep breath. "You smashed some bottles. So you got the rep already. They will remember you. Did you see them show respect and take off today?"

"Sure enough. Word up."

"Then you don't have to do it again. Ride on your rep."

"Come on," Mugsy said. "They just swarm over our butts next week. And Food Castle pays some other guarding fools to run these bums off. We lose this account, you blame me."

"Not for doing your job, Mugsy."

"That's what you say now. But you making good coin off this job, while we can't get anywhere on our pay."

"I'm putting in a rank system with a new title," I said. "If you take additional training and pass my written test, you get a pay increase and the new title."

"Okay, what's the new title?"

"Special Agent."

Mugsy shot me a look.

"Like the FBI?" he said. "They won't like that. You can't use those words. We security guards."

"We are whatever we want to be, Hart."

He said an interesting word.

"American Express has investigators that they call Special Agents," I said. "So do most of the private railroad companies. The U.S. Government actually copied that title from the railroads. My lawyer says no problem with a private outfit calling employees Special Agents, so long as they do not impersonate government men."

"That's far-out total nuts."

"No, it's not. It's the possibility of the future, if we work for it. Mugsy, I been down, beat-up, disillusioned and fired from a job that I loved. Can I change any of that?"

"Not when you been fired."

"Right. The only thing that I can change is my attitude towards whatever happens. Nothing else. You call yourself a security guard."

"That's what the world says what we do," Mugsy said. "They know that we don't do no Special Agent-ing type of work. We stand in front of crap for crap pay and get crap respect."

"That's because the world likes to use shorthand for who we are," I said. "That way, they don't have to think. So, let's you and me study law, learn security techniques and change how the world thinks."

"Max, yo, with all due respect as my boss, you are some kind of dreamy nut. Where did they find you? And how are they going to keep you?"

By now, all the street people were gone.

"Mugsy, this job can take us all to good places," I said. "Do you agree?"

"Maybe."

"Let me ask you this. Does any other security agency make you these kind of what I admit are crazy promises?"

"No. Others got normal bosses."

"Right," I said. "Not like me. But, if one of these fools makes a complaint on you, it will slow down everything good that you need in your day. The cops will look for independent witnesses. Some wits will lie. That pudgy fella with the beard could call 911, report you and have the cops arrest you. That won't help you."

"You telling me to stop working?" Mugsy said.

"I'm telling you to let your rep and the company's rep work FOR you," I said.

My face burned from saying this.

"Don't get arrested or sued. Look up what the law says about pouring out bottles on the Internet. And let me know what you think about the title Special Agent."

CHAPTER 27.

Park Chit-Chat

Talking with Mugsy wound up the key in my back and spun me through Prospect Park. The homeless still squatted outside Lefferts House.

Buzz had called my cellphone and left a message that made absolutely no sense, with saloon noise and jukebox and laughter and confessions in the background. It was something about my pals, the Playpen Irregulars, and a fishing trip from Canarsie.

Lone men and boys swirled through the park walkways. This was after five and to my eye, they were doing nothing. They hung out by the thicker trees and shrubs off the East Drive.

Inside Prospect Park, the waters of Lullwater Lake reflected the ivory-colored Beaux Arts. Boathouse as they lapped against the piers. Images of the red terra-cotta grooves arching over the Tuscan columns rippled in the lagoon's dark surface.

The Boathouse had stood here since 1904 and had seen Flatbush flower, then sicken and waste away.

A gremlin of mischief rose up in me, and I watched one youngster hang by the Boathouse for a few minutes. He walked behind an Asian couple and asked for money.

The Asian man shook his head. The couple strode away.

The youngster padded away and hopped up on the metal fence near the Carousel. He wore a red jogging outfit with short pants and sneakers without shoelaces in them. An arm tattoo read "Crip Killer." That tattoo made him a member of the Bloods gang. His red clothes underlined that fact.

He had a broken nose and scarred face. When he stretched, metal glinted under his shirt, perhaps a knife or a screwdriver. He might be planning a mugging.

An RMP passed by. Neither cop inside gave us a look. Maybe they were heading for the coffee pot inside Flatbush Secure's office for the free cup with sugar and milk substitute. By now, the coffee would be stale.

"Hiya," I approached Fence Hopper. Fear pitched my voice higher.

Part of me wanted to keep walking. But I had started this dance.

"I'm checking on a mugging that went down right near here yesterday. Did you notice any suspicious characters nearby?"

My nerves pulled my feet away from him. But he did not notice.

He shook his head and slithered off the fence and adjusted his belt all in one move.

Then he stopped.

"Are you a cop?" he asked.

That stopped me.

"No, I'm not," I said. "My brother-in-law Nick was attacked here and lost a watch with sentimental value. I am willing to pay to get it back."

His face set into hard lines.

"Why would I know anything about that?" he asked. "Just because I'm hanging out where your bro got jumped, you think I did it? 'cause I'm black?"

He was turning everything around. That included me.

"'course not," I said. "I didn't say that."

"Maybe you should think about what you are saying," he said. "There's a whole lot underneath those words."

Articulated speech coming from someone with the gangsta look flummoxed me more.

"I told you why I'm here," I said.

"But there's another agenda," he said. "You're not telling me everything."

"Nobody tells anyone everything."

"True that," he said. "I got to wonder if you're gay and looking to pick someone up here. 'cause these 'woods are lovely, dark and deep'."

Forcing a smile but trying to make it masculine, I shook my head.

"Now you're quoting Robert Frost," I said. "You're just full of surprises, aren't you?"

"Aren't you?" he said. "I bet that you know lots of tricks."

With that, I smiled again and tried to appear casual. But my body betrayed me. Nothing felt right.

"Where you going?" he asked.

His unlaced sneakers, the kind we cops call "felony shoes," edged towards me. Now he was back in the thug mode again. There was no more Robert Frost.

"What about your important mission? Your brother-in-law Nick's sentimental value wristwatch? Where's your family values?"

Silence followed.

"Okay," he said. "I'm going. I'm not hanging out here with crazy people lurking about."

He moved away. That was what I wanted him to do. Maybe he was a good fella who was carrying the metal in his belt for protection. Maybe I would never know.

CHAPTER 28.

The Daily Round Dances a Rumba

"Royster, I don't believe it," Piva said. He stood in the Flatbush Secure doorway. "Downtown says that crime in our precinct has dropped way down. Theft, burglaries, rob-ohs and even homicides. The Conditions Sergeant says that it's because of your toy cops."

"I agree with him," I said.

"You would. There's money in it for you."

"And facts. In the past two weeks, my Special Agents –"

"Your WHAT?"

"Special Agents. We have a new rank here. Our Special Agents called 911 fourteen times and had twenty-two arrests made by your cops. Seven of us made citizen's arrests. Word gets out."

"It's all bullshit," Ted said.

"You ought to know," I said. "It's also what keeps you employed, Ted. Or else you would have to open up your own charm school."

"Guards do NOT stop street crime," Piva said.

"That's not what you mean," I said. "What you mean is that you have not seen it happen. Not yet. Until this month."

"The stats will go up again," Piva said.

Some of our Special Agents tilted towards our talk, listening in. Fresh coffee smell flowed from our pot. Piva did not look like he wanted a cup.

"Don't be such a crêpe-hanger," I said. "Working at something usually works. Sooner or later. My Special Agents have been working at preventing crimes."

Some Special Agents nodded.

"I know how you think, Piva," I said. "That me and my flat-badge stumblebums are playing Secret Agent 007 games in our hideaway tree-house and pretty soon it will blow up in our faces."

"With someone dead," Piva said.

Someone snorted.

Patso's reddish face unslouched to scrutinize Piva.

Jason stepped out of the supply room that he taught in.

In the last few weeks, Jason had brought in law books. So I had him teaching our guards.

"Do you have any suggestions, Officer?" Jason asked. "Anything that we might do better?"

"Another country heard from," Piva said. "Yeah. Resign. Find some guard job with a normal boss."

With Jason's record, I did not want Piva talking with him.

"These agents had normal bosses already," I said quickly. "And nobody advanced. We're going to change the security business with what we do here."

"With our academy," Jason said. "My academy."

"Like you say, tree-house games," Piva said.

Jason stomped a boot onto the floor. The vibration knocked a *Time* magazine off the table.

"Instead of talking trash about 'another country heard from'," Jason said, "why don't you tell us about what you did on that dead brother's murder? You arrest anyone yet?"

"Who you, pal?" Piva asked.

"Concerned citizen," Jason said.

Jason's face heated with passion that I had never glimpsed before.

"And I've scoped you out in uniform around here, goofing off for years," Jason said. "Now, when we're improving this hood, you say that it's impossible. What's your magic formula?"

"Jason," I said.

"What are you, a wise guy?" Piva asked. His eyes dulled and went dead. I had seen that look before. My feet stepped between Jason and Piva.

"Piva, take a walk with me," I said. "You and me, we never liked inside work, and right now, I need today's *Times*."

Piva shook his head at Jason and stepped outside. I joined him on the sidewalk, feeling stirred up inside and not knowing why.

"I ain't talking," Piva said.

"Ease up," I said. "Anything new on the Lutz kill?"

Piva snapped his head back and forth. He walked away without saying anything.

"What's with him?" Jason asked, stepping outside.

"I'm wondering why Piva came here," I said. "As a white-shield detective, he wouldn't have to give us lower crime stats . The Conditions Sergeant deals with all ups or downs in crime reports. Piva came for some other reason. He had wanted to see us again, to see something for himself."

"Maybe he's after your job," Jason said.

♋

"Max?" Dr. Sunick, our therapist asked. She was coming along the sidewalk from Empire Boulevard. "May I speak with you a moment?"

She craned her head. If people were animals, she would be a terrier, frisky and friendly and lithe. Short blonde hair graying swirled around her heart-shaped face. Deep brownish-green eyes, the color of pond water, drew my attention.

"That employee, Hart," she said. "He's going through some home difficulties now. By ethics and law, I cannot go into specifics at this point. But his stress is such that I would not feel good about him carrying a firearm."

That stopped me.

"You think that he might shoot himself?" I asked.

"I've said all that I can say."

"He's got one of our armed posts," I said. "I'll have to switch him with another agent. Should he be working at all?"

She thought and then shook her head.

"Okay, Doctor," I said. "That's why I talked you into volunteering. I appreciate your helping us."

"You are my very own community service, Max," she said. "And I'm getting some experience here that I could get nowhere else."

"How so?"

"Many of your employees had never had a psychological make-up done. In my view, that's neglect. The only ones who were ever reviewed are veterans or the ones incarcerated when they were young."

∽

Hart was sitting outside, talking with the others, when I went back to the office. He looked up when I entered.

My nerves screamed at me. I tried faking a smile.

"Mugsy, can you come on in a minute, please?" I asked.

He came inside my office. His eyes rimmed red. That was the only thing unusual that I saw today.

"It's vacation time, Mugsy," I said. "What do you say to two weeks with pay? No worries. Dr. Sunick available by phone 24/7. And this does not come off your vacation time. It's just down time. You're carried on the books as working. Sleep until noon every day that the Lord sends."

Skip was going to scream about the two weeks pay. But Dr. Sunick seemed sure about this problem. Looking at Mugsy, I agreed with her. Something was eating him.

"This from the Bug Doc?" he asked.

"It's from you, Mugsy," I said. The fake smile felt sillier now. "What would you like to do?"

He leaned forward. His belly heaved.

"I don't know," he said.

"Do you have any friends or kin outside of Brooklyn?" I asked.

"My son lives in Jersey City. I can stay with him a bit. We get along okay."

I breathed out. This might get easier than I thought. The Jersey angle was a lucky one.

"Good idea. I'll drive you back to your place to pack a bag. Then we get to good old Jersey City. How's that sound?"

"Okay."

"Your gun carry permit does not work in Jersey," I said. "Travel legal and light for my sake. I don't want to lose you or your issued weapon to some corrupt Jersey cop. I'll never get it back. So unbuckle your Sam Browne belt and it will be here when you get back."

He leaned forward in the chair. Traffic noise quieted outside. It seemed like Flatbush was holding it's breath outside. I knew that I was.

"Okay," he said. He took off the heavy gunbelt with the old Colt .38 revolver in the NYPD holster and put it on my desk.

"Nothing will change, Mugsy," I said. "In two weeks, I put you back to making me rich. Let's all just get through this period. Okay?"

ℰⅅ

Traveling to Jersey always wore me out. The Transit Department posted road signs like the Red Chinese were about to invade and wanted to make sure they got snarled before they could ransack the state.

Finding his son's home was another ordeal. But we got there.

The father and son grunted at each other. They probably wanted me to leave before they talked.

But Mugsy looked more collected when I drove away.

ℰⅅ

When I got back to the office, I sat in on Jason's training class. He was a natural teacher. Nine agent trainees were answering his questions and adding their own stories.

Some had struggled through worthless school systems in New York or Alabama. This might be the first time that someone actually reached them in a classroom situation.

Skip showed up after four.

That day he wore a beautifully cut midnight blue suit, white-on-white shirt with French cuffs and a hand-painted red silk tie. His shoes were wet-looking, glossy black leather with tassels.

My ensemble today was the usual thrift shop bulletproof finery. Dark jacket that did not show dirt, dark blue shirt and pressed black jeans with my old Patrol shoes. The outfit made me look like a hardworking knockaround guy.

"I was just on the phone with Edna Hughes, the Assemblywoman for this district," Skip said.

His words sounded faster than normal. Something was exciting him.

"She wants to see both of us ASAP. The monthly crime stats are way, way low for this precinct. She is very happy. We don't want to make her unhappy, do we?"

"I hadn't really thought about it."

"But we have to fly to get there on time. Don't you have a tie?"

"Let me check," I moved to the training room. "Wild Root! Your tie, please, sir!"

Root smirked, unclipped his uniform black necktie from the new guard uniform and flung it across the room to me. He enjoyed disrupting anything organized.

∾

Skip ushered me to his black Lexus, illegally parked in the next door loading zone. He zoomed us through the sluggish Flatbush Avenue traffic, babbling about how happy our clients were today. Their properties were safer than ever before.

"It's because we are treating all our people better," I managed to say. "The new uniforms, shields, pay grade advances, classes and the title of Special Agent."

"Seems impossible," he said. "And childish. Kid stuff."

"I'm no headshrinker wizard," I said. "But we are childish. Not just us security kids. But everyone. We never change too much. We just grow fatter and get more credit cards."

He zinged us into another illegal parking spot off Church Avenue and was out of the car like a dancer. I had never seen him move so fast.

He brought me into a storefront office similar to Flatbush Secure, gave our names to a fashion-model receptionist and stood by, too nervous to sit.

A show-biz type man in a suit opened a door to the inner office. Skip practically dragged me inside.

Assemblywoman Edna Hughes rose from her desk. She stood about two inches over me. Her dark high-cheek-boned face held beauty that commanded respect and needed no make-up. She could have been the mother of the beauteous receptionist outside. Perhaps she was.

Her hair was pulled back, emphasizing her face's strong bones. She wore a clingy, dark green cotton dress and was built generously, strong, slim legs and long tapering fingers.

This scene had all the trappings of Serious Business Between Adults. I prepared myself for euphemisms and boredom.

Classical music played from a system somewhere. A scent of patchouli gifted the room. Framed oil paintings of Haitian folk art and Brooklyn landscapes filled the walls. In one photo, a much younger assemblywoman, in an Afro hairdo and miniskirt, shook hands with the President of the United States. The President seemed to be looking down her peasant blouse.

"It's a happy day for all of us in this community," she said. Her Islands accent lilted gently. "The Citizen's Crime Commission called to ask why misdemeanor theft reports were down eighty-seven percent, burglaries down thirty-three, robberies twenty-nine, and murder down by eleven percent. There has got to be an explanation."

"Maybe the cops stopped answering the phone," I said.

"Max," Skip said.

"Mr. Skip says that you did a lot of ideas that have never been tried before," she said. "Especially in the security business. It has been called a non-industry for some time. A dumping ground for those who have nothing going for them. Mr. Skip, my staff will coordinate media releases with you. This word has to get out fast."

"Before the stats go up again," I said.

"Ms. Lauten outside needs to speak with you now, Mr. Skip," she said, smiling. "That will give me a precious moment alone with Mr. Royster."

"Max," I said. "Mr. Royster is my father. I'm just a guy, is all."

Skip beamed, seemed to bow and melted back to the outer office.

೮

"Please close the door, Max," she said. "Intimacy is better."

"Almost always," I said.

"Your talents seem extraordinary," she said. "Flatbush needs thinkers like you. We have such a crime-ridden, dangerous image."

"Hard as a curbstone," I said.

"But you've managed to soften that image," she said. "Continue to do that over the next two months, there's a job waiting for you."

"Tea-boy at the Shangri-La Massage Parlor?" I asked.

"Better than that. I know what Skip is paying you. This new job will double it. It will be in the hospitality sector in hotels in different Caribbean islands. You will oversee security, among other things. How does that sound to you?"

"The next two months?" I asked. "The start of October? All that just for softening Flatbush?"

An image formed of me strolling along a beach underneath palm trees, barefoot in white duck pants holding a milky coconut with one hand and Cooper in a sinful black bikini with my other. Our skins were tanned, and our bodies rippled with muscles. Alligators in a nearby lagoon bowed their heads as we passed.

Somehow, I pulled myself back to Flatbush.

"This is a job that you will never see advertised," she said. "Many of my constituents are from the Caribbean. As am I. Brooklyn brothers and sisters call us 'coconuts' because we say nothing, hang from the trees and then finally drop without speaking. We respond by calling them 'mainlanders' or 'mains'. But we coconuts have a much higher standard of living than the mains. Most of own property and businesses."

"I've observed that," I said.

"So we'll say nothing more of this. Surely not to Mr. Skip."

"I might not take it," I said. "I like Flatbush."

"Nevertheless, the offer stands."

"And if crime slides back up, I lose the job."

"We both know that won't happen," she said, bursting into another smile that promised all good things.

✌

Skip smiled and fawned and got me safely away from the assemblywoman's sofa. We drove back to Flatbush Secure. I made him slow down.

"You're as jolly as a sand-boy," I observed. "Just let me follow my instincts and crime will keep dropping."

"I'm meeting the Mayor with some media people, as you heard," Skip said. "This is just the beginning. Do you realize the money that you and I can make together, turning this into a safe, landmarked area?"

Back at the office, I saw Manry. He sat talking with Jason and Ted and Buzz. He was still on a leave of absence with pay under the Family Medical Leave Act. He seemed loose and relaxed as he chatted with me about his trip.

I wondered what Skip would do with him when his four months of leave was up. Maybe Skip would toss me and re-instate Manry. It would save Skip a lot of cash to cut the classes and run things like before.

Leaving the office, I walked across Flatbush and up Lincoln Road. Maple Street Academy was near Prospect Park, and teachers were speaking with their kids on the sidewalk. Flatbush Secure had the contract here.

The janitor rattled on as I checked the guard log in the front room, and then the windows and doors. Everything looked okay.

∽

Back at the office, Manry was telling Jason and Buzz about Haiti and how beautiful the jungle was. He smelled of rum and was talking freely. Whatever the family emergency had been in Haiti, he seemed cheery.

Playing Boss Man of the Guard World, I took Ted, Manry, Jason and Patso out to dinner at Dino's.

Through dinner, I let the others talk away while I schemed.

Afterwards, we split up.

∽

I kept Manry with me as we walked up to the Maple Street Academy.

"Let me show you what's happened here since you left," I told Manry. Again, fear rasped my voice higher.

"*Wouch*," he protested. "I am way tired out with all that heavy food. Let's forget security for tonight, okay?"

"It'll just take a minute," I said. "I've got the security code in my head."

At the door lock, I punched in the numbers and Manry followed me inside. With my fingers shaking, I switched off the alarms.

"*Sa derezonab!*" he kept saying. "What are you showing me?"

Lights switched on automatically as we walked.

Then we came to a small room with an opening between it and the dining room for the kids.

"Look in the corner over there," I said. "And tell me what you see."

Manry entered the small room. I clicked the door shut behind him and locked it.

He looked in the corner and then straightened up.

"There's nothing there," he said. "What are you talking about?"

"On the contrary, there is everything there," I said. Now my voice climbed.

Manry tried the door.

"Hey, this is locked!"

"That's right, Manry," I said. "You are in your own little jail here. I've seen you in action. Threatening others with jail. For being poor. Or homeless. How does it feel?"

"Royster, what you playing at?"

"Real games tonight, Manry. You ever been a cop anywhere?"

"Haiti, *ma bête*. You know that. But I don't take no bribes as a cop. Too much hassle for bit of money."

"That's where you learned to slam someone on the thigh with your police baton?"

He frowned.

"We all learned that," he muttered.

"You are a hardworking man, Mr. Manry. I seldom saw anyone work harder. You take the job home with you."

"Yeah," he said. "Now let me out."

"The sale begins when the customer says, 'No'." I said." You got no limit to what you can do, here or in Haiti. And you're braver than I am. If you saw the cops chasing a mugger, what would you do?"

"Knock him on his *bouda*," he said.

"And that's what you did. You saw the cops losing that mugger on the foot race. NYPD can't run. We all know that. So you used your police training to baton him across the leg. Good, smart technique. Didn't you just mean to stop him?"

"I didn't do it!"

"In five minutes, I'm going to leave you here. You can't break out of that room. There's not enough room to kick or shoulder your way through the door. Then I'll break off the front door lock. Alarm will call 911. The cops will come, find you there and arrest you for burglary. And crack possession."

"Max, what crack? I don't even drink coffee!"

From the pocket of my thrift shop blazer, I shook out a plastic bag. Tiny chunks of rock candy lay inside the bag. It looked like crack, but it was just candy. Street people would think that it was crack. So would Manry.

"Manry, you tried to stop a mugger. Nobody blames you for that. You made an honest mistake. Please admit it."

"You frame me, *ak touye ou*. I kill you!"

"How will that help your own case?" I asked. "If you kill an ex-cop, they really come after you. We both know that."

I reached through the opening and emptied the bag at his feet. The chunks hit the floor. They sounded like gravel bits. He bent down, searching.

I sprinkled the rock candy residue from the bag onto his head and shoulders.

"Now the residue is in your hair and your jacket," I said. "Don't waste time trying to blow it away. Or find it on the floor in the dark. You can't. The cops will see it. They'll hit you with a drug charge, too. Under the law, that can be three to six years more in the joint."

"I tell the cops you put me here!"

"How often do they hear excuses like that? You and I both want to be running Flatbush Secure. We are rivals. They will still lock you up. It's a felony. They have to arrest you."

"I didn't do it!"

My belly buckled. Fear made me want to hurl.

Shaky legs walked me to the admin office. From my tours here before, I knew where they kept the petty cash. Holding it by the edges to avoid fingerprints, I picked up the gray metal tin with the cash and walked back to Manry. He was trying to kick the door. But the space was too small. Coins and dollar bills spilled onto the floor.

"Listen, I got family problems!" he said.

"Sorry for that."

"No, I mean, that night that guy got killed, I visit my brother. He in Chicago, man! How do I be here killing this fool? I got the email on my phone now! I didn't fly back until that morning."

Something like wind went out of me.

"Show me," I said.

He took out a pricey-looking phone. He punched in codes. His own fingers shook. This was making both us professionals fall apart from nerves. If my first heart attack hit now, Manry would go to prison but I might die.

"Look!" he said. "This page in my e-mail. Trip details, man! It shows my flight leaving at 12:30 a.m. and getting into New York at 4:30 a.m. Then, they ask me to comment about the flight! How do I kill somebody in Flatbush while on a plane from Chicago?"

"Aw, raspberries!" I said.

The screen showed what he was telling me.

It seemed time to re-negotiate.

"Okay, then we make a deal," I said. "Hand me your driver's license."

"No way!"

"Goodnight, then. I hope that dinner filled you up. Jail food tastes like someone is frying a cat."

"Here it is."

"Smart move. If you tell anyone about our little talk, I will plant some drugs in your house where you can't find them, call the cops and have them make the happy discovery."

It was a fantasy. But, in a crisis, nobody thought things through. Manry looked like a fella in crisis.

"I've scared you and taken ten minutes of your time," I said. "And this helps you."

"How this helps me?"

"Because you convinced me that you didn't kill Lutz. So I don't feed you to the cops. Ever. They don't watch you and maybe see you impersonate a cop and beat up the homeless."

"I never do that!"

"Manry, a while back, I videoed you," I lied. My voice slowed down like a negotiator, like the Dutch captain buying Manhattan from the Lenape tribe in 1624. "And so did some folks living near the park. You don't want that kind of attention from the cops. Homeless people find a clinic lawyer, sue you and you lose your house."

"Okay," Manry said. "You talk too flipping much, man. What do you want?"

"In a minute, I'll give you a screwdriver. Twenty minutes work and you can chip away the door and leave here. No cops. Make sure that you lock up. You're on leave with pay. Go home and enjoy it. Don't come near me or the office. I see you, I shoot you."

Guns and me hated each other. But Manry did not know that. Like everybody, he thought that ex-cops like me needed guns near my pillow to get to sleep. But my life had no guns.

"If you stay smart and cool," I said, "I'll get you a better job in security. Leave Flatbush behind you. Somewhere in corporate Manhattan."

"Royster, I'm not leaving here!"

"Don't forget those videotapes of you whamming the homeless. If you want to blame someone for that, look in the mirror."

My screwdriver bobbled in my hands. I gave it to Manry.

"I feel like the worst detective in Brooklyn," I said. "Sorry for the drama. But stay away from me, or I'll drop you."

He was chipping at the wood to get free before I left the school.

CHAPTER 29.

Heavy Eddy

Even holding Cooper's flanks, it was difficult sleeping that night. Images of Manry sawing down a shotgun and blasting me from behind filled my head.

ↄ

The next morning, I got to the office first, built myself a cup of coffee from our cop-trap percolator and thought about the case.

The janitor from Maple Street Academy called to gripe about their wrecked door and damaged petty cash box. But nothing was missing. While they spoke, I thought about Lutz's death.

Two uniforms from the Seven-One, stopped in, guzzled black coffees, swapped clichés with me, and then went back on patrol.

Deirdre, one of our woman guards, filled the doorway, holding onto Leo's bicep. She grinned at me, showing a gold tooth, her strong, full body bursting in the dark blue uniform. Her short hair waved as she hauled Leo, now wearing his new guard uniform, through the doorway.

"Leo, honey," Deirdre said. "Get your paycheck. I gotta get on post."

"'Honey?'" I asked.

"Yeah, that's me," Leo said. "I today's honey. For now."

"Leo," I said. "We just hired you yesterday. You're already chasing women?"

It was tough trying to play the Heavy Boss with Leo.

"Leo, you two both work together," I said.

"We sure do!" Deirdre said. "All night."

"Remember the rules about ro-mance in the work-place?" I asked. "No hanky-panky."

"Ay, *jefe*," Leo wailed. He muttered something in Spanish that I could not catch.

"Well," I started to crumble.

Leo hopped on one foot.

"No hanky," I said. "Maybe a little panky."

Leo stopped breathing hard and looked like an angel again.

"Hanky-panky," I said. "Where does that expression comes from?"

"It comes from men," Deirdre said. "And what they do with women."

"Where?" Leo asked.

"Under they pants, sweetie," she said.

"Excuse me," I said. "Can I help either of you with anything?"

"No thanks, *jefe*," Leo said. "We got it made."

"In the shade," Deirdre said. "If that ain't a racial remark."

Ted came to the doorway, sour face, steaming coffee cup, a folded *New York Post* tucked under his arm.

"It's all bullshit," Ted said when he glimpsed the happy couple.

Leo and Deirdre deigned not to hear.

"Ah, the morning benediction," I said. "What you gonna do, Ted? Just two crazy kids in love."

Ted watched them cavort down the sidewalk and squeeze into Deirdre's small Pinto.

"He's hopping the black lady fence?" Ted said. "Why don't you stop him?"

"Why don't you tell me how?" I said.

❧

Later that day, my desk phone rang.

"This is Piva," a familiar voice said. "Like I said, you are playing tree house games for kids with your Special Agents and that crap. One of your whiz-bang crime fighters took on two cops last night and almost got himself killed."

My legs flopped me into my chair, making me feel like my own grandfather.

"Don't drag it out, Piva. Gimme a name."

"Flat-badge jerk guard Hart," Piva said. "On the nick-name line, he calls himself Mugsy."

"Then he's okay?"

"Jersey City cops saw him hopping around drunk and then he challenged them to a quick-draw contest. He dug around his spongy beer gut. They thought he had a gun. You remember how that usually goes, Royster?"

"But he didn't."

"Lucky thing. He realized that, too, and charged them. Cops got in a little stick time but he'll live. You better fire him right now to cover yourself. Or else someone can sue you for hiring and arming him."

"He's unarmed," I said. Piva usually churned my gut and made me clip my words. "And on leave. And I don't fire work-ers to duck lawsuits. I leave that up to the Department."

"And the Department did just that. Everyone knew that you were a funny bunny. It's a miracle you're not in the nuthouse."

"Keep those prayers coming," I said. "Otherwise, I might still wind up in the ha-ha hotel. Anything on the Lutz kill?"

"Nothing really."

"Since me and my Special Agents are chasing away your thieves, maybe you can re-work your cold cases."

"I always keep working."

"Coming from you, Piva, that is a bowl of steam. Your idea of re-working a cold case is to take a nap."

He hung up.

❧

Dr. Sunick sounded melancholy when I told her about Mugsy's wild carouse. But she surprised me and volunteered to see him again for free. Professionals like her seemed rare to me.

Ted was busy gossiping with Root and another agent about Leo's seduction of Deirdre.

"Was you there, Charlie?" I asked Ted.

"I'm not 'Charlie'," Ted said.

"'Was you there, Charlie?' is an old line from burlesque, Ted," I said. "It means that you were not there. So you can't ever know who seduced who. They may not even know. And it's not our business. Leave it lay."

"She should keep it in the race," Ted said. "Instead of giving it to a Puerto."

"It ain't your problem," I said. "So, now for something completely different. Talk baseball or something."

Ted and the other two talked baseball. The Yankees were suffering.

⌁

A grizzled tree trunk of a black man about seventy years old filled my doorway. He must have topped close to 300 pounds. White beard covered his lower face over very dark skin. His nose looked broken and rebroken and mashed down. He wore a long and loose-hanging denim jacket, like something from 19th century plantation country, matching jeans and square-toed jodhpurs.

"I'm Heavy Eddie," he said in a deep rolling voice. "I would like to talk with the head guard man here."

Ted thumbed at me.

Watching Heavy Eddie's hands, I nodded my head and pointed to the chair in front of my desk. It creaked when he sat in it. So did my nerves.

"Some men, black and white both, been knocking over the crates where we keep our stuff. They got no badge or uniform. I'm the talk man for us brothers and sisters sleeping near Lefferts House. You the security there, right?"

Somehow, he commanded respect. I felt myself straightening up my desk and aligning papers.

"They used a police club on one of us. If they are your people, this jazz got to go. Or we will use what we got against them."

"Heavy Eddie, it's not my people," I said. "We fixed that problem weeks ago. Do you have a cellphone?"

"You must be joking. Everybody got a cellphone."

– 208 –

"Take my card then." I handed it to him. "Anything else happens, call me."

"You get there fast?"

"Before you finish folding your phone."

"Playing fair, I tell you that I'm going to the Precinct now to report it. And Channel Eleven News meeting me there."

"Go ahead, Heavy Eddie. My conscience is clean. It wasn't my guys. I have tightened up internal controls a lot since I took over."

⌇

The rest of the morning, I pushed papers and sat in on Jason's training class. At noon, he gave a Special Agent test.

Six guards passed the course. Nine others washed out.

"You can re-apply to our class in thirty days," Jason announced.

He looked over at me to see if he were following the plan that we had agreed on.

I nodded.

"But you gentlemen and ladies signed up," Jason said. "You agreed that if you did not pass our academy, you could not advance to the Special Agent rank."

"Man, that's crazy!" one washout said. "This is just supposed to be a make-believe deal. No guard agency has you study for a week and then flunks you."

"This one does," Jason said. His temper showed again in his voice. "And you saying that I waste my time running a fake? I don't respect that coming out of you. Some of you passed. Others didn't. You blaming me for that?"

More of them grumbled. Three quit.

"I flunked out," Patso told me. "Jason's questions were hard."

"You griping, too?" I asked. "Maybe you want to quit as well?"

Patso made a horrid face of pained innocence.

"You washing out shows everyone that we don't play favorites," I said. "It's probably the most valuable thing you've done this year."

CHAPTER 30.

Philosophers Say "Property Is Theft."

That night, Cooper and I dozed after making love. She woke me as fiddle music unrolled from the music system.

"Mister Free Spirit," she whispered. "I've got something important to ask you. Are you all awake now?"

"Parts of me feel happily dead," I said. "But my ears still work."

"There's a house for sale at 116 Maple Street," she said. "It's got a backyard with trees. Three stories. The quietest block in Flatbush. I'd like you to look at it with me tomorrow and then co-sign the lease with me. But only if you want to."

Flatbush got very quiet.

Me and my exhausted body sat up in our bed. Suddenly, I felt all shaky.

"Own a home?" I said.

"Rent money just goes down a rathole and we never see it again. A thirty-year mortgage puts us in a whole other world."

"The American dream," I said. "Owning your own home."

"Are you so in love with your Manhattan apartment?" she asked.

"Hardly."

"I'm worried, too. A gazillion things could go wrong. But this could be our common goal. We could work for this together. What have we been working for together so far?"

"Love."

"Stop trying to be funny all the time, Max. If you can't give me a cogent answer right now, what does that say about our relationship?"

I was getting the feeling that playtime was over and someone was forcing me to grow up again.

Once we were in this house, the marriage question would rise up. It would follow like a cup of coffee with breakfast.

Another question was how much I had in the bank now and how long could I tread water there.

My plot to rejoin the Job might need the cash that this new house idea would take. Some business types might be furious with me for risking this. But I was not naked in bed with them now.

"Deal me in," I said to her. "We'll look at the house tomorrow."

She hugged me then straddled me. I don't remember who fell asleep first.

※

The next morning, sirens split the air outside the office. It sounded like a 10-13, the most serious radio call, meaning a cop was in trouble. Out of habit, I stepped out of the doorway and looked north towards Prospect Park.

Two RMPs streaked up from Ocean Avenue, alongside the park. Three Fire Department ambulances came over from Empire Boulevard.

After last night's business-in-bed conference, this might be my last chance to play teenager.

"Hold the fort, Ted," I said. "I need a walk anyway."

Striding across Flatbush Avenue in street clothes, I got past the looky-loos coming off the front stoops and heading towards the ambulances.

Just inside the park's gray stone wall, uniforms were stringing up yellow crime scene tape. The Fire Department ambulance paramedics were getting out of their rigs.

Two bodies lay next to the wall. Blood and gore covered their faces. Their hands were black. The clothes and bulky doubled-up socks marked them as homeless. Now they were lifeless.

A police baton lay next to the bodies. Blood gleamed on it.

Something sick rose up in me. Manry had not been around since our little night-time jaunt together. If he figured that I might shoot him, he would not be playing around this close to the office.

※

At noon, I broke my own rule and watched the TV news. There was no mention of the bodies. It might be too new. But Heavy Eddie the Homeless Talk Man filled the screen. A young blonde reporter with a white porcelain smile held the mike to get his word out.

"Nobody wants us around," Heavy Eddie said.

The TV camera shot his ebony skin against the snow-white beard. It gave him the dignified look that he wore in real life.

"But we need to live, just like you. We will not bow down before the brutality that slaughtered our dear friends, Reen and Harry. May they rest in peace. And I accuse the 71st Precinct police of turning a blind eye to this. They don't want us here, either."

෩

That afternoon, I met with Cooper, walked through our dream house. Two stories, three bedrooms done up in a white-and-black color scheme that reminded me of Boston cream pie.

The agent quoted us the price.

It was a steal. I could see why it excited Cooper. The place was catching onto me as well.

෩

"My friend Brigden wants me to meet you," a woman's voice crackled from my cell. "This is Professor Spingles from Medgar Evers College. Meet me at the gun store, in the basement of 6716 Fort Hamilton Parkway. I've got some papers to give you."

"You can't come to my office?"

"Not today. I'm on a most strict super-tight schedule today."

෩

I drove the Flatbush Secure van to the address: the Bay Ridge Fish and Gun Club, I followed the sound of gunshots downstairs. Man-sized combat targets papered the walls. Display cases of nickeled revolvers, sleek foreign automatics, target pistols with dark hardwood grips and blued steel drew my eyes.

Gunpowder smell wafted around me. For some reason, I had never been in here before.

"The Professor's waiting on you in Lane Three," the Italian grandfather with a hook nose and beautifully capped teeth said in his foreign accent. "She's on a most strict super-tight schedule today."

"So I hear."

The ear protection headset seemed to pinch my ears. Shaking a bit from memories, I pushed open the range door.

Professor Springles was alone in the indoor range. She wore a red baseball cap reading "I'll Give You My Number – Maybe." A wiry blonde woman with wide eyeglasses that covered most of her face, she looked like a jogger.

Her ear protection was two brass shell casings jammed into her little-girl ears. She was handling a blued-steel German Luger 1908 model with a swastika on the rubber grips. She slammed a magazine into the butt of the gun, sighted and fired eight shots. Her paper combat target bucked and danced at the twenty-five-yard range as the slugs hit it.

"Brigden keeps bugging me to meet you," she said. "Says that you have some nutty ideas. So we'll be pals."

"Life laughs that way," I said.

"Therefore, snookums," she said to me. "I've got a real cool paper for you."

"I am only called snookums by my intimates," I said.

"Hoo-rah. The man's still in the game. Brigden said that you were practically married by now."

"Impractically. What have you got?"

She loaded a fresh magazine of brass-colored 9mm shells into the Luger.

"Okey-dokey, sports fans. A Stanford professor named Zimbardo wanted to study how jail affects inmates. So he took two groups of young normal college students. One was guards, one group inmates. Everyone was tested and proved to be normal before the experiment began."

She fired a few more rounds. Her hands were steadier than mine during qualification. She shot better than I could.

"Here," she said. With her free hand, she gave me a thick sheaf of paper. "Read about the experiment. They all play-acted. The experiment was supposed to last just two weeks. But, right away, the fake guards acted like real sadists. The fake inmates forgot that it was just an experiment. They started freaking out from stress. The headshrinker running the experiment had to shut it down after just six days. And these were normal college kids."

"Professor, you're not making no kind of sense. What can this cuckoo experiment have to do with my Brooklyn business today?"

"Think about it."

"Are you on some kind of medication? There is no connection."

"You just don't want to see the connection. Stop playing dumb. Stop ignoring what is right in front of you. How do you think that some security guards might act if their job rests on pleasing those folks that you call Flippers?"

"I don't know," I said.

"You better find out. Before someone gets killed."

೧

That evening, Cooper and I went to a meeting of the Flippers. Everyone knew about the drop in crime statistics. Some praised Skip and me. I spoke up and said that the agents, guards and support staff should get the credit.

"This comes from increasing their image, pay and uniforms," I said. "As I said, you get what you pay for. Treat the workers like trash, and you get trashy performance. Show them a future with respect and training, a career path to get promoted to boss, and you will get a safe neighborhood for you and your children."

"That may be," Breathless Brigden said. "Most of you know me. I'm Brigden, and I live on Empire Boulevard. I and several others have tried pointing out to you that we seem to have lost the true meaning of this group. We are not working with the community that has lived here before us. Instead, we are dictating to them."

My thrift shop jacket swelled in the chest at her words. Brigden was talking truth.

Then my head dipped because I could not speak up and agree with her.

"We choose to do this publicly," Brigden said. "This is the only way to do this effectively. Some of us seem to put property over people."

"This is stupid talk," Epps said. "We care about the total picture."

"I cannot convince myself of that anymore," Brigden said.

She led a group of five others to the street door and beyond it to Flatbush Avenue.

My face burned as if someone had slapped me. Stealing a glance at Cooper, I saw that she looked bored.

❧

That night in bed, Cooper and I did not talk about the day's meeting.

❧

The next morning, as I got to the office, Wild Root and three other agents were inside. Root held up some folded papers and waved them before me.

"What's that?" I asked.

"We need you as a reference," Root said. "Me and six others are applying to the police. NYPD. For next year's class. But, first, we followed your advice and registered at Medgar Evers Community College. That way, we can say that we are college students. Helps us in the process, right?"

I could not stop my smile from spreading.

"Helps everything," I said. "That's great news. Why did you do it, guys?"

"Your influence," Root said. "And that pension of half pay after twenty years. We can talk some of these other fools into applying. You just watch us!"

CHAPTER 31.

With Tash

After downing a Razadyne to greet the day, I subwayed up to Tash's liquor store in the Playpen, my term for the Upper East Side.

I padded into his book-clogged office, where I found him behind his rolltop desk.

"Good afternoon," Tash said.

As always, Tash looked like a well-fed Washington fat cat. A midnight blue pinstripe suit covered his round belly and huge shoulders. He wore the whitest shirts in the Playpen. They acted as a kind of barrier against the world of chaos outside his office and wooden roll-top desk. He had sat at that desk and watched the world spin crazily on its axis outside.

A blood-red necktie and matching silk handkerchief completed the ensemble.

His high forehead crinkled in thought above his tortoise-shell glasses. His hair was the color of saddle leather.

"Playpen Irregulars call-up," I said. "I need you and your three cashiers, Mulu Ken, Alem and Lielit, for an afternoon of undercover roping."

"'Roping', you say?" Tash asked.

"Roping."

Down the hall, the whirligig activity of Tash's Liquors kept spinning. Playpenners crowded the aisles to buy a sprightly little Zinfandel that everyone was chattering about.

Four aisles of sparkling bottles looked out onto Lexington Avenue. A carpet brown as buckram ran along the floor. It soaked up spills.

More thoughts about street-corner fascism fluttered behind my eyelids. Black-and-white newsreels from the Spanish Civil War ground out their message. North Korea, Libya and Indonesia showed their colors.

Most countries in the world still had at least two fascist parties. They shied away from the word "fascism" but the melody lingered on.

Perhaps Professor Springles was affecting me more than I knew.

Something churned in my stomach. Maybe it was the jolly little Razadyne, doing its work.

"Max, we're very busy right now," said Tash.

"Busy is a four-letter word. Both of us are Playpen Irregulars. That means that we help each other whenever possible."

"Well, that's a nice cuddly concept when you're ten years old with your other ten-year-old buddies," Tash said. "But when you grow up, you see things differently. Responsibilities, ramifications —"

"AWW, PISH-TOSH!" I hollered.

The store outside seemed to hush.

Tash regarded me from underneath his high brow.

"You emitted an utterance, sir," he observed.

"I did that," I said. "With many more to come."

Tash kept regarding me.

"I believe that you said 'pish-tosh'," he rumbled on. "This is some sort of foul oath or imprecation, sir?"

"One of the foulest, Mr. Tash," I said.

Since I had first met him as our substitute English teacher at St. Blaise's, formality came easy.

"Being an Irregular is childish," I said. "I admit it. That is the whole concept. We help each other with a child's simple outlook. We bond in our secret tree house, away from our parents. We live for each other, and to the outside world it looks like we never grow up."

"And to hell with business?" Tash asked.

"Because this is the Playpen, business is worshipped," I said. "Like a cliff overhanging us, there is always Something More to Do. Everyone acts like they are too important to speak at a normal speed. Making that money. Idleness is considered depraved."

"So you're deliberately setting out to be childish?" Tash asked.

"Absolutely. Again, that's the whole point of us Irregulars: that the adult way does not work."

"Children," Tash breathed out. "I am surrounded by children. Is this really important?"

"Depends on your point of view," I said. "Two people who loved each other, beaten to death."

He rolled to his feet.

"I'm coming," he said.

"Yeah!" I said. "Saddle up, Irregulars!"

CHAPTER 32.

Store Security

Tash parked his Ford Fairlane, a vintage model from the years when Flatbush had been safe, on Flatbush Avenue near my office. Three Ethiopian cashiers from Tash's Liquors sat in the back.

Alem, the youngest, eased out. Great luminous eyes lit her face over full, high breasts, flat stomach and flaring hips. High cheekbones sloped down to a pointed chin. She looked like an Egyptian tomb carving. Hers was a face that commanded attention.

Everyone on the street eyed us. Men clutching cigarette butts or crumpled beer cans ogled her.

The other two women, Lielit and Mulu Ken, wore native Ethiopian smocks that showed their own beauty. All three lit up the gray sidewalk.

"Wait here a minute, please," I said.

Then I strode over to the Flatbush Secure storefront. Ted, Jason and Ivan were discussing the New York Mets.

Inside my office, I unclipped the gold star badge from my uniform and pinned it to the right hip of my jeans. My thrift shop jacket covered the star, but I could pull the jacket back and show it. Then I took a cheap suede holster with an uncomfortable metal clip from the desk drawer. It was the kind of holster than stingy cops wore instead of buying a good one. Gun dealers would sell a pistol and throw this kind of holster in for free.

☙

Back outside, I went across Flatbush to the Phat Albert Warehouse. Rummaging through the toy section, I found the Junior Policeman kit and mumbled something about a present for my nephew. The kit held a silver plastic badge, plastic handcuffs, a whistle and a realistic-looking black plastic gun modeled on a Smith & Wesson 9mm.

The gun could fool anyone into thinking that it was real. It fooled me.

Jamming the gun into my suede holster, I left the kit next to a garbage can to make some kid happy.

I returned to the group, who were busy buttonholing street people and asking them questions.

"Let's go, Irregulars," I said. "Tash, you've got your lines down for our little play?"

"Let us avaunt and perform," Tash said.

We found Brooklyn Beverage at Flatbush Avenue and Maple Street, a storefront between a superette and a barbershop.

The store was about thirty feet long and narrow, with a back room. Two rows of neglected bottles ran on dirty shelves along one wall. A paunchy black man in a loose-fitting red T-shirt lounged near the register. Smoky bulletproof glass separated him from us. My heart knocked against my rib cage.

"Good afternoon," Tash said. "I'm Bob Tash of Tash's Liquors in Manhattan. Who do I have the pleasure of speaking with?"

The man at the register looked at the women.

Mulu Ken smiled at him, her perfect teeth showing, her eyes heated.

"Name of Bruce," the man said.

"I've had the same location for my outlet for the past twenty-six years," Tash said. "I want to expand into emerging neighborhoods like this one. In five years, this will be a very different kind of area."

"Whites?" Bruce from the cash register said.

"Not necessarily," Tash said. "Just more money. Blacks and Latino families who want to keep their city culture. That's good news for both you and I, Bruce. Now I know that you have deep roots and trust bonded in this community here."

Bruce stared at Tash.

"They rupture heads here," Bruce said.

"So you're might consider selling this business for the right price?" Tash said.

"Quick, fast and in a hurry," Bruce opined.

My body started to unkink. Bruce was warming to the topic.

"Very good," Tash said. "I'm going to have to speak with other proprietors nearby, of course. But you get first opportunity at this sale. Ms. Alem here will stay with you and go over your recent sales figures and customer volume. You have a security system here, I assume?"

"Cameras."

"Anything else?"

"Oh, yeah," Bruce said. "Real good one, too."

Bruce turned away.

"ROLAND!" he shouted.

Another man limped out of the back room. He held a sawed-off double-barreled shotgun held together by gray masking tape.

By training, my right hand snapped to my hip. Unhappy memories echoed.

Roland the Shotgunner showed a sad, fat scarred face, smoked green eyeglasses and a huge belly.

"Roland, put up that sawed-off," Bruce said. "This is business."

Roland obeyed. My breathing eased.

"So you're shooting the robbers?" Tash asked.

"Look like this," Roland said. "Dude come in, say he want the register. Bruce say, 'No, bro. Can't do that. This store all we got.'"

"Bet they love that," I said.

Bruce smirked and kept explaining Life.

"So, I say to him, 'Look, bro, I know that everyone got to make a living. So I give you five out my own pocket and everything be mellow, okay? We all friends and no police or nothing.'"

"What if he doesn't go with that idea?" I asked.

"That's when I come out with my sawed-off," Roland said. "That's all I do, all day. Wait. I say 'C'mon, bro, you hear the man. See this shotgun? Take the five and go, or I blow your butt away.'"

"Did you ever have to shoot?" I asked.

Roland smirked.

"Only once," he said.

"Who you, man?" Bruce asked me.

"Executive Protection," I said, trying to sound dangerous.

My hand lifted the jacket, showing the gold star badge. A security guard had no arrest power. But it impressed some TV addicts.

And Tash sure looked like an executive.

"Yeah, I see the gun," Bruce said.

"We have other properties to look at," Tash said. "So we will leave Alem with you to go over the books and watch your customer videos."

"Why the videos?" Roland asked.

Tash smiled.

"To determine customer volume, time of day, demeanor and service requests. Believe me, that can make a big change in sales."

"What's all that truck?" Bruce asked. "You think you can tell us any kind of smart-talking smack and we gonna swallow it? Most our customers, they want a short dog of Old Hickory Whiskey or a pocket bottle of Night Train."

"All that is going to change," Tash smiled. "We'll be back in a while."

Roland hoisted his sawed-off back into his lair.

Mulu Ken, Lielit, Tash and I took our leave.

We were back out on the sidewalk.

"We've got six more stores to check, for my plan to work," I said. "But this one, Brooklyn Beverage, is the closest to the park and our best bet."

"Are you sure?"

"Give him some time alone with Alem, and he will inhale her aspect, her beauty, and tell her anything that she wants to hear," I said. "She's a great Irregular. He will reveal to her all the secrets of the Universe. Whatever he's got will come rolling on out."

CHAPTER 33.

We Get a Hit

We were canvassing our third liquor store when Tash's phone buzzed.

Alem's voice came over the phone's speaker. "*Tuhru,*" she said. The call ended.

"'*Tuhru*' means 'good' in Amharic," Tash said. "That means that she saw videos of the dead homeless people."

"Reen and Harry," I said. "That's a relief. With all these liquor stores near here, I was afraid that we were going to run out of Ethiopians."

"What do you call this kind of undercover work again?" Tash asked. "Pretending to want one thing but getting another thing?"

"Roping," I said. "Giving them enough rope."

We hustled back to Cut-Rate Liquors to find Alem sitting close to Bruce and drinking tea with him out of plastic cups.

The video screen behind Bruce's counter was frozen. Alem chattered something at Tash in Amharic. Tash answered her back in the same language.

"Go, Mr. Tash," I said, like we were in Saint Blaise's sixth grade English class. "You're speaking Amharic now? Very domestic of you. Maybe you'll be getting married next?"

Tash formed a face to make a pit bull weep.

I came around the bulletproof glass and stood near Bruce to watch the video playback. His desk smelled of spilled beer.

"Hey, man," Bruce said. "What the hell?"

"Mellow, Bruce," I said. "I come in peace."

The video screen showed a black man and a black woman shambling away from the front of the store.

The man looked bulky and slow-moving with a limping left leg. He picked up each foot and put it down like he was trying to build up his leg muscles.

The woman boasted a blonde wig piled high on her head and moved differently, with a dancer's grace. She wore a huge floppy purple hat and tan leather gloves.

"Yo, why we stopping my tape here?" Bruce asked.

Something in his tone made me step next to the video machine. He reached for the black button marked 'delete. '

My body blocked his arm.

"What's all this truck?" Bruce asked. "Really want to buy me out? Or this some flimflam?"

"Absolutely," I said. "Would this face lie?"

"Yup."

"You got customer relations program?" Lielit purred from the doorway. Mulu Ken wafted in behind her.

Tash had texted them to come to the store. I wanted all the bodies and their looks bearing down on Bruce. With this sales pressure, Bruce would not be thinking logically.

"How people in your neighborhood feel about your store?" Mulu Ken asked.

They were stalling Bruce.

On the video screen, Reen and Harry were carrying their shopping bags across the sidewalk out front. Another figure passed after them. I could not see the second figure's face. But he wore a peaked eight-point hat and a jacket. It looked like a Flatbush Secure uniform. Then the guard figure was off camera. Others took up the screen.

"The two people, they wear the same clothes," Alem said. "So I recognize them from the pictures you show."

Her head dipped down.

I tried shaking off how I felt. She should not have to go through this.

"Who's that guard?" I asked Bruce.

"Roland!" Bruce shouted.

Roland came out. The shotgun hung in his hand, pointed at the floor. He looked scattered, as if he had been asleep or sampling the stock.

It was time to try my most steely voice.

"Roland," I said. "Put that monster back in the room. We're still talking business."

Bruce and Roland looked at each other.

"That shotgun is under the legal length," I lied. "Dump it somewhere else, or the cops'll put you in the joint."

"It's legal, this long, okay," Roland said.

"They changed the law on shotguns," I lied. "Didn't you hear?"

Roland shrugged and put the sawed-off back in his outpost.

"Man, I know you a guard like the other guards," Bruce said to me. "I see you around here all the time. What's the game, dude?"

"No game," I said. "Just like you, I'm trying to clean up my business. Don't you lose your chance to leave this neighborhood and start over in someplace better. Who was that guard on the tape?"

"I'm not talking no more," Bruce said. "Roland, you stay there with that gun. These guards protect us better than the cops do. They clear them bums from in front of my doorway. So I get more customers that way."

"It ain't legal," I said.

Even to me, that sounded silly.

"They clear my spot, I let them pick out what they want to drink," Bruce said. "That's my right, huh?"

"What if the guards get a little too wild?" I asked.

"Man, get out of my store!" Bruce shouted. "What I care if they get too wild? I got these bums come in here, steal my stuff, damage the front, cost me a fortune in insurance all the time. Say they gonna burn me out. And kill me. Piss in my door. Break my windows. Why should I care about stink-finger old bums and their rights? Can't I work like a normal fool? What about MY rights?"

CHAPTER 34.

Nightwalking

The next day came gray and windy.

Cooper and laziness kept me in bed until evening.

"I'm sorry, my sweet," I muttered. "But I must away."

"I want you to stay in bed with me forever, Max," Cooper said. "Where are you going?"

"Just a little inspection tour of my sites," I said. "Saturday night, and everyone tends to goof off some."

Since I wanted to look different from before, I ignored the uniform and dressed in an old white suit from a thrift shop.

My sites did not worry me anymore. But something made me think that the same person killed Lutz and Reen and Harry.

That killer might have worn a guard uniform. He had used a baton. I could not tell Cooper that right now. Tonight, I might have to move someone around or wreck something to get more facts. It was better that she did not know what I was going to do. Or else, it might surface in court.

With secrets like this, we were growing farther apart.

Three steel ball-point pens went into my back pocket. They served well for stabbing in the eyes, throat or gut. No cop would ever arrest me for carrying them.

"Why must you go?" she asked.

"America," I answered.

A Native American bone dagger with a handle wrapped in dried deer gut went against my calf, attached by the elastic surgical band under the jeans. Dealers sold them at the Native American bazaars at Inwood Hill Park.

The dagger could kill.

Most hooligans or cops just frisked the chest and belt areas. They ignored the legs.

This felt risky. Goosebumps from fear scored my skin.

Leaving Cooper in bed this way felt wrong.

But I pushed myself out of the bedroom and down the steps.

Saturday nights worked well for farming cases. Witnesses drank and talked loudly. Everything loosened up.

My fingers stabbed Jason's cell-phone number.

Jason answered on the first buzz.

"Boss man," he said.

"Jason, how's by you?"

"Righteous, boss man."

"If you don't need the unmarked van tonight, I want to wheel around the hood a bit," I said. "Can I pick it up?"

"I'll bring it to you. Right now. Where are you?"

"Lincoln and Flatbush, in five minutes."

"See ya."

Saturday night crowds were already thickening along the sidewalks. It reminded me of the Patrol days. Some locals would get cut, robbed or raped tonight just because it was Saturday night. Some might die.

It formed an American tradition. Experts called cheap pistols "Saturday Night Specials".

Jason bounced over in the unmarked dark green Ford van.

"Been hearing some jackass talk," he said. "They saying that you a racist who can't stand black folks."

"I'm a naive fool," I said. "Because I like everybody."

"I know. Anyone with eyes can see it. But that's talk going around. So I'll be your Saturday night date tonight, keep you out of trouble."

"Jason, you can't do that. Might get you jammed up in some stupid street fight. Locked down with your record."

"You want these keys, boss man?"

"Come on."

"If you get beat down, that sucker Ted be running the agency. Or that fat-mouth Skip. Rather have you there, driving us crazy with Special Agent lectures and your other dreams."

"More mutiny."

"You promote me to Trainer, right quick," he said. "Tonight, I'm just protecting my investment."

"Okay, okay. Let's stop wasting time."

"I'll drive," Jason said. "Seen you drive."

"In-sub-ord-ination," I said.

We cruised down Flatbush Avenue and checked on the Maple Street Academy.

Carpenters had fixed the damage by now.

We took coffee and at Toomey's and scanned another spot on Empire Boulevard.

Night came.

As Jason wheeled past Cooper's house, the light still showed on in her bedroom window. My body ached to be there with her.

I thought about The Softness of Men.

છ

The cellphone buzzed in my hip pocket.

Annoyance surged through me. Whenever I started thinking, my phone interrupted me.

"Hey, Boss," Leo's voice gurgled over the phone. "I can't guard Erasmus School tonight."

"Leo, you have my fullest attention," I said.

"I drunk, Boss."

"Like my Uncle Ba-Ba used to sing the song, 'Somebody Put Something in My Whiskey that Made Me Drunk.' How did you get into this condition?"

"Deirdre make me this way. We in a motel. Oh, yeah. Something *más*. She say she don't can work her shift at supermarket tonight."

"Leo, we're trying to raise up the guard business here."

Leo giggled.

"You never," he said.

"There's a lot in those two words," I said.

"Before I help you, remember?"

"You only crank this up when you're pounding down booze and driving me cuckoo. And it works. Good night, Leo. Don't hurl on the hotel carpet."

Leo giggled and clicked off.

"Jason, let's hit Erasmus fast," I said. "It's about to be unprotected. We got any weapons in this truck?"

"Just one baton. Me being ex-con, I can't even carry that on the street."

"I know. So, don't. Please. I can't stand losing my trainer."

We rocketed down Flatbush Avenue.

✌

It was time to phone the good gray government in the form of Sgt. Lipkin.

"What is it, Royster?" Lipkin grunted. His voice implied that he was Being-a-Professional that day. And he had no time for aging kids like me.

"Those two homeless ones killed in the park, Al," I said.

"You mean Reen and Harry?" Lipkin asked. "I talked to a uniform who had locked them up for years. Reen was a juice-head and a flirt. Harry was always protecting her honor. And getting collared for it."

"True love."

"Seems like."

"Don't knock it. We don't see much of it anymore."

"How's the new girlfriend?" Lipkin asked. "Speaking of true love."

"Arghhh. Al, when did Harry and Reen get beat down?"

"Remember that was a cold night, some drizzle, there. So the M.E. could fix the time of death around 8:30, 9:00, something like that. Why?"

His voice sounded like he was losing interest. That should not happen.

"Because it may be connected with the Lutz kill," I said. "Can't you canvass the area unofficially? As a favor to me?"

"Max, how did you survive on the Job?"

"I didn't."

"Why should I do you this favor?" Lipkin said. "Become your personal detective. Department punishes cops every month for doing what you're begging me to do, mister square-badge guard boss. Teach your guards to play detective, huh?"

"Some guards would make good cops," I said. "Gotta guy named Jason here who is everything that you could ask for. Among others. They just need some luck, to take the test and get through the Academy."

"Yeah, yeah, just unlucky," Lipkin said. "Whatever you say. This other rookie cop is off-duty and walking home near the murder scene.

"Sees someone going through the bushes close to the bodies. Rookie is a hot head. He braces a perp. Perp ran like a deer. This Rookie lives on pizza and corn nuts, and this character left him winded. But the Rookie saw him run into the Ebbets Field Houses. How many of your guards live there?"

"About half. That's the only big housing complex in Flatbush. Lower rents than most. But just because the client was hanging around the kill zone doesn't mean that he did the job on Reen and Harry."

"Sure, it ain't a great lead," Lipkin said. "Agreed. Sounds hokey, yeah. But killers do return to the scene in real life."

"You the murder expert," I said, trying to soften him up. "Why do they return?"

"Mucho reasons," Lipkin said. "See if they dropped something that might ID them. Some to gloat. To enjoy the memories. Some dig watching us root around in frustration. So I'll check who lives in Ebbets Field Houses. I mean, what else do we got to work with?"

Chapter 35.

The Battle of Erasmus Hall School

We reached Erasmus Hall School with its Gothic turrets looming over Flatbush Avenue.

Root stood by in his uniform, chain-smoking and dropping the butts in a tin can by the guard hut.

We sent him away and called Mugsy Hart at home. Mugsy cussed some wild words but said that he would cover the site in an hour.

"Something scraped, just now," Jason said.

"I didn't hear anything," I said.

"Around the corner there," he whispered. "Erasmus Place."

"Rest easy here," I said.

Jason darted along the school front and around the corner. He moved without making any noise, in his sneakers.

I locked the van and followed behind him.

"Don't move!" Jason shouted. "Citizen's arrest!"

My feet pumped.

Around the corner, two big black men in rough clothes grappled with Jason. The two men looked familiar for some reason. But adrenaline gave me tunnel vision.

Jason slammed one on the neck. The other punched Jason and grabbed him in a chokehold.

Jason gasped.

My heart jumped up.

Spray paint showed on the Erasmus wall behind them.

The pair were tagging the wall with graffiti.

The choker pulled Jason back.

The puncher hit Jason again and turned to me.

He was Manry, my old pal.

My jaw dropped.

Manry dodged my strike, spun and slugged me.

Everything exploded.

The sidewalk hit my face, scraping it.

My vision clouded and then cleared.

Jason whipped to his right. His left hand chopped the choker below the belt. The choker yelped. Jason hit again, stomped the foot and spun out of the choke. He hit the choker's throat.

The choker spun back.

I tried rolling up.

The choker was Alvin Cobb, the guard who had slugged me on my first day.

Manry kicked me.

His foot hit my ribs.

I fell back down.

Cobb knocked over a paint can. Bright green oozed.

Manry's foot blotted out my sight.

Blood filled my mouth. It tasted bad.

"You going down, sucker!" Jason shouted.

Cobb kicked Jason in the groin.

Jason screamed and folded.

Manry kicked me again.

"Bad, bad," I whispered.

I fell back down again.

Nobody went by on Erasmus Place.

Traffic stayed on Flatbush.

Manry reached down and grabbed my neck.

"We trash Erasmus, we trash your agency," he said. "Call it Flatbush Un-Secure."

I could not move.

Manry yanked my head back.

He bared my Adam's Apple.

Jason pushed himself up off the sidewalk. Cobb hit him twice.

Jason took the hits, rolled with them and held his groin with one hand.

Jason's foot lashed out. It hit Cobb's knee. Cobb hopped backwards. Jason hit him like lightning, against the face, three times.

"Get my gun!" Cobb shouted.

Manry's hand went back to strike my throat.

Jason threw himself through the air.

Jason crashed into Manry.

Both went down.

I got up on an elbow. Manry banged into me.

I put my free elbow against his jaw twice. My weight got behind it.

Manry got to his feet.

Cobb was already running down Erasmus Place, moving jagged on his bad knee.

I lunged at Manry. My hands missed him.

Jason threw two more strikes that pushed Manry back.

Manry spat blood and ran.

"Jason, watch out!" I shouted. "Cobb's going for a piece!"

Manry ran like an athlete. His shoes flew.

"He ain't getting no kind of piece," Jason wheezed. "Cobb a stone punk."

Jason's eyes shut. Tears oozed. He bent over, breathing hard.

Cobb was already moving a Toyota out from the curb.

He was about fifty feet from us.

Manry caught up to the car and wrenched open the passenger door.

"Hey, mister!" I shouted. "You forgot your paint!"

Manry fell inside. The car jerked away, turned a corner and was gone.

"Ooooh, baby," Jason breathed. "That hurts."

"Jason, thanks," I panted. "Tell you what, I'll cancel your rumba lessons."

"They were gonna tag up all over the school," he said. "Paint gang stuff on the walls. Break some windows. Hurt the agency. Show their power. But they ain't no gang. They got too much ego to be in no gang."

CHAPTER 36.

Showdown

"Jason, do you need a doctor?" I asked.

"Hell, no."

"After tonight, everything comes easy. And we are knocking down crime. Cooper and I will have our new home next month."

"Why don't you tell Cooper all this happy stuff?" he asked.

A crazy thought nested inside me. Then it would not fly away.

"I'll tell her on our honeymoon," I said. "And I bet that she'll accept my proposal. I used to say that I would never try marriage again. But she is too good and lovely to let slip away."

"You sound pretty sure," Jason said. "Wowie zowie!"

"Because I am sure," I said. "Feeling light-headed now, yeah. But this is something that I must have been thinking about for weeks now."

An image of Cooper naked in bed spurred me on now. She was more passionate and inventive than anyone before. Her heat delighted me. It would be wonderful being with her forever.

"Big change, Max."

"Even if I get back on the cops, I can still work as a consultant for Flatbush Secure. Cooper can help me with my memory problems. With her, I can handle them. And the bank will let me sign for our new house. Banks love civil servants to sign thirty-year mortgages. Hot damn, I'm in love like a kid walking on air!"

My cellphone buzzed.

"This is Heavy Eddie," a deep voice on my phone said. "You better remember me, player. Because about a dozen fools with nightsticks telling us to move off Lefferts House grounds here. I bet that they are your goons. After you, I call 911."

That chilled me. If the cops found my guys slugging the homeless, Skip would fire me to duck lawsuits. He would have to.

"Don't call 911, Heavy," I said. "I can get over there and make it right. Get you safe."

"These fools are gonna hurt my people. I'm calling the Man."

My palms wetted. The Razadyne spun me dizzy.

"Heavy," I said. "I got keys to an empty warehouse in Canarsie. It's a good place for you and your people to winter when it gets cold. Just maintain there, no cops, and I'll put you inside that warehouse."

"Then hurry up, dude," Heavy Eddie said. He ended the call.

"Kick this thing in the ass!" I shouted to Jason. "Lefferts House! 10-60!"

As we rocked through potholes, I told Jason what we had.

"Call 911, Max," he said. Even now, his voice stayed calm. He drove like an expert, better than I ever could. "Don't mess in this without a piece. All I got is my training baton."

"If these are our guys, I got to squelch it," I said. "No cops, no media. Or else, Flatbush Secure is through. And us with it."

"It's going to be some hard pipe-swinging brother-muggers looking to get paid," he said. "Crips, maybe. Not our cats."

We were streaming up Flatbush Avenue. I lowered the window to listen. No sirens sounded yet.

"Faster, Jason."

"Naw, Max," he said, slowing. "You'll get messed up, jumping into this."

We were at Flatbush Avenue and Maple Street. He stopped the van.

"I can't fight you for the keys," I said. "You're too young and tough for me."

It was like Patrol again, when my partner did not want to answer a call. So I did what I used to do. I hauled my gut onto the sidewalk and ran towards trouble.

"Max, I'm trying to protect you!"

My feet slapped the sidewalk past our office. I cut across Lloyd Sealey Square. Maybe Lloyd had done what I was doing right now.

A gypsy cab braked and skidded as I ran. The front fender just missed my kneecap.

The forgotten landmarks flashed past me. The Ebbets Field Apartments formed a hulk off my right shoulder. This was where Jason had saved my life years ago.

My lungs burned. The body screamed in protest. This could kill me.

Nighttime traffic slowed to let me gallop into the park. Behind me, Jason's van gunned the engine. He was following me. But he did not want to. My lazy Patrol partners had done the same thing.

"Jason!" I shouted over my shoulder. "I need you!"

Just inside the park, I ran past the Carousel and onto the Lefferts House grounds.

Men in George Washington masks slammed clubs against cooking fire grilles. Red sparks exploded against the spiked fence. Homeless children screamed. Their parents clutched them.

"That ain't right, man!" Heavy Eddie boomed. "Take that somewhere else, brother man!"

More than a dozen Masks out-numbered the homeless. Heavy Eddie had about ten total, with some kids, wailing and scrabbling duffle bags out of the way.

The Masks ripped down a pup tent.

Shavey, the homeless man, climbed the dangerous spiked fence and ran into the trees.

"Somebody help us!" the same grandmother that I remembered cried out. "Help us, Jesus! Is this America?"

It was time to run a bluff.

"Police officer, ma'am!" I shouted. "You're safe. We got units rolling."

It the Masks were hip, they would run now.

But two Masks turned and bulled me down to the dirt. One hit my ribs with his baton. The pain crumpled me in two. My heel flailed and caught his shin.

I rolled and kicked again and missed the other one. He raised his club. My hand flashed down to my leg, snagged the bone knife from the elastic and threw it at him.

As a kid, I used to practice knife-throwing.

The knife flew without turning over and sank into his gut. He bleated and dropped to his knees. I grabbed for his club but he fell on it. I yanked out my knife. Two more Masks stomped me.

Jason appeared. He swung his baton against the man's thigh. The Mask fell against Jason. Jason sidestepped and dodged the Mask's arms.

Three Masks knocked Jason down.

I tried rolling into a ball. A club hit me. My hand went up and stabbed the Mask in his leg. The knife handle broke off. My hand still gripped the broken bone hilt. More Masks crowded me. I was going under.

"Help!" I shouted. "Lefferts House! 10-13! Jason!"

Feet blocked my sight. I tasted my own blood. I tripped one Mask to the ground. He swung at me.

I grabbed the mask and yanked it down to blind him. The mask came off.

It was Epps, the black Flipper from the group. He spat at me and punched, smashing my lips.

"You, Epps!" I shouted. "Are you nuts?"

Over his shoulder, I saw Jason run into the park.

Epps pushed to his feet. He reached under his jacket. Another Mask blocked him. I knew the Mask's body shape and size.

"Hart!" I shouted. "Mugsy! Stand fast!"

The Mask turned and stripped off his cover. It was Mugsy Hart, out on bail from Jersey.

"No witnesses!" Epps shouted. Orange gunfire bucked his hand. Explosions hammered my ears. Epps was shooting at me. I felt something whip past me. Mugsy slammed into Epps, jolting his arm.

"Lose that gun!" Mugsy shouted. "We agreed on that! Just muscle!"

CHAPTER 37.

Chaos

Epps jumped on top of a packing crate to take the high ground. He bobbled near the spiked fence around Lefferts House.

He aimed the gun out at me, a silver pocket automatic, made for close work.

Epps sighted and shot again.

BAM!

Dirt kicked up a few feet away. It hit my eyes and went into my mouth. A club from below smashed Epps across the thigh. He wobbled and shot again. The club flailed. Jason was swinging it. He reached up and hit the thigh again.

Epps fell backwards against the spiked fence. He screamed. His body impaled. A metal spike came bloody through his belly. The spike pointed up. The gun fired at the sky. His head sagged.

Blood gushed from his screaming mouth. He flopped like a fish.

The gun dropped. By habit, I jammed it into my pocket.

"I killed him," Jason said.

"Had no choice," I panted. "Thanks."

"Run, Max," Jason hissed. He yanked me to my feet. "You don't need this."

"Thigh shot!" I shouted. "You just used it on that Mask! The same way that Lutz got it. You hit Lutz. You saw the cops chasing someone and you had a baton somewhere. Why?"

"Like I told you," Jason panted. "I always wanted to be a cop. But I hit the wrong guy that night."

"And you knew OB!" I shouted. "Flatbush dudes, running hustles. Betcha hated him."

"He another punk!" Jason said.

"So you wrote 'OB' by Lutz's body," I said. "To put it on him."

"That's what OB deserved. Degenerate gangsta scum!"

"Why you doing this, Jason?" I asked.

"Policing my turf, man," he said. "You wouldn't understand. You're cultured.

But having that power feels good to a loser like me. No laws stopping you. Direct action."

"Let's git!" Heavy Eddy shouted.

He pulled his group out along the path. The kids screeched. Some Masks followed them, waving batons.

"This will break you, Max," Jason said. "Take off. No need for me to hurt you more. You tried fixing me. But it don't work."

"Jason," Mugsy shouted. "What do we do now?"

"They're your muscle now," I said. "They follow you. Not me."

"The Flippers promise us the Kingdom," Jason said. "Jobs. Homes. A piece of the pie. If we stay with you, we get nothing."

"They're just using you," I said. "Like always. Money uses the poor. For once, you got the power."

"Yeah, Max," he said. "Direct action."

"Then why'd you beat those two homeless in the park?"

"Because they tried to snitch on me," Jason said. "Just for moving them off corners. Said I had no right. What could I do, Max? Cops would love busting me, convicted felon."

"More bullying," I said. "You're under citizen's arrest, Jason."

He kicked my leg out from under me. I went down, rolled up and caught his shin with my foot. He stopped.

He threw a jab, cross and hook. All connected. Blood smeared my eyes, blurring my sight. He could box me to death. So I went down again and rolled low. I hit his legs, put my shoulder against his knee and heaved forward with everything I had. I used the ground for traction. He kept punching. But nothing stopped my tackle. His fists pounded my neck.

He yanked the gun from my pocket and crammed it into his belt.

"Gimme that gun!" I shouted.

Jason kept hitting. I flung him backwards. He hit a tree. His head snapped back. He sagged and slid down the tree.

Sirens sounded. Car doors slammed behind me. Radios gurgled.

"Police!" a cop shouted. "Don't a mother-jumper move!"

Someone's baton lay on the ground. Jason snatched it up and swung at my head.

Terrified, I threw up my wrist. Pain hit me. Bones cracked.

"Drop that club!" Hairy Man shouted. Car lights lit us. Piva, in uniform, leaned against the hood, aiming his Glock.

Jason shook his head.

A shot cracked as Piva fired.

The Masks ran.

"Don't shoot!" I shouted. "I'm Royster, off The Job!"

"Royster?" Piva cried out. "Nobody shoot! Stop it!"

Jason still stood. The club waved in his hand. The shot had missed him.

"Piva, you were right!" I hollered.

"What?" Piva shouted back. "Talk fast or else!"

"My guards went haywire! They hired out to the Flippers."

"You!" Piva shouted at Jason. "It's over now. Just drop the club!"

"AWWW!" Jason roared. His temper broke again. He ran forward. He swung the club.

"Drop it!" Piva ordered.

Jason turned towards the cops and charged them. The club swung. His chest swelled. The handsome face twisted. Teeth gnashed.

He yanked the gun and pointed it at the cops.

"Go ahead and shoot!" he roared. "I don't care no more!"

The first cop, a reedy black man with gold-rimmed glasses, fired. His gun bucked. Two more fired. Jason's shirt spurted. Blood gushed. He fell forward. The club pinwheeled and smacked the RMP windshield. Glass exploded. Jason rolled over. His eyes closed.

"Cuff him!" Piva shouted. "Cuff Royster. Cuff everyone who ain't on the frigging Job! Roll me a boss and a bus. Ambulance. Get the Duty Captain here."

Exhaustion floored me. I sank down to the ground. It smelled of leaves and dirt and felt right to be lying flat.

The Integrity Waltz

Hairy Man and Wide Lady hustled me to the precinct in cuffs. Paramedics checked me and declared me healthy enough.

Piva detained me on a Riot charge and put me in a holding pen.

Hours dragged past. I could feel my whiskers pushing out into stubble.

"Here's your lawyer," Piva said. "But you better talk now."

Skip swept inside the holding pen in a dress suit, white shirt and necktie.

"Where's the Legal Aid lawyer that I asked them to send?" I asked.

"He on his lazy white way," Skip said. "But I'm licensed to practice all this law mess in New York State as well. The police checked, just now. What have you told them?"

"Nothing."

"Good. Then don't."

"They picked up some guards running through the park. Charges of riot and manslaughter."

"They get paid," Skip said. "They're guards."

"They're people, too. Which the Flippers understood. They were paying off Jason, promising him a corporate kingdom somewhere. He fell for it."

"Say fricking nothing," Skip said. His voice iced my insides. "Not a damn word. Our guards made their choices. You

– 242 –

gotta think about your own future. If this gets out, you and the agency are finished."

"Why should I dummy up?"

"Because you wanting to turn cop again, Max. Do nothing. Say nothing. And I can promise you your police shield back on your chest. And a sweet job as security consultant part-time. Is that reasonable?"

"Ask Jason."

"Why not ask Cooper?" Skip leaned closer. My breath caught. "Time to grow up, Peter Pan."

"Time to let you and some of the Flippers take vacations overseas," I said. "Just until your lawyers can stomp out any charges. No extraditions. Slink back to your condos when the hired guns say that it is safe."

"That be a damn poor interpretation of this, Max."

"Very poor," I said. "Like I am going to be soon."

Skip shook his head.

"The fact that some guards went wild and turned sour —"

"Not sour," I said. "Fascist."

"Whatever. That's life. But you, my man, you did something never done before. Made Flatbush safer. Squealing like a stuck pig for some idea of fairness is gonna kill all that. Your good work forgotten. Flatbush will slide back to crime."

"Unless I do some other crime this morning," I said. "Perjury."

I bent over, rocking in the hard wooden chair. My bruises sang. Blood caked on my lips and neck. It flaked off when I shook my head. Paramedics had taped my wrist.

"Baby, baby," Skip said. "You really want to mess up your life. Crushes me to do this, Max.

But I just found out that you bought a fixer-upper Flatbush home from the Government. And you lied all outrageous-like on the form."

My body heaved again.

"I never bought a house!" I said.

"I got the papers in my office. Your signature. Witnessed, too. Maybe you were too busy signing papers every day to examine everything. That's a pity."

"That's a frame!"

"You gave me the deed, baby. Maybe you forgot. But I gotta let you go. You are no longer a part of Flatbush Secure. Fired for making fraudulent statements to the Government. Now, shut up around the media, or else I'll get you prosecuted for that fraud."

"You're bluffing," I said. "I'll talk to the media as much as I want to. Try and stop me."

My chest ached but I breathed out, feeling cleaner.

My bruises sang some more.

Skip left, muttering more threats.

Lipkin got through on my cell phone.

"Jason died without talking," he said. "The case is all blowed up. Tell them whatever they ask. Maybe you'll get through."

Then he cut the call.

Piva and the Duty Captain grilled me. I bargained for them to release me. They brought in an ancient white-haired Assistant D.A. who promised me immunity if I told them everything. So I got all undressed for them and told the whole story. It took a full pot of coffee and a box of croissants from the re-opened new Flatbush bakery. But then it was done.

The media swarmed me on the precinct steps. They peppered me with good sharp questions. Skip's threat hung over me.

The media put me under the lights and cameras.

"Telling the truth today might bring me real trouble," I said. "But me and some of my Special Agents of Flatbush Secure have risked our lives for this Flatbush neighborhood. If I cover things up, Flatbush will suffer. And we want Flatbush to grow. Better and safer and softer every day. So, ask me whatever you want."

They did.

&

When I staggered up the steps to my home, it was sunrise. Cooper was still asleep in bed, curled up like a child.

Bittersweet and gentle, I woke her up. She grasped the story at once. My legs twitched from everything that had happened. I threw my clothes down and washed as I talked.

The dried blood-cakes ruined her good towels.

The whole planet felt like it was tumbling out of control. But I tried to steady myself as the morning moved.

"Somehow, Cooper," I said. "You've managed to change my mind about holy matrimony. For me, that's like discovering that I can fly. Come fly with me into City Hall or a big church fandango with the Sky Pilot reading from The Big Book while everyone worries about how they look. Please, marry me."

She turned away and looked out at the street. I had never seen her look so lovely.

"You're just running wounded today, Max," she said. "Changing your life takes more than just a trauma. You are trying to force something down your own throat for the wrong reasons."

My throat worked. It wanted some new words to get through this talk.

"And you've already condemned some of my friends," she said. "You'll have to testify against others."

"If there's a trial. But I doubt it."

"There will be trials," she said. "Accusations. The press will turn it into us being racists. Flatbush will turn against us on street corners."

"But you ARE Flatbush," I said. "Just a minority group here."

"Not anymore. You fixed that, Max. It's best that you go back to your apartment now, Max. Back to your old life."

My head dropped down and then snapped back up. I felt like a heartsick teenager again. My eyes wetted.

"Sometime this week, I'll drop your things off in Manhattan," she said. "You belong there and not here, trying to build something with me. I'll have to look elsewhere for a life-mate."

❧

Then I was shambling back downstairs and trying not to think. Something felt like a steel splinter in my lungs.

My cellphone buzzed.

"Cooper!" I said. "Calling me back. Making up."

The phone unflipped against my ear.

"This is Buddy," a man's voice said. "Excuse me for calling so early. But I'm shaving and watching you on the news. We had a friend who wanted a city job. Remember?"

My ears moved back as I inhaled, grinning.

"Is it moving forward now?" I asked.

"I'm afraid not," Buddy said. "It's finished. This kind of publicity ends it. No chance at all of a quiet re-entry. Impossible."

"And the twenty thousand?"

"That's used up, too. It went for lunches and other favors called in beforehand. Considerations that will now have to be re-considered."

"I want that money."

"A lot of people do," he said.

And he hung up.

❧

Limping across Flatbush Avenue, I re-traced my run of last night. My whole body ached and creaked. I felt like joining Heavy Eddie's homeless family.

Inside the park, cop cars still hung around Lefferts House. Yellow crime-scene tape stretched. Freshly barbered bosses, faces sleek with rest, conferred with each other and did not notice me.

At the Carousel, Margaret was dismounting from her child's bike. She wore a black sweat suit with little green shamrocks on it. She shook her hands, unlocked the Carousel and started the calliope music. It was some old tune that I had heard as a child.

"Maxy, boy!" she cawed. "What is everyone screaming about, happened here last night? How's the boy? You're a little down about something, maybe? You certainly look it. You want a free ride?"

"Love it," I said.

The music speeded up. It hooked up my nerves and made them stronger.

On a whim, I seized Margaret and put us in waltz position. My feet flew. We waltzed around the Carousel. The cops hooted. A few cheered.

– 246 –

The green park spun around me. My head went back in a laugh. Bones crackled in my hurt neck. Margaret giggled.

"Whatever are you doing, Max?" she asked.

"I call it 'The Integrity Waltz'," I said. I spun her into a waltz twinkle and followed her with a leap. "Because I still got my integrity."

Special thanks once again to:

To Detective-Investigators Mark Baldessare and Fareed "Fred" Ghussin and all the other cops and federal agents who taught me so much about hunting our real-life serial killers.

To the *Spy, the Movie* team – Jim MacPherson, Alex Klymko, Charles Messina and all the rest of the gang for a grand adventure in screenwriting.

To Nad Wolinska for her as always inventive cover illustration and Richard Amari for his equally inventive cover design.

To my editor and screenwriting partner, Lynwood Shiva Sawyer, for his support and encouragement over the years

And my thanks to that wonderful woman, companion and friend from Guangzhou, China, who shares my adventures and my life.

The next Max Royster adventure is coming soon!

When the Whistle Blows, Everyone Goes

Remember me?

Max Royster, ex-cop bounced from the NYPD for mental disease, overweight, divorced and broke.

A Manhattan tycoon frets about his beautiful daughter.

She is cavorting somewhere near Palm Springs, California.

He pays me to find her.

This simple job turns into a hairball.

She leads me astray.

Someone kills her boyfriend.

The U.S. Park Rangers blame me for it and lock me up in a federal prison.

Me being me, I try to stay cheery by organizing swing dances between male inmates.

An inmate hate group tries to rape and kill me.

Other inmates protect me for kicks.

Some enjoy the dances. Anything beats prison routine.

The warden and the guards suspect me of spying on them for the FBI.

Things look grim for our hero.

Can I swing-dance and laugh my way out of lock-down to find the real killer among the Beautiful People in Palm Springs?

Everyone wants to see what happens next.

You will, too.

If you enjoyed reading *Softening Flatbush,* you'll definitely like Frank Hickey's other Max Royster novels:.

Brownstone Kidnap Crackup

When Max witnesses a debutante's kidnapping, he becomes the FBI's prime suspect. Or is he actually their salvation?

℘

It's Christmas in Manhattan.

A blizzard whips the city.

The Beautiful People, in the elite Upper East Side, celebrate in their brownstones.

Until a kidnapper seizes a beautiful young debutante.

Max Royster, fired from the NYPD for mental illness, fights the kidnapper but loses.

The kidnapper flees. Stripped of gun, shield and power, Max has only his wits to save the victim.

The FBI treats Max like a suspect and tramples roughshod on his rights.

During this long sleepless night, an unknown FBI agent cracks up. Over the radio, he quotes J. Edgar Hoover and plants false clues.

To solve the case, Max must smash through the facade and mysteries of millionaires in their snug brownstones.

Exotic women tempt him to give up.

The blizzard worsens.

As the winds howl and snowdrifts deepen, Max risks his life and his freedom in a desperate bid to save the victim.

Once again, Max Royster is back on the street in *Brownstone Kidnap Crackup.*

Funny Bunny Hunts the Horn Bug

To catch a sex killer targeting Upper East Side beauties, misfit NYPD cop Max Royster goes undercover…as an NYPD cop!

The Upper East Side of Manhattan is one of the richest neighborhoods in the world.

But Max Royster, a maverick, outspoken and erudite NYPD foot cop, who grew up working-class in this tony area, calls it "the Playpen." Money protects the bluebloods in this area like the bars on an infant's playpen.

Late one night, patrolling wealthy brownstones, he sees a burglar attacking a rich actress. Max chases him. They fight but the burglar escapes.

The burglar is a sexual predator, known in cop-speak as a "Horn Bug".

For losing the suspect, Max's captain deems Max "a Funny Bunny," too unstable for police work. He strips Max of his gun and badge, then orders Max into Bellevue Hospital for observation and maybe for the rest of his life.

Without any tools or support, Max ten days to stop this Horn Bug.

The Gypsy Twist

Max Royster's hunt for a sadistic serial killer takes a startling turn when he realizes that not all predators are born alike.

One autumn night, someone strangles a teenage boy jogging in Central Park.

In Brooklyn, street cop Max Royster risks his life to disarm a madwoman with a knife without harming her. Nevertheless, her lawyer charges Max with brutality. The Department decides to punish Max a.

Max's protector is Sgt. Lipkin, an expert detective working the Central Park murder. Lipkin knows that a killer like this seeks a new sexual thrill, a "Gypsy Twist," with each new murder. The dead boy is the son of one of the wealthy elite of the Upper East Side. Max is the only cop in the city from that world, and on scholarship years before, Max had even graduated from the dead boy's school.

Well aware of Max's range of knowledge, Lipkin summons Max for the assistance that only Max can provide.

Max probes the tony school and neighborhood, ignoring bosses who, out of jealousy, try to block his progress.

A beautiful, free-spirited reporter, Diana, woos Max to try and make him reveal insights about the case. Denying him nothing, she lures Max onward.

The killer seizes another school-boy who was playing soccer in the park and drags him to death with a car.

Wealthy New Yorkers scream that someone is butchering their sons. The city rocks.

One night, muggers attack Sgt. and Max, who freezes on the trigger. The muggers cripple Lipkin.

The Department moves to fire Max.

But the dead boy's tycoon father hires Max to track down the killer. Max and Diana live below the radar in the New Orleans and San Francisco underworlds, hunting the killer until a shocking conclusion reveals their identity.

CPSIA information can be obtained
at www.ICGtesting.com
Printed in the USA
FFOW01n1907020814
6584FF

9 780984 881062